Chiseler in Jade

Also in This Series

That First Heady Burn

True Vermilion

The Dark Shill

A Stack of Sawbucks

The Hillside Roble

The Peroxide Pomp

The Incidental Twin

Brawl in Bardo

The Window-Shade Job

The Convenient Patsy

The Artisanal Grifter

Shrink in the Shadows

Project Chartreuse

From a Desert Playa

The Tired Canary

A Desperate Frame-up

Trail of the Blue Agave

The Saucer-Heads

The Satin Squeeze Play

Chiseler in Jade

Subscribe to the Slater Ibáñez Books newsletter: slaternews.dagmarmiura.com

Chiseler in Jade

Chiseler in Jade

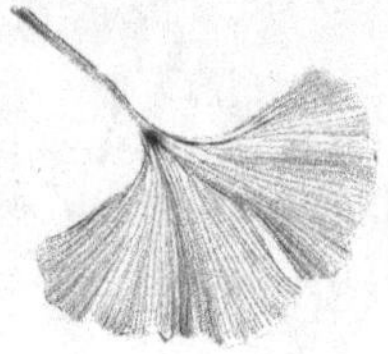

George Bixley

DAGMAR
MIURA
LOS ANGELES

Published by Dagmar Miura
Los Angeles
www.dagmarmiura.com

Chiseler in Jade

First published 2024

ISBN: 978-1-956744-41-5

ONE

T HE MIDDLE SEAT WAS always a drag, but at least it was a short flight, and he'd be on the ground at LAX in an hour. Slater knew it was his own damn fault, as he'd made a last-minute decision to bolt, claiming he had work to do. He didn't really need to get back to LA, and Pike was only staying another couple of days, but Esther stressed him out, made him feel like he had to be on good behavior all the time.

The guy in the window seat had been dozing since Slater had sat down, and now he woke up, and stretched, and turned to him.

"Where are we?"

Slater eyed him sidelong. "Row 24."

"OK, but … where is this plane going?"

"It'll come to you," he said, and looked away.

"Seriously—I don't know."

"Are you kidding me?"

"I'm not," he said, his tone rising.

"We're headed to LAX."

"From?"

"Albuquerque." Slater frowned. "How can you not know that?"

The guy gestured to the window. "And it's night-time."

"We left at eight. We're getting in at nine fifteen."

"What's your name?"

"Slater."

"That doesn't sound familiar."

"Why would it? I never saw you before I boarded this tub."

"I don't actually know what my name is."

"Wow." Slater gave him the once-over. From the look on his face the guy wasn't messing with him. In his early forties, maybe, he was dressed up, in a sharp brown suit that looked tailored. His Black hair was in tidy curls with a fade above his ears. That wasn't cheap to maintain either.

"Did you take something?" Slater said. "One of those blackout sleeping pills?"

"How would I know? I don't remember anything."

"You wouldn't have made it past the TSA without an ID."

He patted his chest, then pulled a wallet out of an inner jacket pocket. Not opening it, he handed it over.

Slater scoffed, and flipped it open, and dug through the contents. There was two hundred in cash in the main pocket, and a little window pouch with a driver's license.

"The State of California says you're allowed to drive." He studied the card. "Buckminster Mainwaring. Ouch. If I had a handle like that I'd want to forget it too." Slater eyed him. "Does that sound familiar?"

The guy furrowed his brow and shook his head.

"It has your picture and your address. I know this street. It's up the hill from the reservoir in Silver Lake. That means you have money. I can tell that from your clothes too." He held up another card. "This gym is totally bougie. You have more than one high-end credit card, and a national park pass." Folding it closed, he handed the wallet back. "You're a fancy lad, Buckminster."

He tucked it into his jacket. "None of this sounds familiar."

"Does your head hurt? Maybe you fell and banged it on something."

Once he'd groped his hair with both hands, he said, "My head is fine. Maybe it's a vortex. If I really was in Albuquerque, maybe there's a vortex there that messed up my brain."

"A vortex."

He swirled a finger in the air. "A concentrated area of psychic power. They're all over the Southwest."

"That just sounds like bullshit. It has to be drugs. You took something. You know, a really good rule for dopers is to stick to one drug at a time. Mix the wrong ones and you stop breathing." Slater raised his eyebrows. "Or lose your memory."

"What am I going to do?"

"I'd go to urgent care."

"I don't want to do that. They'll lock me up."

Slater sighed and closed his eyes for a moment. He knew it was probably a mistake to get involved, but this guy, this situation—it was just too compelling.

"I can drive you to your address in Silver Lake. It's not far from my place. Maybe somebody there will be able to explain things."

———◆———

AS THE PASSENGERS UP front started to deplane, Slater said, "Did you bring a carry-on?"

"I'm not sure."

"We can wait for everybody else to get off, then see if there's anything left."

Once the last passengers had shuffled past their row, Slater rose and pulled down his satchel. "I'm not seeing any other bags."

"I must not have one."

When they were outside the terminal, Slater led him across the roadway to the parking structure. His Continental was right where he'd left it. It was a classic '70s model, in a beautiful shade of cloudy blue, moody even under the fluorescent lights. He hadn't had it for long, as it was a replacement for his beloved Thunderbird. It had breathed its last after someone had sabotaged the brakes on a previous job. This baby had the same engine, the same chassis, so it felt comfortably familiar. He unlocked the passenger door and then walked around to the driver's side.

"This is quite the car," Buckminster said, as they both climbed in.

"I know."

At the kiosk on the way out, Slater rolled down his window and handed over the ticket.

"Two hundred forty-eight," the attendant said.

He dug his wad of cash from the front pocket of his jeans and handed over some C-notes, then folded his change and stuffed it away as the arm swung up.

"How long were you in Albuquerque?"

"Four days," Slater said.

"That seems like a great deal of money for four days of parking."

"That's the cost of parking right at the terminal."

"Maybe you're a fancy lad too."

He shoulder-checked as he merged onto the roadway. "Only when it comes to my ride."

"It doesn't really fit with your Mexican vibe. The jeans and the leather jacket."

Slater heard it all the time—he had his father's dark Latin coloring, his black hair, and the assumptions started from there.

"It's vinyl, not leather. And I'm not Mexican. Obviously you haven't forgotten how to be a racist dick."

He looked over at him and frowned. "I'm not racist."

"How would you know?" Slater said intently.

He got on the 105 and merged left into the carpool lane, the big vehicle's engine humming contentedly, serene and confident at highway speed. While they were rolling through downtown, he gestured to the office towers.

"Does any of this look familiar?"

"I guess so. I mean, I know where we are."

As he turned into the driveway at the address on Buckminster's license, a sprawling low-slung house with Spanish roof tile came into view. The yard had well-established ficus hedges and an island of birds of paradise, the orange flower spikes briefly illuminated by his headlights as he pulled in.

"There's no cars here," Slater said.

"You have to come inside with me."

Shifting into Park, he killed the engine and climbed out.

"Do you have keys on you?" Slater said.

He patted the pockets of his suit pants as they walked to the front door and eventually pulled out a jumbled ring of them.

Slater tried one of the keys in the deadbolt, then the one next to it. "If there's an alarm and you need a code, we're screwed."

"Well, you can't stop now."

Eventually one of them fit, and he twisted it in the lock, and pushed open the door. No alarm sounded. Slater led the way in and flicked on the room lights.

"Hello," he called, and they both stood there listening, but there was no answer, no sound of movement, only silence.

This was the living room, he saw, looking around, with adobe-colored tile floors and dark beams across the ceiling. Inside and out it was a classic Spanish colonial.

"I know this place," Buckminster said.

"You should. You have a key, and it's where you told the DMV you live."

He pulled off his suit jacket and tossed it on the back of one of the club chairs as he walked deeper into the house. Following him, Slater watched as he reached for a switch and flicked on the room lights. This was the kitchen. Buckminster opened a cupboard and pulled out a bottle.

"You like scotch?"

"I'm not going to lie to you," Slater said, resting his hands on his hips. "I like it a lot."

He grabbed two lowball tumblers from another cupboard and poured a finger into each.

"You knew where the lights were," Slater said, "and the booze, and the glasses."

"I think things are starting to come back."

He handed one of the tumblers to him, and Slater tapped it against his glass, then stepped back into the living room and over to the picture window. Taking a sip, he relished the delicious nutty burn. This was quality stuff.

Down below the dark sprawl of the reservoir spread out, and beyond it the glittering lights of the houses on the opposite hillside.

"This is quite the view, Mainwaring. Whatever else you've got going on, you're rich."

"It's pronounced *man*-wearing, not *mane*-wearing. And I'm not rich. I'm comfortable."

Slater stepped back to the lounge furniture and dropped into a club chair. "Rich people always say that. It just means you're not megarich."

"I'm remembering more."

"Like how to pronounce your name."

He sat on the sofa across from Slater and sipped from his glass. "Everybody calls me Bucky. I'm in real estate."

"You sell it?"

"Right. And help people buy it."

"That explains the big house."

"I remember my family, and my car."

"It wasn't in the driveway."

"I must have left it at the airport. Or maybe it's in Albuquerque. Is that a long drive?"

"Twelve hours."

Bucky frowned. "I couldn't have done that."

"You don't remember anything from today?"

"Not yet. I remember what's stressing me out, though. It might be connected. Maybe I tried to block it and lost everything else in the process."

"What's stressing you out?"

"Why would you care?" He threw up a hand. "We just met."

Slater waggled his tumbler. "I'm not done with my scotch, and it sounds like it might be an interesting story. Don't take this the wrong way, Bucky, but you're a pretty intriguing person."

TWO

Bucky scoffed. "There's this guy. Chad. The fucker is blackmailing me."

"Blackmailing you for what?" Slater said.

"Sex and drugs. He took photos of us naked together, and now he's threatening to send them to people at my church."

"Your church doesn't know you're on dick?"

"They know I'm gay, but I don't want them to see me having sex and shooting up in a toilet stall. I'm a deacon."

"Show me the photo."

Bucky shook his head. "No way."

"Where did this happen?"

"I was at a nightclub. It's mostly a straight place but it's mixed."

"Do you make a habit of shooting up? Maybe the

dope is what erased your memory."

"I'm not a junkie," he said, raising his voice. "It was a setup. We did some ecstasy, and I was feeling great. He took me into the men's room to make out. The next thing I know he's got a syringe."

"He injected you?"

"He just handed it to me. And then there was a flash of light. Someone took the photo while I had my pants down, my dick hanging out, and a syringe in my hand."

"Then he sent you the photo and demanded cash," Slater said.

"That's about it."

"I can look into this guy. It's kind of what I do for work." He waved at the room. "Obviously you can afford to pay me."

"What kind of work do you do?"

"I'm an insurance investigator," Slater said. "It means I dig into fraud and the lowlifes who do it."

Bucky shook his head. "There's no point. You'll never be able to get the images deleted. He'll have copies in six different places."

"Even so, I can mess him up, and threaten him. Maybe he'll back off. Does he carry a firearm?"

"I've never seen him with one." His eyes flicked up and down Slater's form. "I bet you can be intimidating."

"When I need to be. Where does Chad work?"

"I have no idea. I met him in that nightclub, but when he wanted payment, he summoned me to a dive bar on Wilcox in Hollywood."

"The Blue Dragon?" Slater said.

"How do you know that place?"

"It's been there forever, and the beer is cheap."

"Well, Chad holds court there."

"What does he look like?"

"I have a photo of him." Bucky pulled out his phone and tapped at it, then sat up and handed it across the coffee table.

The image on the screen was a man's head in profile, and slightly blurry, but there was enough detail that he could definitely identify the guy. The bland Anglo type, he was in his twenties, with dark hair and a flat nose.

"This is in the Blue Dragon," Slater said. "I recognize the wallpaper."

"I took it surreptitiously on my way in to meet him."

"Do you know his last name?"

"No idea. I ran that photo through one of those facial recognition sites, but nothing came up. It's not a very good photo. The software asked for a full-face one."

"Can I text this to myself?"

"Knock yourself out. You really want to go after him?"

"I can poke around and see what's what."

"Just don't spook the guy so that he sends that photo to my church."

"That's the last thing a blackmailer wants to do," Slater said, tapping at the phone. "It would instantly cut off his revenue stream, and it would make it a whole lot more likely that you'd go to the cops. He'll avoid doing that unless he has no other options."

Handing the device back to Bucky, he pulled out his own phone and opened the text, adding a contact for Bucky Mainwaring. He texted back "Slater," then looked up.

"What else do you know about Chad?"

"I'm not sure." Bucky folded one leg over the other. "Maybe I'll be able to tell you something else when more of my memory comes back. What's it going to cost me?"

"Two grand to get started. We can reassess in a couple days. I don't need it now. It can wait till you remember where your bank is."

Bucky chuckled and waggled his glass. "Do you want another drink?"

"I do, but I can't. I have to drive."

"I was hoping to lower your inhibitions a little, and get a look at what's under that shirt."

"Are you hitting on me?"

Bucky raised his eyebrows. "You're not into guys? Or am I too swishy for you?"

"I don't mind swishy guys. They're usually conscientious in the sack." He waved a hand. "I'll fuck you, Bucky, if that's what you want. I don't need the Dutch courage. But I wonder if I could get charged with assault because you have diminished capacity. I don't need to be on the sex-crime registry."

"I'm the one who suggested it. Besides, who would call the cops on you?"

"How would you know? Can you be sure there's no husband or wife or side piece who's going to bust in and cap me?"

He chuckled. "I'm almost certain. I'm more concerned about that ring on your finger. Usually that means you're exclusive with somebody else."

Slater absently rubbed it with the tip of his

thumb. "It's true that I'm deeply embroiled in a multidimensional narrative complex. But one of the rules is that I can hook up with guys if he's out of town." He raised his eyebrows. "And he's out of town."

"What the hell is a narrative complex?"

"It's what squares would call a relationship, but it's much more intricate and meaningful. It operates in visible and unseen dimensions, ever expanding, its tendrils extending through time and space."

"OK, then." Bucky chuckled. "What's your man like?"

"Let's not talk about him." Slater sat up and drained his glass, then rose. "I want to talk about you. What do you want to do?"

"I kind of like the take-charge thing. That you're a little pushy."

"I can do that." He stepped closer as Bucky got up. "How pushy?"

He held his gaze. "No bruises. But I can handle it rough."

"I feel you, Bucky." Moving fast, Slater slapped him hard, right and then left, a rapid kovac.

Bucky inhaled sharply. "You're a damn bully."

"You'll take it and you'll like it," he growled.

Slater grabbed his wrist and spun him around. Bucky yelped as he shoved his arm up his back. It was hard to weasel out of that position, and it gave him control of the guy. He frog-marched him a few steps but then stopped.

"Where's the bedroom?"

"I think it's that way," Bucky said, and jutted his chin toward the hall. He chuckled. "I guess we'll find out."

Pushing him down the hall, Slater spotted a bed in one of the rooms, and shoved him onto it, then pulled off his own shirt.

"What are you going to do?" Bucky said, leaning back on his elbows, his eyes wide.

"I'm going to fuck you till you scream." He stooped to untie his boots and pull them off.

"Please—be gentle with me."

Unbuttoning his jeans, Slater jutted his chin. "Shut your damn mouth."

Once he was undressed, he climbed on top of him, and slapped him again, and massaged his pecs through his shirt.

"This feels expensive," Slater said. "I kind of don't want to rip it off you."

"It does have buttons."

Slater growled and unbuttoned the shirt, then leaned back as Bucky sat up to pull it off. Soon he had his pants off, and grabbed his cock, already thick and engorged. Pressing their lips together, Slater forced his tongue into his mouth, and spent a minute in the intensity of it.

He sat back and squeezed their cocks together. "Do you have lube?"

"Can you wear a condom? They're in the drawer."

Reaching for the bedside table, he scrabbled to find one, and rolled it on his rock-hard cock, then grabbed the lube and slapped Bucky again.

"Stop it," he yelped, pushing on Slater's chest.

Shoving his knees up, Slater loomed over him and slowly started to penetrate him, watching his face to gauge his reaction. He took his time, easing into it, and eventually was deep inside him. He grabbed

Bucky's wrists and held tight as he started to pound him. As he got into it, Bucky struggled with him, then yelped, his head arching back.

He'd climaxed, Slater realized, and pounded harder until he came himself, straining into him. Flopping beside him on the bed, he folded his arm over his eyes.

"That was amazing," Bucky said, breathing hard.

"You popped when I was inside you. That doesn't happen very often."

"It's because you're so handsome."

Slater chuckled. "You haven't forgotten how to lay your mack down."

"I think it's about being bullied. Like in high school. Somehow it turned into a turn-on. You've got the dick-swagger to pull it off."

He grunted but didn't respond, trying to tune him out. The debrief, the processing, the yap-yap-yap—he hated this part.

A while later, Bucky said, "Want to shower?"

"I just need a towel."

"Through there."

Slater got up, and once he'd cleaned up, walked back into the bedroom, and snatched up his shirt, and pulled it on. A huge chunk of milky quartz sat on top of a dresser near the bathroom door, and Slater picked it up to look it over.

"That's to keep the energy in the room positive," Bucky said. He was stretched out on his side, head propped on his arm, watching him.

"Who knew a rock could vacuum up bad vibes?" He set it down again.

"It doesn't vacuum them. It channels them into

different kinds of energy."

"Of course. I should have noticed that happening." He pulled on his jeans. "Are you going to be OK alone tonight?"

"I'm fine. Maybe I'll remember more after a good sleep."

Once he'd tied his boots, Slater walked out and climbed in the Continental, then drove to his house. It was nearby, off Sunset, down the hill from the stadium. A big obnoxious box, it was out of step with the historic neighborhood, built by some idiot gentrifiers who'd soon gone broke. He'd never admit it out loud, but he knew he counted as a gentrifier too, since he'd bought the place from the bank. He was just another cog in the perpetual mechanism of displacement.

The ground floor had a garage, and he nosed inside, killing the engine and climbing out as the door rolled down. A flight of stairs led up to the bedrooms, and another flight above that was the kitchen and living space and an outdoor deck.

Slater trudged up to the top floor and pulled open the kitchen cupboard where they kept the booze, his own cheap-ass bourbon and Pike's better-quality scotch. He couldn't afford to buy that regularly because he drank so damn much of it. In the big picture he was cutting back, and there was a plan for that, complete with booze rules, so for now he had to stick to the applejack.

He'd already had a snort tonight, but technically that was a work meeting, so the booze rules were reset, and he poured his daily ration into a glass. The paltry half inch made him scowl.

At the other end of the big empty room, near the

French doors to the deck, was a set of lounge furniture, and he carried his tumbler over and sat on the sofa to pull off his boots and his socks, then wriggled his toes in the patch of artificial grass that stood in for an area rug. It felt pretty close to real Bermuda grass except that it had no moisture in it.

Taking a sip from his tumbler, he relished the heady burn, and coughed a little at the sharp vapor. Even the cheap bourbon warmed his belly and made him smile.

Digging out his phone, he called Pike.

"Did you make it home?" Pike said when he picked up.

"I miss you. I had to go into the laundry basket to sniff your dirty clothes."

"You could have just stayed another day or two, and gone back with me."

"I can't stay away from LA for too long," Slater said. "Out there I felt like I was going to dry out. Like I'd wind up a carcass out in the desert."

"Plus my mother makes you nervous."

"There's that."

"Deep down I think she likes you," Pike said.

"I was trying hard to be civil. It's not something I normally do."

"She respects the no-bullshit approach."

"That's because she's the same way," Slater said. "Esther doesn't have time for fools and stupes."

They talked a while longer, and Slater told him about how he'd met Bucky, and driven him home, omitting the part about hooking up. Finally Pike said, "I should go to bed. It's late here."

"As you're going to sleep, I want you to visualize

me rock hard and deep inside you. My mouth on your neck, my hands on your pecs."

"Stop that," Pike said, lowering his voice. "You'll get me all wound up."

"I'm wrapping my hand around your cock. My other hand is on your neck."

"Oh, man. You want me to have to rub one out before I go to sleep? Is that what you want?"

"Whatever it takes," Slater said. "Just don't forget me. Don't forget what's waiting here for you."

Once he'd ended the call, he got up and went to the kitchen and poured more bourbon. It was beyond his ration, but he needed it—he was all dehydrated from flying. Taking a satisfying slurp, he walked back through the big empty room to the French doors. People had told him he needed to put furniture in here, fill it up with something, but he liked it just fine with nothing in it, bare wood floors and lots of space.

Standing at the French doors, he looked out at the tops of the towers of the Financial District glittering in the distance and took a long sip. It felt good to be sated, the smell of that loopy guy still on his skin, the bourbon on his palate. For a while, anyway. Then it started all over again, as predictable as the sunrise.

THREE

WHEN SLATER WOKE, HE was in his bed, with bright morning light streaming in the windows. His head didn't hurt—he must have stuck close to his ration.

His business partner, Max, had asked him to sit in on a meeting, but that wasn't until the afternoon. Mostly they shared the office and other resources, and worked their own cases, but once in a while they collaborated. He regularly wanted to punch Max in the face, but then he felt that way about most people. They'd built a rapport, him and Max, and trust. Max had saved his ass more than once.

Forcing himself out of bed, he got dressed and headed upstairs, and grabbed a frozen bagel from the Frigidaire. Once he'd split it in two, and shoved it in the toaster, he fired up the coffee machine. When it had brewed he carried his mug and the bagel outside and sat at the patio table on the deck. It was cold out here, even in the late morning, with the sun blazing low in the sky on its winter arc.

Eventually he hustled down to the garage, and got behind the wheel of the Continental, and twisted the key in the ignition. He loved the sound of its engine, throaty and calm and always consistent. Backing into the street, he waited for the garage door to roll down, then drove downtown to the Fashion District and parked in the surface lot across from his office.

The century-old building had once been exclusively offices, but the neighborhood had changed, and today it was mostly a warren of small garment factories. Nobody was around the lobby, and the hallway upstairs was quiet, as Sunday was the only day the factories were idle.

As he twisted his key in the deadbolt, he admired their names on the office door:

SLATER IBÁÑEZ
MAXIMILLIAN CONROY
INVESTIGATIONS

The suite was three small rooms, a front desk that their operatives sometimes used plus an office for each of them. Slater stepped into Max's to find him sitting behind his desk. Beefy and with the mousy brown hair so many white guys had, Max was wearing his brown suit and a dark-red necktie. His sidearm bulged under his jacket—unlike Slater, he was a licensed PI, and had a carry permit.

Slater dropped into one of the guest chairs. "I hate that suit."

"I have to wear it sometimes. I have a system." He whirled a finger in the air. "It's in the rotation."

"I'm going to have to take you suit shopping."

"Christ, not that again. It really stressed me out."

He raised his eyebrows. "So burn that suit, and I won't have to force the issue. You know Vanessa will back me up. She has to look at it too. I bet she'd be down for a clothing intervention."

Max laughed. "The last thing I need is you two ganging up on me."

"So what are you working on?"

He sat up. "The City of Lennox hired me to look into a person they're planning to honor with a street sign. They're naming a square after her."

"I've seen those. They put up a sign at a plain old intersection and call it a square."

"Exactly. There's really no squares in this town. The city is comfortable with that little lie, but some conflicting facts came up in their research into her background, so they called me in."

"Who's the pigeon?"

"A drag performer named Gladys Rayon," Max said.

Slater chuckled. "That's a good one. 'Glad it's rayon.' Like you can afford to ruin that dress because it's not a more expensive fabric."

"It makes you wonder what she's up to in that dress."

"A hint of sleaze. It's clever."

"The people at city hall said she was a smart cookie," Max said.

"Is that who we're meeting today?"

"I actually hired a historian. She'll be here soon."

Slater frowned. "How old is this drag queen?"

"She's no kid. The sign is going up next to a doughnut shop where she led a sit-in during the early 1970s. The location of it is where the facts don't quite line up. Today it's a car wash, but there's evidence that the shop never existed."

"So the sit-in story could be bullshit."

Max spread his hands. "We'll hear what the historian has to say, but the city wants a deeper background check. Arrests and felonies are easy to look up. They want the other stuff."

"The desk jockeys want to know if there's dirt on her that never made it to court."

"I figured this is your world."

"I definitely know a few drag queens," Slater said. "I can make some calls. If she's been around that long, people will know her."

"Are you working right now?"

"I picked up a lulu," he said, and told Max about meeting Bucky on the airplane.

"That's nuts." Max frowned. "It has to be drugs. Why else would your mind just go blank?"

"I hear you, brother."

There was a knock at the door, and Max rose and stepped around his desk, out to the front office.

"Iris," he said as he pulled it open.

Slater got up and stood outside Max's office, watching as Iris beamed and grasped Max's hand. Tall and imposing, she was wearing her Black hair in neat little dreads, and a caftan in a sky-blue print over her bulky frame. In one hand she was carrying a slender brown zippered briefcase.

"I thought I had the wrong address," Iris said.

"This building is all sewing factories."

"I know it's gritty," Max said, "but it allows us to keep a low profile."

"It's probably good for me to come down out of the ivory tower once in a while."

"This is my business partner," Max said. "He's helping me out with research."

"I saw your name on the door," she said, and greeted him, then waved at the room. "I love the deco furniture."

"It's vintage," Max said.

Slater had to suppress a smile. The guy wouldn't even have known what that word meant when they'd first met. This business had brought them both a long way.

Iris pointed to the little plaster statue on the front desk, next to the computer monitor—a skeleton wearing a crown and holding a scythe at the ready. "This fellow is Latin American."

"He's become something of a mascot for our office," Max said.

"His name is Rey Pascual." Slater put his hands on his hips. "People always think he's the narco saint, but he's not. He's the king of the graveyard."

Max beckoned her into his office, and Slater waited for her to sit, then shifted the other guest chair on an angle so that he could see them both.

"I asked Slater to sit in because I wanted to get his insights as well as yours," Max said, rolling his chair closer to his desk.

"The part he's not saying is that I'm queer," Slater said, "so I should know something about drag queens."

Iris leaned toward him to briefly touch his knee. "I'm so happy to hear you use that word. Academia is like an echo chamber. I'm never quite sure what's going on in the real world."

"Max and I definitely specialize in keeping it real. Where's your ivory tower?"

"I'm a professor at Cal State Dominguez Hills."

Slater nodded. "Good school."

"Not everyone would agree with you."

"It's a public university. By definition that's a good thing."

Iris raised her eyebrows. "Where would a guy like you get an idea like that?"

His instinct was to snap back with an angry retort, something like *The same place you learned to typecast people, brainiac*, but he swallowed that. "My mother is all about public education. She says that schools should educate people rather than reinforce the establishment. For her that makes UC and Cal State the greatest educational achievement in history."

Max eyed Iris. "In addition to being an educator, she's evidently also a pinko."

Iris laughed and turned to Slater. "Did you go to UC or Cal State?"

"I went to community college to learn how to do the gardening for people who went to UC or Cal State."

"Tell us about Gladys Rayon," Max said.

Iris shifted in her chair. "It's a clever stage name. Like many drag pseudonyms, it's a play on words. Gladys Rayon," she said, and then slowly, "'Glad it's rayon.' That's a reference to fashion."

"Lo, the truth revealed," Slater said. "I never

would have been able to figure that out."

Max sat up in his chair, stifling a smirk.

"I did some reading in the archives," Iris said. "The city thought there was a contradiction." She looked from him to Max, holding their gaze in turn. This woman had clearly spent time in front of a lecture hall. "They concluded that the doughnut shop wasn't where the sit-in was supposed to have happened. Their records showed the shop's address to be several blocks away, technically in an unincorporated area outside the City of Lennox. That made the whole story suspicious."

"You wouldn't want to put up a sign for something that didn't even happen in your town," Max said.

Iris nodded. "In reality there was a doughnut shop there until the fall of 1973, when it moved to the better-known address."

"So the city got their wires crossed."

"Correct. The story still holds together." She lifted her briefcase and zipped it open. "I made copies of the source documents for you."

"What was the sit-in about?" Slater said.

"The place was open all night," she said. "The drag queens and other queer folks would go in there after the bars closed to sober up and socialize. The police would regularly come by and arrest people."

"For what?"

"Well, people got arrested for cross-dressing until 1974, and lewd conduct was a pretty vague charge. They could put you in jail for the weekend even if the DA decided there wasn't enough evidence to prosecute."

"So they rioted."

"More like they refused to leave the shop when the police showed up. That got them media attention, and things started to change."

"Is Gladys Rayon still performing?" Slater said.

"Surprisingly, yes, even though he retired from his job with the DWP."

"They have extremely good benefits," Max said. "You can collect your pension and your salary at the same time for years and years and years. They live like royalty."

They listened to Iris outline more details of her research, and finally she handed Max a sheaf of paper.

Once she'd left, Slater stepped over to his own office, its walls painted turquoise in contrast to Max's warm yellow, with a matching deco-era desk. Resting his arms on the blotter, he eyed the plaster statue next to his monitor, a rendition of Pollux standing with a horse. Normally he wouldn't have put up with a second tchotchke cluttering up the office, but it had been a gift from Pike. The corresponding statue of Castor was on Pike's desk.

Scrolling through the contacts on his phone, he found Jack, a hookup from a while back who also did drag. He listened to it ring, glad that the guy picked up.

"Hey, handsome. I haven't heard from you in ages," Jack said.

"Yeah, it's been a while. Listen, I need some information on a local drag queen."

"Ooh, gossip. I love it."

"It has to be factual. I'll pay you for it if you need to do any work."

"Who are we talking about?"

"A performer named Gladys Rayon."

"I don't know her, but I think I've heard that name. Is she around my age?"

"Much older. Like war surplus. She has to be in her seventies."

"What kind of tea do you need?"

"Don't worry about legal stuff," Slater said. "I'm interested in what the legal system never heard about. Sexual abuse, thievery, anything shady."

"People love to keep track of all that," Jack said. "Give me a couple days."

Rising, Slater stood in Max's doorway. "I set the wheels in motion."

"Thanks, buddy."

He waved an arm. "It goes both ways."

FOUR

OSING THE CONTINENTAL OUT of the parking lot, Slater headed toward Silver Lake, and soon pulled into Bucky's driveway. He'd seen the birds of paradise last night, but in the dark he hadn't noticed the plumeria growing next to the house. It was almost completely defoliated.

Looking around at the sky, he took a second to get his bearings. This wall faced south. It was surprising the shrub was doing so well here. Usually they could only handle full sun at the coast. Inland like this they had to be planted in the shade.

Squatting for a moment, he probed the soil around its trunk with his fingers. It was bone dry. Whoever was taking care of Bucky's yard knew enough not to water it in winter.

He rose and slapped the dust off his hand against

his jeans, then rang the bell. A minute later Bucky pulled open the door. He was wearing chinos and a navy-blue polo shirt with an obnoxious prominent logo on the breast.

"Remember me?" Slater said.

"Of course." He flashed a smile. "Come in."

Slater followed him into the kitchen.

"I'm just having a sandwich. Do you want something?"

"I don't. Unless the java's on."

Bucky pulled a mug from a cupboard and handed it to him, gesturing to the coffeemaker on the counter. Even that was upscale looking—brushed metal, a milk-foaming attachment, a hopper for whole coffee beans on top. He poured himself a mugful from the carafe and sat across from him at the little kitchen table.

Bucky held his sandwich with both hands. "Thank you for taking care of me last night. I felt quite lost."

"It was pretty damn odd. Do you remember hiring me?"

"Of course I do. I knew you were OK. Your aura was intensely red."

"You could see that," Slater said, "but you couldn't remember your own name?"

"My doctor said the memory loss was transient." He gestured with his sandwich. "I saw her this morning."

"Is she the kind of doctor that takes your blood pressure, or the kind that uses the *I Ching* and a psychic plunger to unclog your aura?"

He frowned. "She's a medical doctor. I think she's right. Other memories are coming back."

Slater slurped at his coffee. "Fuck me—that's good joe. I bet that coffeemaker cost more than my car."

Bucky chuckled. "I like beautiful things."

"Does your doc know why it happened?"

"She doesn't think I was affected by a psychic vortex either. Like you said, it was likely drug-induced. I have to assume that Chad drugged me. He's that kind of person."

"Was he in Albuquerque too? Do you remember why you were there?"

"I don't know that. I remember all about my life before, but there's still a couple of days missing before I woke up on that plane."

He folded his arms. "Did you use your credit cards? There'll be a record of where you were."

Bucky's eyebrows shot up. "That's such a good idea." He took a bite of his sandwich, then set it down and pulled out his phone, and tapped at it for a minute. "I haven't used my cards since early last week," he said finally.

"What about the location history on your phone?"

"I have that switched off. I don't need big tech keeping track of my whereabouts."

"They're still collecting the data and selling it. Turning it off just means you can't see it. They still can. Give me your phone."

"Why?"

"I want to check something."

He hesitated, but handed it over, and Slater tapped at it, quickly connecting to a server run by his Russian tech supplier. It took a second to log into it, and download the tracking software, and then override the phone's security settings. The tracker was designed to run in the background, invisible to Bucky, and report the phone's location to Slater.

"What are you doing?" Bucky said.

It was taking a long time, but the install finally finished, and a bubble popped up with the words "окон. скрытый." When he tapped it, it disappeared.

"You definitely have location tracking turned off," he said, and handed it back.

"So how do you plan to go after Chad?" Bucky said. "You don't know anything about him."

"I'll start at the Blue Dragon. If he hangs out there, somebody will know him. The bartenders and the regulars."

He nodded. "Just keep me in the loop. I have some money for you."

Taking another bite, he rose, and through a mouthful of sandwich, added, "I'll be right back."

When he returned, he had a sheaf of C-notes, and set them on the table. Slater rose and scooped them up, folding them in half, and tucked them in the pocket of his jeans.

"You're not going to count it?"

"If you're messing with me, I know where you live."

"A veiled threat. So ominous." He cocked his head. "It fits with your aura. That kind of energy is exactly what Chad needs." As he walked him to the front door, Bucky added, "I had a lot of fun last night. Maybe we can do that again."

"Maybe. I can't get sticky about it. You know why."

"That ring on your finger."

"You don't need to be interested in me anyway. I'm trouble."

"A bad boy," Bucky offered.

Slater paused on the doorstep and met his gaze. "Real bad."

"That just makes you more interesting, not less."

"If you're such a dick-hound, why is there no man in your life? You're smoking hot, and you have money. That's like gay catnip. Or maybe you just haven't remembered him yet?"

He guffawed, his tone deep. "There's no man. Mostly I like things the way they are."

It was too early to go to that dive bar to ask about Chad, Slater decided, climbing into the Continental. Instead he drove to his house, even though the place felt empty and lifeless with Pike out of town.

In the garage he grabbed a hand trimmer and a leaf rake, then pulled a trash bag out of the box of them on the workbench. Climbing two flights to the deck, he spent some time in the fading daylight pruning the California fuchsia he'd planted in wooden boxes along the low wall that surrounded the space, trimming it up for spring. He needed to get his hands in the dirt once in a while. It was contemplative work, and gave him time to think, and balanced out all the dealings with lowlifes.

Bucky wasn't especially annoying, and he hadn't wanted to punch the guy in the face even once, despite the cluelessness and the crystals and the assessment of his aura. Maybe he was getting soft, getting too tolerant, distracted by Pike and their narrative complex. It wasn't really unethical to put tracking software on him either, despite the fact that Bucky was his client, as the guy didn't keep track of it himself. Having access to that information might illuminate things.

Eventually he had the fuchsia looking tight, and as twilight faded he raked the detritus into the leaf bag, and carried it down to the green bin. After he'd washed up, he climbed in the Continental and backed into the street, and got on the freeway, headed for Hollywood.

The Blue Dragon had a long bar at the back and a couple of booths and tables, he remembered. It should be easy enough to position himself where he could interrogate the bartender about Chad. He found a meter up the block on Wilcox and pulled in, then walked toward the bar. As he passed the walkway next to the building, in the shadows farther in, he caught sight of movement. There were a couple of people there. It wasn't an alley for vehicles, just a wide passage to a courtyard and some businesses. Those were offices and shops, he knew, and they'd all be shut down at this hour.

A woman, he realized, peering into the darkness, and she was trying to pull herself away from a man. He had a hand tight around her wrist, and yanked her closer, the pair of them spinning around like dancers. The guy slapped her face.

Stepping into the walkway, Slater strode toward them and balled his fists. The man was absorbed in the conflict, growling something at her, and facing away from Slater—he never saw it coming.

As he stepped up, Slater barked, "Hey."

The guy turned toward him, and seeing him in profile, in the instant before he struck, Slater recognized the ratty hair, the flat nose. This was Chad. Slater threw a fast right hook, connecting with his jaw, and Chad's head spun. He stumbled toward the wall and lost his balance when he connected with it, tumbling onto his butt on the concrete.

The woman took a few steps back and shouted, "Prick."

As Chad got to his feet, he stayed low, in a crouch, his eyes wide and darting around the space. Slater knew that look: disorientation and raw fear, just before the anger set in. Suddenly Chad bolted, rushing past him, and ran out of the walkway onto the street.

Slater watched him go, then turned to the woman. Lean and Latin, she pushed her dark hair back with a hand, and took a breath.

"You OK?"

"What did you do that for?" she demanded.

"Why did I punch him? So that he wouldn't break your arm. He's a damn lowlife."

She jabbed a finger at Slater. "It's you. You're the lowlife." And louder, "You. Stay out of my business."

He scoffed as she strode toward the street. At least she went the opposite way from where Chad had gone. The walkway wasn't lit, and he looked around, peering into the gloom farther in, but no one else was here. No one had seen the altercation. Before he walked out, the glint of glass caught his eye, in the shadows against the wall where Chad had tumbled, and he stepped closer to look. Someone had dropped their phone.

Stooping, he scooped it up. It had a purple silicone case, and the screen lit up when he tapped the power button. It hadn't been here long—it had to belong to Chad or that ingrate with all the hair. This was way more valuable than any interview with a bartender, even if it was the woman's. He stuffed it in his hip pocket and walked back to his car.

Once he was behind the wheel he looked over the device. The lock-screen image was a logo, the word VOLES in stylized blocky purple letters. That had to be a sports team. It was the same color as the phone case. It was Chad's phone, he realized—the woman had her own in her hand when she'd chewed him out.

It was still early enough, he decided, and dug out his phone, and dialed Andy, his operative who did what he claimed was "deep research," even though objectively it mostly amounted to hacking.

Andy picked up the call. "I prefer text communication."

"Fuck that," Slater said. "Can I come by? It's work."

"It's late."

"So charge me your evening rate. You're going to chisel me anyway. You know you will, and I know you will."

"You get excellent value for what you … pay me, Ibáñez. I'm at my place. Come on over."

Starting the engine, he pulled into the street, and headed back downtown to Broadway, and parked in the surface lot behind Andy's building. The attendant made him pay the ridiculous flat rate. In the daytime it was priced high for people visiting offices and retailers in the neighborhood, but at night it was even higher for all the bars and restaurants.

He walked around to Andy's building, and up to his loft, and knocked on the door. When Andy pulled it open his wild brown hair was a perfect mess, and his face bore several days of stubble. He flashed that easy smile. Such a beautiful man.

Andy was wearing his usual T-shirt and boxer shorts, even though he kept the place cold, because his metabolism ran hot. Slater followed him into the lone room with tall multipane windows that looked onto the square. Those and the scuffed board floors dated to the last century, when it had been a textile warehouse. Dropping into his gaming chair, Andy scooted closer to his array of computer monitors, and Slater stood nearby, between the desk and the bed.

"Are you working tonight?" he said.

"Mostly just messing around."

Slater handed him the phone. "This isn't mine. I want to get into it."

"The easiest way to do that is to … guess the PIN or the password."

"I don't know the guy, so that's impossible."

"You must know something about him."

"I know he's a lowlife. I think he's straight—I saw him roughing up a woman tonight."

"Straight guys are simpleminded," Andy said. "Look at his … lock screen image." He turned the screen toward him.

"Voles. It has to be some kind of sports team."

"I think it's football. Not pro ball but not … high school either. The owner is obviously a fan. What do … fans say?"

"I'm stupid and I waste time on pointless bull-shit?" Slater said.

"That's what you say. Think about sports people."

He pursed his lips for a moment. "They say stuff like 'Batter up,' and '*dee*-fense,' and 'Go team.'"

"Or 'Go Voles,'" Andy said. "Try that." His lack of fine motor control made it laborious for him to do, and he handed the phone over.

"It wants a PIN."

"Tap 'Forgot PIN' and it'll ask for a … password. Wait—and type 'Go Voles' in all lowercase. Guys who obsess over … sports don't have time for capital letters."

Andy was right—when he hit the button marked FORGOT PIN, a password window came up.

"Wait," Andy said. "He might have an app that photographs … anyone who enters a wrong password. Turn it away from your face."

Slater angled the screen toward the windows, then typed the phrase, looking at it sidelong. When he tapped ENTER, the screen resolved into a grid of icons.

"Fuck me. Ha!" He held the screen toward Andy.

"It worked." Andy laughed, his random muscle movements intensifying for a moment. "Right on."

"You're a freaking genius, son. I knew you'd know what to do. 'Go Voles.' People are so fucking stupid."

"I'd say people are predictable, not stupid. Are you … going to give it back to the guy?"

"I think so."

"Before you do that, I can … copy all the accessible data, all the … texts and the contact list."

"That would be great," Slater said, and handed it over.

Andy connected the phone to a cable, then spent a minute at his computer, focused on his screens. Eventually he swiveled to the desk drawers, jand rolled one open, and dug out a padded brown envelope. Disconnecting the phone, he tucked it inside.

"This has an RF-blocking lining," he said. "That

way the guy won't be … able to track it and come knock on your door."

"I never even thought of that. Can't we just put it in airplane mode?"

He handed it over. "That doesn't always switch off … all the radios."

"What if he tracks it this far?"

"It's a big building," Andy said. "He won't be able to figure out which unit it was in."

Slater folded the top of the envelope closed. "So where's spouse B? Is he staying late at the office already, and not answering his phone, and coming home drunk? You haven't been married that long."

"You're the only active drunk in my life, Ibáñez. He's having … dinner with his parents."

"They didn't invite you?" He frowned. "That seems harsh. Do you think Kyle poisoned them against you?"

Andy raised his voice. "I was invited. I chose not to go. We all … get along fine."

"I wonder, though. Sometimes when you look at the perfect porcelain vase up close, you can see all the little cracks."

"Stop talking about my in-laws. You should … focus on that hunk of man meat you've got smoldering at home."

"He's in Albuquerque with his mother for a couple days." Slater shifted on his feet. "When he's not around, I feel kind of sad. And you're on your own tonight too." He waved his arm. "Here we both are, and there's your bed."

"You are so full of bullshit. You just adapted your … sex addiction from mindless hookups onto

Pike." He raised his voice. "I'm not going to … let you break my heart again. I will not do it."

Watching him, Slater could feel his temples throbbing. He was breathing hard. That was the first time Andy had said it. Even though he knew that's what had happened, knew he'd hurt him, now that he'd actually spoken the words, somehow it was more real.

"Bye, beautiful," he said, and walked out.

———•———

NOSING THE CONTINENTAL OUT of the lot, Slater drove to his house, and hustled up the stairs, and grabbed his laptop. On the sofa he pulled off his boots and felt the fake grass under his feet. It still made him smile, the way Pike had chosen that to go under the coffee table. The guy was so perfectly odd sometimes.

He looked through the data that Andy had sent from Chad's phone, focusing on the texts. Tonight he'd been messaging someone named Liz. The terse exchange started with Chad's "Where you at" and then the response "On my way." The last message from Liz was "I'm outside." From the time stamp, she had to have sent it just minutes before Slater had pulled up at the Blue Dragon. Liz was the woman this putz had assaulted.

Next he scrolled through the photos. Lots of them were of football players, guys running around the gridiron wearing white and purple uniforms emblazoned with VOLES. These weren't taken from up in the stands. For some reason Chad had access to the field. He'd been standing on the sidelines.

Another series were photos of a group of people, Chad not among them, standing around a tall table cluttered with cocktail glasses and beer bottles. They were in a bar, with the harsh light of the camera flash illuminating their faces and highlighting the fact that most of them were glassy-eyed and wasted. All of them looked to be in their twenties, and strictly gender binary, the women dressed hoochie and the men dressed nightclub sleazy.

Slater quickly swiped through a long series of photos of plated food, then paused at a photo of a sheet of paper. It was a note, written in thick Sharpie, "IOU $500," with a scrawled signature. The top of the sheet was cut off but it looked like letterhead, with "Los Angeles 90017" in flat formal type with a simple ornament below it. He took a second to look it up. That zip code covered part of downtown, the Financial District. The signature on the note was an illegible scrawl, starting with a *W*, maybe, but no way could he parse the name.

Was Chad's surname in any of this stuff? Andy had sent the phone's contact list, and he scrolled through it, scanning the names, until he found the entry for Dad. There was another one for Mom, but neither had their names listed, or addresses, just phone numbers. Dad's entry had an office phone number too, and when he did a web search, the first result was a business-card entry on a job-networking website for William Newkirk-Sloane. It didn't get much Waspier than that. The listing said William was an actuary, but it didn't list an employer. Maybe that was a gig you could do freelance.

The shortcut to getting Chad's address was to

look at the phone's navigation app—most people had "home" marked. But taking the phone out of the radio-shielded package was risky. Maybe he could do it inside the envelope.

Sitting up, he opened the top and pulled it as wide as he could to reach inside, tapping at the screen and peering in at it. Chad did have a marker for home, and it was in Pasadena. He zoomed in on the map to get the street number. Sealing the envelope again, he pulled up a map on his computer. The address was near the Arroyo, and a street view showed a whole block of sprawling mansions. The house he'd marked as home was mostly hidden by shrubbery, but a trio of upper-floor gables was visible. This was an old-money house, from early in the last century, not a crib for a penny-ante grifter who hung out at a dive bar.

Property ownership was public record, and he dug around for a minute to find the details on that address. The owner was listed as William Newkirk-Sloane—that was Dad. So lowlife Chad was living with his parents.

Next Slater did a search online for that ingrate Liz and her phone number, but it didn't bring up anything useful. He sent Andy a text:

> Can you put an identity to this cell number? Owner's name is Liz.

Taking a breath, he folded his laptop closed, and rubbed his eyes, then dug out his phone and called Pike.

"Hey, forty-niner," Pike said when he picked up.

He asked about Slater's day, and Slater told him

about coming across Chad and Liz and finding the phone.

"I can't believe you went after the guy."

"She weighs like a buck forty," Slater said, "and this baboon was roughing her up. I wasn't just going to watch."

"One of the old-timers in my unit once told me, 'Never interfere in a boy-girl fight.' That seems like salient advice. What if he'd been armed?"

"I didn't think of that in the moment."

They talked a while longer, then ended the call, and Slater set his phone down on the faux grass. In the BP era, before Pike, this was the time of day he'd arrange a hookup. It was as easy as opening the app. Even though it fit with the sex rules they'd agreed to, he knew he shouldn't. It still pissed Pike off. That guy was everything, and everything should be enough.

Instead of grabbing his phone, he got up and padded over to the kitchen. Pulling out the fifth of bourbon, he poured his ration into a tumbler.

Fuck it, he decided. If he couldn't do a hookup, maybe he could bend the booze rules. Pike didn't love the fact that he drank a lot either, but he didn't push too hard on it. And he wasn't freaking here. Pouring another inch into the glass, he took a slurp, relishing that first burn in his throat, the heady fumes in his nose.

He went out onto the deck and stood at the low wall that surrounded the space, swirling the contents of his glass. It was cold out here. In the distance a police helicopter had its spotlight trained on the ground, the beam blue-white in the hazy air. It was far enough away that he could just hear the beat of the rotors above the dull background noise of the metropolis. Somebody down there was going to jail tonight.

Taking another slurp of the amber liquid, he watched the helicopter travel its slow orbit around whatever desperado or crisis it was focused on. He could feel the warm glow in his stomach starting to radiate outward, slowing things down. The energy-cleansing crystals, the flighty bullies, the relentless spotlights. Soon all the bullshit would be dialed down, muted, temporarily obscured.

SLATER'S ALARM DRAGGED HIM up to consciousness, and he sat up so that he wouldn't fall into sleep again. His head hurt, and when he swung his feet onto the floor, it pounded even worse. At least the room wasn't spinning. He didn't remember going to bed, but yesterday's clothes were strewn on the floor over by the closet.

"Damn it," he growled.

Eventually he forced himself to stand up, breathing deeply to keep his balance. In the bathroom mirror he glanced at the dark circles under his eyes, then popped some ibuprofen, and washed up, and got dressed. Upstairs, sitting at the dining table, he texted his Russian tech supplier, Svetlana:

Can you see me today?

Her response came a moment later, as Slater was hunched over with his elbows on the table, massaging his temples:

I do nothing but work.

Forcing himself out of the chair, he took the envelope with Chad's phone down to the garage. It still caught him off-guard sometimes to see the sleek blue Continental parked here, as his brain expected the Thunderbird. He missed that sweet ride.

After a few deep breaths, he popped it into Drive and backed into the street, and waited for the door to roll down, then headed for Glendale.

Svetlana's workshop was a low-slung structure on a gritty back street that hadn't yet been hit by the wave of gentrification. He parked the Continental in front and climbed out, taking a minute to look over the foliage climbing the front. He'd helped her find a landscaper to cover the aging building's peeling paint and sagging roofline. It was cheaper to plant fast-growing cedars and evergreen ivy than to rebuild or add some bogus facade. The ivy had grown in really well, completely covering the wall up to the roof, and the row of cedars fronting the sidewalk was neatly trimmed. That would keep the local bureaucrats off her back for a while at least.

Slater walked to the side street and around to the alley behind the building, where the real entrance was. As he rang the bell he looked up into the camera mounted overhead. The door lock snapped open, and he stepped into the gloomy antechamber and waited while he was scanned.

This was all tech Svetlana had built herself, outside

any industrial standards or government inspections. Hopefully it wasn't serving a Chernobyl level of radiation every time he did this. Soon the inner door lock snapped open, and he stepped inside.

The dank room had workbenches around the sides, littered with circuit boards and wire and plastic housing. Only the top few inches of the windows were exposed, and even then they were covered with heavy metal mesh. The place smelled like machine oil.

Standing near a computer on the workbench, Svetlana greeted him as he stepped in. Curvy, with her hair pulled back, she always wore bright colors. Today it was a yellow flower-print skirt and a pastel-blue top that showed a lot of cleavage.

"You have a new car," she said, her Slavic accent flattening the vowels, "and it's again an old car."

She must monitor the street out front with cameras, he realized, and she had to be watching closely if she'd seen him park.

"The Thunderbird died. I crashed it on the Newhall Grade."

She raised her eyebrows. "You weren't injured?"

"Lucky for me, I wasn't."

"Well, the blue is a lovely color." She waved at the thick envelope in his hand. "You have brought me a smartphone."

"You could tell from the scanner?"

"It's safe to take it out of the shielded envelope here. My whole building is an RF-proof Faraday cage."

"So you already know why I have it shielded," he said, and pulled it out of the envelope.

Svetlana shrugged and took it from him. "It's an

effective technique to hide the device."

"Can you install software that lets me see the texts and voice messages? I don't care about anything else."

"Do you know the unlock code?"

"I do."

"Then half the work is done. Give me your phone too. I'll add an app that lets you watch the user."

She shifted her ample butt onto the stool at the computer monitor, then plugged both phones into cables on the workbench. Slater couldn't see exactly what was going on, just a glowing blur where the screen was, as Svetlana had a directional privacy filter on it.

Glancing around the space, there was another person working today, a woman perched on a stool at the far end of the room. Her blond hair was bundled up, and she was wearing headgear with magnifying lenses, and working on something with a soldering iron.

Eventually Svetlana disconnected the devices, and handed over his phone, and slipped Chad's back into the RF-shielded envelope.

"Open the app," she said, and waited for him to do it. "It won't connect until the target phone is on the cell network again, but you will be able to see the phone's texts and recordings and the emails. You can also see anything he types into an app, with the name of the app, but not images of it, and not the screen taps. The phone's location is shown anytime."

"Such great access," Slater said. "Clearly you've done this before." The app looked clunky, he thought, as he tapped through the screens, but the esthetics didn't matter. Svetlana's stuff always just worked. "What do I owe you?"

"Let's say three dollars. No change to your subscription price."

"Excellent."

He dug out his wad and peeled off three C-notes. When he handed them over, Svetlana tucked them into her bra.

"When I came in," Slater said, "your door unlocked as soon as I looked up into the camera. There used to be a delay."

"You notice things." A smile played on her lips. "I automated the process. Facial recognition. No need to worry—my software remembers your face but it won't be distributed outside this building."

"I'm not worried."

"Constant upgrades, and constant expenses. The fire department made me put in the emergency exits. One in every room." She gestured to the door in the middle of the wall. It did look new, and the door looked heavy, with a crash bar wired into a box mounted on the wall next to it.

"Once they've approved it," Slater said, "at least they'll quit bugging you."

"So how is it going with your *menty* federal agent boyfriend?" Svetlana said.

"He hasn't dumped me yet, so I'd say it's positive."

"We need to think of a way to use his connections. He's a valuable resource that you're ignoring." She raised her eyebrows. "It's like the expression, you're leaving money on the table."

"Messing with the federal government seems like an awfully big risk. And I have to be careful—if we got caught, he wouldn't hesitate to bust me."

"I've been in this business a long time. I've never had trouble with the police. I don't work with foolish people, and I don't work with desperate people. You're neither one of those. It's possible to be smart about it."

"I'll keep it in mind." He tapped his temple with his finger. "*Spaciba.*"

Svetlana chuckled. "Nice pronunciation. I'm happy that you're practicing."

He walked out, through the antechamber and into the alley. She always pressed him about Pike. He really didn't want to break that trust, hijacking his laptop or bugging his phone or worse. Maybe she'd get the hint eventually that he just wasn't going to do it.

Once he was behind the wheel of the Continental, he set the padded envelope on the passenger seat, then navigated to the freeway. Once he was cruising, he reached for it and pulled out the phone. Almost instantly it started binging with notifications and messages. A minute later the phone rang, an obnoxious staccato tweedle.

Slater picked up and said, "Who's this?"

"I've got a better one for you, pal. Who the fuck are you and why are you answering my phone?" Chad's voice was nasal, and reedy, not like what he'd imagined.

"Oh, I'm so glad you called," he said, affecting a light tone. "I wondered who belonged to this. I found it on the street last night."

"Where are you? I'll come pick it up."

"I'm out running errands today. Maybe I can drop

it off. I'm in Glendale and Pasadena."

"There's a coffee place on Colorado Boulevard," Chad said. "By the museum. Bring it there."

Slater ended the call. He knew where that coffeehouse was. The idiot had likely picked it because it was the closest public place to his house.

A few miles down the freeway the phone rang again, jarring and migraine-inducing, like bagpipes playing circus music. The caller ID said SPIEGEL-RUTHERFORD LLC. Slater held the phone at arm's length to distort the sound of his voice, and deepened his tone when he answered.

"Who's this?"

"It's Walter, you blockhead. Who did you think it was? Look at your caller ID."

Slater hesitated. "Oh, yeah?"

"Are you still in bed? I've got your money. Come and pick it up."

The line went dead. When he pulled up at the coffee place, he thumb-typed a note on his own phone:

Walter
Spiegel-Rutherford LLC
blackmail victim?

Next he dug in the glove box for his stealthy glasses. They had clear lenses, and the frames bore a vibrant abstract pattern. They were heavy because of the batteries inside the thick arms. Svetlana had built them to jam security cameras. Tiny lamps studding the frames around the lenses generated ultraviolet and infrared light that was invisible to the human eye, but cameras picked it up as glare. The vivid pattern on the frames added mathematical noise to facial recognition software, so even if it could see past the light interference, it would still register him as a different person than when he wasn't wearing the glasses.

Taking a second to click on the little power switch with a fingernail, he pulled them on his face and climbed out of the car.

When he stepped into the coffeehouse, he saw that it was hopping, with a line of people waiting to order and most of the tables occupied. Chad was here, slouching on a stool, his back to the front window, elbows on the counter behind him. An angry red shiner encircled his left eye. He'd hit him good and solid. Last night he hadn't noticed it, but Chad had a pencil-thin mustache on his upper lip.

Slater stood near the entrance and took a moment to gape at the room, then pulled out the purple phone and held it in the air. Chad sprung off his stool, and stepped over, and grabbed it from his hand.

"Finally." He started tapping at it, not looking up. "Where did you find it?"

"It was in an alley in Hollywood."

"I'm so glad I've got this back. I was going nuts without it."

The upside of the guy's disinterest was that he didn't recognize him as the one who'd clocked him last night and given him that shiner. That wasn't too surprising, as it had happened fast, and it was dark, and Chad had been spooked.

"It took you long enough," he said, finally meeting Slater's eye. Frowning, he added, "What's with the glasses?"

The less attention this guy gave him the better, he

knew that. He knew he should let it go, rise above it, take the high road, all those pretty words the shrinks had laid out for him in his youth. But in the moment he just couldn't resist, and he slapped Chad hard, left and right, a rapid kovac.

"Why do you make me do this to you?" Slater demanded. "Why do you do it?"

Chad stumbled back a few steps and touched his face, with that familiar look of shock morphing into anger.

"What the fuck, man? You can't hit me."

"Somebody has to. You're a self-involved idiot."

There were a lot of eyes on him now, he could feel it. He knew Chad wasn't going to come at him—the guy was a backroom lowlife, not a street brawler. He turned and walked out.

Before he stepped into the street behind the Continental, he looked back to make sure nobody had followed him to get his plate number. Chad was too skittish to do that, but bystanders in pricey neighborhoods like this were more likely to have that kind of third-party moral indignation, to be shocked by a petty disagreement, to try to get him popped. But no one was paying any attention to him.

SIX

S LATER NAVIGATED TO THE 110 and headed downtown to his office. The day laborers who hung around the lobby waiting for gigs cutting fabric and grading patterns and transporting garments had mostly cleared out already. Upstairs he could hear the sewing machines humming in the other suites as he walked to his office.

As he flicked on the lights he double-clicked his tongue to greet the statue of Rey Pascual, posed to watch the front door with his bony empty eye sockets. Briefly sticking his head into Max's office, he made sure no one else was here, then went to his own office. He heaved his boots up on the desktop and pulled the keyboard into his lap.

Spiegel-Rutherford was a law firm, it turned out, and they weren't ambulance chasers like all the ones on the billboards. The pitch on their website was low-key and aimed at other businesses. Digging around the site, the only Walter he could find was Walter Yan. The guy was a lawyer, it seemed, and not a partner, but not an intern or a new hire either, based on his brief bio. The portrait photo showed a man with some lines around his eyes, maybe still in his forties, with his hair in a conservative side-part like military guys wore. He had a decent smile. Fuckable, Slater decided.

Yan—had he seen that name before? The image of the handwritten IOU for five hundred bucks. He switched to the info dump from Chad's phone and looked through the photos. The cropped letterhead bore the same zip code as Spiegel-Rutherford's offices. It was hard to read the signature, but that could definitely be a *W* up front. The second part was short, and it started with a *Y* if he looked at it right. It read more like Yeu or Yim but it could be Yan. Definitely close enough, he decided. This was the guy.

A web search for that name brought up his law firm and then a site for a classic car club. The name was on a page of photos from their rallies and events. In one of them Walter was posing with a classic Barracuda, a broad smile on his face. Even wearing sunglasses and half hidden behind the door of his car, this was definitely the same guy—that jawline and that haircut. The car was a beautiful third gen, a '73 or '74, bright green with a black hardtop.

Slater knew where his office was, and it was still business hours. If Walter drove that rig to work, he knew exactly where to find it. Before he could sit up and get on with it, he got distracted scrolling through the photos of the classic rigs and restomods from the car club. There were some beautiful vehicles in this town.

A sharp knock at the front door pulled him out of it. He got up and went to unlock it, and pulled it open, one boot firmly planted against the inside in case somebody planned to rush him. Standing there was a lanky guy with blue eyes, and gray hair, and serious wrinkles, wearing a maroon cardigan and baggy chinos.

"What do you need, son?" Slater said.

"Are you Max Conroy?"

"Might be. Who's asking?"

"Can I come in?" he said, and waved his arm.

"Why?"

He scoffed. "I want to talk to you. You're investigating me."

"Did you cheat on your wife, or did she cheat on you?"

"It's not about that. My name is Bill. I'm the performer known professionally as Gladys Rayon."

"Of course." He pulled the door open wider. "Max is my business partner. He's not around."

"So you're Ibáñez. Your name is on the door."

"I'll cop to that." He put his hands on his hips. "You could call him."

Bill frowned. "No one answers your office line, and no one calls back when I leave a message."

"Yeah, we're short-staffed. I know a little about the investigation. What do you need from Max?"

"I need him to know that I'm not a liar," he said intently. "I understand that's what he's looking into."

"Max is good at what he does. If you're not lying

about your past, he'll figure that out."

Bill frowned. "That sounds like what the cops say. 'If you haven't done anything wrong, you have nothing to worry about.' But they're still going to slam you on the hood of the prowl car, and snap on the handcuffs, and do a full cavity search."

He had to chuckle. "Max won't be getting up in your cha-cha."

"Can you ask him to call me?"

Slater raised his eyebrows. "Have you got a number?"

Reaching into his pants pocket, Bill produced a business card and handed it over. Slater glanced at it. Written in large script was GLADYS RAYON, and below that a phone number and a web address.

"I'll pass it on."

"Thank you." He gave Slater a pointed once-over. "I like the look you're working, by the way. You've got the body for it."

"Your mother should have named you Frank."

"I'm too old to be indirect. It's a waste of time."

"Well, it's not a curated look. It's just what I put on in the morning."

"You know that saying: We're all born naked, and the rest is drag."

"The wisdom of the ages," Slater said, and moved to close the door.

In Max's office he put the card on his blotter, then snapped a photo of it, and texted it to Max:

This bird dropped by the office. Wants to talk to you.

A minute later he killed the lights and locked up the office, and headed down to his car, and drove to his house. Once the door had rolled down behind him, he went to the back of the garage and spent a minute unlocking his gear cabinet. It was actually an armored gun safe, built to look like an office-supply sheet-metal storage cabinet, and it had a serious locking mechanism. Slater didn't have any weapons, but he kept his surveillance gear in here, all the stuff he got from Svetlana that was technically illegal. Any junkie who broke in to steal copper and tools would soon give up trying to open it.

Once he was in, he pulled one of the vehicle trackers off its charging cable. A black plastic box about the size of a thick cell phone, it had no markings, and magnetic ribs studded one side. Thinking about it, he took a second one. Maybe he'd put one on Bucky's vehicle too. Stepping around to the trunk of the Continental, he tucked both devices in the space behind the spare tire. That wouldn't prevent a cop from finding them in a search, but at least they were out of plain view.

Svetlana built the trackers to use terrestrial cell towers and Wi-Fi signals to calculate their position, not using the much weaker GPS signals from space, so it didn't need a view of the sky or an external antenna, and the battery lasted for ages.

Cruising back downtown, in the Financial District, Slater turned into the garage under the office tower where Walter Yan's law office was. He paused for a second to look over the small patch of sandy ground between the ramp he was descending and the one leading up. A sprawling agave was planted in the middle. It had bloomed and was dying now, starting to dry up, and someone had cut down the stalk, but at least they'd left several of the pups. In a year those would be much bigger and look great.

Down below, the parked cars were thinning out as the end of the day approached. He prowled the lanes on the first level, then nosed the Continental down to the next one. And there it was: that beautiful green Barracuda, gleaming and dramatic, parked nose-out.

He rolled past and pulled into a stall, then reached into the backseat and fished a pair of black latex gloves from the box he kept there, and wriggled his hands into them. Climbing out, he opened the trunk and retrieved one of the trackers, wiping it against his shirt to remove his fingerprints. His DNA was still all over it, of course, and there was nothing he could do about that. But it seemed unlikely that anyone who found it would go to the trouble of looking for DNA and analyzing it. Prints were much easier to find. Peering at the device, he found the little recessed power switch and clicked it on with a fingernail.

Once he'd closed the trunk, he scanned the garage, but no one was in view. Walking over to the Barracuda, he squatted at the rear tire on the driver's side and reached up into the wheel well. The magnetic ribs quickly found purchase, attaching with a satisfying tug. Rising, Slater peeled off the gloves, and went back to the Continental, and climbed in.

Before he started the engine, he thought about it. There was no reason to avoid the guy. Maybe he could just talk to him—if he could talk his way past the firm's reception. Walter wasn't a partner, so he'd be less insulated than the higher-ups.

He got out of the car again and strode over to the

stairwell, hustling up to the lobby. When he stepped onto the elevator he hit the button for 42. Spiegel-Rutherford was almost at the top of the building. The higher the floor, the more pretentious they were bound to be, and the less likely that he'd be able just to stroll in.

The double doors to the firm's suite were propped open, revealing a roomy front office with dark wood furniture. At the front counter sat a woman wearing a sharp red suit and a mike headset. An expensive-looking bejeweled brooch sparkled on her lapel, and her blond hair was in a carefully coiffed updo, her makeup subtle and flawless. This was the kind of frontwoman you paid a premium to make sure your business looked upscale.

Slater braced his hands on the counter and leaned toward her. She was ignoring him, looking to the side, toward the hallway that led deeper into the office. Her eyes bright, she flashed a smile. Slater followed her gaze and saw that she was looking at a guy walking toward them, in a sharp gray suit with a dark-red necktie—Walter.

In the brief moment that Slater glanced at him, he saw that Walter's eyes were fixed on Slater's butt. But he quickly looked away, and avoided his gaze as he strode by, and instead flashed a smile at the receptionist.

They both watched Walter walk out toward the elevators, and then the woman looked up at him. Her smile faded and her eyes went dead.

"Can I help you?"

Slater stood erect. "I doubt it," he said, and walked out.

Walter was already gone from the elevator lobby, but it didn't matter. He had to grin to himself as he stepped into the car and rode down. He'd learned a lot—that look. He knew exactly what that was about. The way he'd leaned on the counter had emphasized his butt, and Walter had been admiring it. He was a man's man. That was his way in with this guy.

The Barracuda was gone from the garage. As he climbed into the Continental, he dug out his phone and opened Svetlana's tracking app to check on it, but there was no cell service down here. Nosing the vehicle up onto the street, into the fading daylight, he pulled over at a red curb and looked at the phone again. The tracker was up and working, and showed the Barracuda's location as a few blocks from here. Thank you, Svetlana.

He saw that Andy had texted earlier:

> I found the name that goes with that number. Liz Delgado. She's in IT. Works at Fosfor Petroleum.

Oil companies were bad news. For some reason they employed lots of yahoos and lowlifes. Maybe it was like that invasive teasel. It looked reasonable enough early in its life cycle, but after it went to seed, it got all prickly and ornery and then died. Maybe the oil industry was like that, rough and grubby as it entered its death throes.

The company's head office was right here in the Financial District, he saw when he looked it up. But the workday was over, and he had somewhere to be.

Slater set the phone in its dash mount and pulled into the street, then headed to the 110, and merged into the sluggish late-day traffic. By the time he was on the horseshoe at LAX it was completely dark out. Pulling up to the right terminal, he spotted Pike, already at the curb, standing with his little wheelie bag. Slater's heart soared just seeing the guy.

His dark hair slicked back, Pike was beefy, with a perfect little paunch over his belt. Even wearing that fugly green polo shirt the guy was beautiful, even the way he stood there, feet planted apart, watching the traffic.

When Slater stopped at the curb, Pike opened the door and folded the seat forward so he could lift his bag into the back.

"It's hilarious that a car this size is a two-door," he said as he climbed in, and took a breath. "Man, this airport."

"I know."

Slater leaned over, running a hand into his hair, and they spent a moment with their mouths locked together. Eventually Pike pulled back and chuckled.

"You should drive. We'll get popped for blocking traffic."

He checked his side mirror and pulled into the roadway.

"How's your case going with the amnesiac?" Pike said.

"I tracked down the blackmailer. It looks like he comes from money. I think I found another victim too."

"You have to be careful with crooks like that," Pike said. "If they think they have nothing to lose, they can lash out. Like a cornered rat."

Slater eyed him sidelong. "I've actually been doing this for a while."

"I get it." Pike laughed and reached over to squeeze his shoulder. "You know what you're doing."

Once they'd pulled into the garage, Pike dropped his bag in the bedroom, and ditched his shoes, then climbed the stairs.

"Thai or burritos?"

"You pick," Slater said, and watched as he tapped at his phone to get food delivered.

After they'd eaten, and dumped the wrappers in the trash, Slater pulled his boots off and sat at the end of the sofa. Pike shifted next to him, leaning back and lifting his feet onto the cushions, and Slater wrapped his arms around his torso.

"I've missed you," Pike said.

"You're so warm. It feels freaking perfect." Slater mouthed his neck and spoke under his breath. "I'm going to fuck you so hard."

"I'm counting on it. Want to read to me first? Just until my burrito settles."

Pike reached for the copy of the *Odyssey* on the coffee table and handed it back to him. It had become a thing for them, reading the classics. When they'd met, Pike had been reading a primer, then they read the *Iliad* together, and now they were slogging through the *Odyssey*. Slater was surprised that it actually held his interest. It likely wouldn't have if they weren't doing it together, a mutual endeavor that built something beyond either one of them or the books.

"So what's happening?" Pike said.

"Odysseus and his son just decided to murdertize all the men who are hanging around the palace trying to get with his wife."

"Weren't there like a hundred of them? It doesn't seem realistic that he'd go after a mob like that."

"I'm sure he can handle it," Slater said. "He's a total badass. What's unrealistic is that Penelope didn't sleep with any of them for ten damn years. She must have superhuman willpower."

"It's also a stretch that she doesn't recognize him, even disguised as a bum. It's her own husband."

"He probably aged a lot in those years, with all the stuff he went through. What did you look like ten years ago?"

Pike turned his head to meet his gaze. "I think you'd recognize me."

"I bet you were still so fucking hot."

He chuckled. "Read on."

"After Telemachus retired for the evening," Slater began, "Penelope emerged from the women's quarters to talk to her mysterious guest. He'd claimed to have met Odysseus on Crete, and Penelope asked him to describe her long-missing husband ..."

Eventually Pike's breathing took on the regular rhythm of sleep, and Slater set the book aside.

"I'm fading," Pike said, stirring as Slater shifted position. "We should go downstairs."

Slater followed him down to the bedroom, and pulled off his shirt, and watched Pike undress.

"You're hard," Slater said.

"Of course I am, with you standing there in those jeans." Naked now, he climbed on the bed and sat back on the pillows, and stroked his cock, and raised his eyebrows.

"I'm thinking you're going to have to fuck me with that thing," Slater said, unbuckling his belt.

"Don't take off your jeans. Let me."

As he climbed onto the bed beside him, Pike groped his crotch, massaging his swelling cock through the denim. He met his mouth, warm and intent and perfect, and Slater ran his hands over his bare chest and his arms.

Sitting up, Pike popped his fly and yanked the jeans off, then took him into his mouth. Arching his back, Slater relished the intensity of it. Pike grabbed the lube and massaged a finger into him, mouthing his neck, running a hand through his hair. Shifting closer, Pike pressed into him, and Slater winced at the intensity. Pike knew him, knew what he could handle, and soon he pushed harder, and built up to pounding him.

As he climaxed, Pike yelped and strained into him, then lowered his weight onto his body.

"Don't move," Slater said, and grabbed his own cock.

Pike batted his hand away, and grabbed his cock, and started pumping him. He met Slater's eye and held it. He knew what that did to him—it pushed him over the edge, and his body shuddered as he came.

As he stretched out beside him, Pike was still breathing hard. Slater shoved an arm under Pike's sweaty neck. It didn't matter how many times they did this. It never got old.

SEVEN

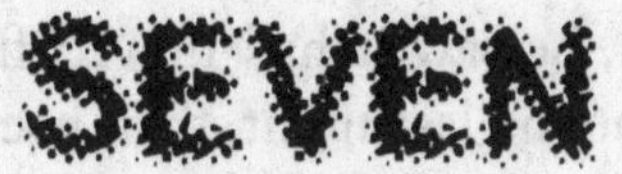

PIKE WAS ALREADY GONE to work when Slater woke. He pulled on a clean pair of jeans and a dark shirt, then trudged up the stairs for some java and fruit, and to think about what he needed to do. Sitting at the dining table, he checked Svetlana's apps for his trackers.

Chad's phone had gone to the Blue Dragon last night, no surprise, then moved to his place in Pasadena. The route history showed he was moving on the 134, and in Hollywood the marker entered a parking garage near the Blue Dragon. That meant he was driving himself, not taking rideshares. Driving your own rig was the default in this town, but the map history confirmed that's what Chad was doing.

The other activity on Chad's phone was a bunch of meaningless texting, and thirty minutes on a social media app, but he hadn't written anything, so Slater couldn't tell what he was up to. Next he spent six minutes on a banking app, also without typing anything. He probably logged into it with a fingerprint or his ugly face.

None of that was particularly informative. When he looked at the vehicle tracker on Walter's beautiful Barracuda, he saw it had moved from his office to South Pasadena last night, then back to the same spot in the Financial District this morning. That tracker wasn't nearly as precise as the one he had on Chad, with the phone's robust location capabilities, but when he zoomed in, he could see that the place where the Barracuda had spent the night in South Pas was a house on a residential street. The green circle for its estimated location overlapped four different properties on two streets, but it was centered on the driveway of just one of them.

A search on his phone showed that the owner of that address was W. J. Yan—it was Walter's house. That seemed boring, using such a beautiful vehicle just to drive home and then back to work. But at least now he knew where the guy lived.

Next he needed to talk to Liz at that oil company. Hustling down to the garage, he backed the Continental into the street and drove to the Financial District. Cruising the block where the company's office was, he lucked out when an SUV pulled out of a street space right in front of him. He nosed in and plinked some coins in the meter, then walked up the block to the office tower.

The lobby didn't have card-key barriers to the elevators, like some buildings did now, as the wealth gap gradually widened and security inevitably grew tighter at places like this. The directory on the wall listed the floor for Fosfor Petroleum, and he rode up and walked into the company's office. The reception space was simple, with a few chairs and the company logo plastered on the wall, not flashy like the digs of the bankers and brokers, or conservative like Walter's law firm, or folksy-casual like the tech bros on the Westside. Oil was an old industry in this town, and this place felt like that—functional, traditional, not overly concerned with appearances.

The front desk was staffed by a woman in a dark sweater and long stringy hair.

"I need the IT department," Slater said, standing in front of her.

She smiled and pointed down the hall. "Second office on the left. You can't miss it."

The unmarked door was closed, but the handle was unlocked. Inside he found a few feet of grubby carpet in front of a service counter, with half a dozen desks beyond it, each with a big computer monitor, only a few of them occupied. At one side, through a double doorway, he could see a server rack and the forest of cables connecting them.

Standing next to a desk just across the counter was a guy with short black hair and spotty skin. He looked like he might still be in his teens. The guy looked up as he stepped in, unsubtly giving him the once-over, his gaze lingering on his jeans.

"You like what you see down there?" Slater said, and briefly grabbed his crotch.

His face went red. "Uh—what can I help you with?"

Slater leaned on the counter and held his gaze. "Is Liz here today?"

He turned and shouted toward the doorway to the server room. "Delgado."

A moment later Liz appeared, dressed differently today, in dark trousers and a striped blouse, wearing black-framed glasses. But the mass of dark hair was the same—this was definitely the woman from the alley outside the Blue Dragon. Frowning, she approached the counter.

"Remember me?" Slater said.

"Refresh my memory."

"I ran into you and Chad in Hollywood the other night."

Her eyes went hard. "You." She subtly looked sidelong at the young guy, now sitting at his desk just a few feet away, absorbed in his computer screen but clearly within earshot.

"Have you had lunch yet?" Slater said. "I'm buying. Unless you want to talk here, that is."

Liz pressed her lips into a hard line, studying him. Finally she turned to the guy at the desk. "I'm going for lunch."

With the key card dangling from a lanyard around her neck, she unlocked the gate at the end of the counter and stepped through, and Slater followed her down the hall to the front office.

"So where are we eating, big spender?" Liz said, once they had boarded the elevator.

"I don't really know the neighborhood. I'll leave it to you."

She scoffed, not meeting his eye, and stepped aside as the doors opened on a lower floor for other people to board.

Once they were in the lobby, she led Slater out to the street, then around the corner to a Cali-fresh place, where they joined the line to order. It wouldn't have been his first choice, as Pike had ordered burritos just last night.

Liz said something in Spanish, waving a hand.

"I don't actually speak the language," Slater said.

"You look like you should."

"Yeah, I get that a lot."

"I just said my father laughs at this chain. He says, 'Who would pay twelve bucks for a burrito?'"

When they got to the counter, Slater paid for both of them, and they found a table along the side wall. Liz ate a few bites from her bowl before she spoke, waving her fork.

"So who the hell are you, and what do you want with me?"

"The name is Ibáñez. I'm an insurance investigator."

"What does insurance have to do with me?"

"I saw you get assaulted," Slater said. "Chad shouldn't get away with that. I can make a statement as a witness."

Looking at her bowl, she dug around with her fork. "You don't know me, and you don't know Chad."

"So he's your boyfriend?"

"God, no. More like a business associate."

Slater set down his burrito and folded his arms. "He works with you at Fosfor?"

"He doesn't. Chad has a side hustle. I help him out with it sometimes. That night we had a small disagreement. The details of that are none of your business. Whatever you think you saw, you don't need to take it to the cops."

"I couldn't care less about your boy-girl bullshit, or your disagreement, or whatever it was. There's no point in me doing that anyway. You're the only one who can get him busted."

"Good answer." She set down her fork and sighed. "I loved the *putaso*. Seeing you deck him. *Bam*. He needed that."

"What's Chad's main gig?"

"I don't actually know that. I know he hangs out a lot. He goes to strip clubs. I'm sure he hassles the sizzlers. He's definitely the type."

"The side hustle you're talking about is the blackmail racket, I'm thinking," Slater said. "Why are you working with him?"

Her eyebrows shot up. "What blackmail racket?"

"You know exactly what I'm talking about. So far I've tracked down two people he's put the squeeze on."

"Are you taking that to the cops?"

"Not yet, but it might involve them eventually. You can get on the right side of it, Liz, and be a witness. Or you can go down with Chad as a fraudster. Blackmail is a felony. We're talking decades in the hoosegow."

She held his gaze. "I don't know anything about his racket."

"You just told me you work for him," he said, and louder, "Sing, sister."

Liz pursed her lips and watched him for a moment. "How about this. I started out as a victim. They blackmailed me, but I don't have any money, so instead they use me as a honey pot."

"You lure in the straight guys."

"I've only done it once or twice. Lots of guys don't care about sex photos. One guy asked for more of them to show his wife. One woman they tried to scam used the picture to rack up followers on her social media account. She pretended to be victimized, but she's actually the one who released the photo. She never paid Chad anything. The whole thing was hilarious."

"But some people are willing to pay."

"Older people," Liz said. "When they're rich, it's more lucrative."

"They have more to lose." He watched her for a moment. "You said 'they.' Who else does Chad work with?"

"I just meant Chad."

It didn't wash—he could tell she was lying, the way she averted her gaze, scrambling to think fast. But she'd already told him a lot.

"What clubs do you work?" Slater said.

"Straight clubs in Hollywood."

"Even to pick up gay guys?"

"Closeted gay guys go to straight clubs."

Slater sat up and crumpled his burrito wrapper.

"Before you go, can I ask you a favor?" Liz said. "In exchange for everything I just gave you."

"You can ask."

"If the cops are coming for Chad, give me a head's up so I can get out of the way."

"On one condition—that you don't tell Chad anything about me."

She smiled. "That's easy."

"Give me your number," he said, and thumb-typed it into his phone as she recited it. He texted her "Slater," and a moment later heard a muffled *ding* in her pocket.

"You gave me your real number," he said, looking up at her.

"Why wouldn't I?"

"Well, now you've got mine."

———◦———

ONCE HE'D WALKED BACK to the Continental, Slater drove the few blocks to his office, and parked in the lot across the street. A couple of day laborers were hanging out in the lobby, even though the full-day gigs were taken early. Upstairs the lights were off, and Rey Pascual was facing the front door, watching anyone who came in. Their operative Etta used the desk sometimes, and she always positioned Rey that way when she left.

As he was walking in to his desk, his phone buzzed in his hand. The caller ID said it was Jack. He dropped into his chair and picked up.

"People know Gladys Rayon," Jack said. "She's been around quite a while. One guy called her a drag grandmother."

"That sounds like her."

"I'm told that as a performer she's cutthroat, and won't hesitate to step on your toes to get better lighting. But she's not a crook. Apparently she dated some other queens over the years but never got the reputation as a user or an abuser."

"Is she partnered with anybody now, or sleeping with somebody specific?" Slater studied the statue of

Pollux as he listened, admiring the little guy's lush head of hair.

"I didn't hear anything like that. Sorry."

"Don't be sorry. You heard plenty."

"I talked to a guy who knows her quite well," Jack said. "I'll text you his name and number so you can interview him yourself."

"Excellent. What do you want me to pay you?"

"It wasn't really work at all. Just gossiping with old friends. Maybe you can buy me dinner."

"Deal," Slater said, and ended the call.

Pulling his keyboard close, he started an email to Max: "I got the dope from the drag network on Gladys Rayon," he wrote, and added all the details of what Jack had said, and copied the info on the contact he'd dug up.

Once he'd sent that, Slater looked at his phone and opened Svetlana's app to check on Chad. There were several new text exchanges, including a terse one with someone listed only as T: "Where you at" and "Here" and "Waiting." Chad had also texted someone named Mara: "Where's my effing money?" The response was "Come by the store," followed by a second text, "Fuck face."

Mara was obviously another blackmail victim. It was an unusual name—maybe he could find them without paying Andy to do it. A web search for the name with their phone number brought up an eyewear shop on Melrose, owned by someone named Mara Ortiz. Their texts with numskull Chad had mentioned a store. This was the right Mara.

Locking up the office, he went down to his car and drove west, out to the Fairfax neighborhood, and found a meter up the block from Mara's shop. In front of it, deep wooden planter boxes lined a stretch of several storefronts, blocking half the sidewalk. They were planted with rosebushes. Slater paused to look them over. Scrubby and spindly and overwatered, they needed fertilizer, and pruning.

The shop next to the eyewear place was a tattoo business, and a guy wearing a tank top with heavily inked arms stepped out and stretched his back. He had a lush mustache with the tips waxed into curls and wore a stupid flat-top kepi cap.

"You like the roses?" A cigarette dangled from his lips, and he cupped his hands to light it, a cloud of smoke billowing up around his head.

"They look like hell. Who's supposed to be taking care of them?"

"The shopkeepers do it. I water them sometimes. They're not really meant to beautify the street." He gestured with his cigarette. "It's to stop the homeless from moving in."

It was effective, Slater saw, as the boxes left enough space between them and the gutter to walk but not to set up a tent.

"It might keep them away, but the flip side is you're attracting rats."

The guy frowned. "I've never seen rats here."

"Just because you're a slack-jawed half-wit doesn't change reality." He raised his voice. "The sky is still blue even if you refuse to look up. There's rat droppings, and marks where they've gnawed the wood."

Not waiting for a reply, he walked over to Mara's shop, the little bell over the door tinkling as he stepped in. It wasn't very big. Racks of frames and sunglasses hung on the walls, and near the counter was a stand with some little handbags and clutches. Most of it looked like it was aimed at women.

From the counter farther inside a woman called a greeting. Her tangle of wavy black hair was pushed back, and she wore dark-framed cat-eye glasses.

Approaching her, Slater said, "You're Mara."

She smiled and braced her hands on the counter. "Are you shopping for your girlfriend?"

Before he could answer, the desk phone next to the register rang, and she held up her index finger at him as she picked up. Listening, her demeanor quickly shifted, and her brow furrowed.

"I don't really care if he changed his number," she said into the receiver, then snapped, "Fine." As she listened she jotted something down on a yellow notepad that sat on the counter.

Slater could almost read it from where he was standing, even though it was upside down: the name Gonzalo, and under that a string of digits that started with 323. A phone number. Pulling out his phone, he feigned studying the screen, and briefly glanced up at Mara, but she was ignoring him, engrossed in the call. He zoomed in on the notepad with the phone's camera and snapped a photo. The name and the digits were legible in the image, he saw when he checked the photo, and he tucked the phone away.

"Where were we?" Mara said, replacing the receiver and looking up at him.

"You're being blackmailed by a lowlife named Chad."

Her eyes hardened. "Are you here for the pickup?

I can't believe anyone on his crew isn't frat-boy pasty white."

"I'm not working for him," Slater said, and put his hands on his hips. "I'm investigating him. Who else is on his crew?"

"The fuck are you?"

He dug a business card from his hip pocket and handed it over, and watched as she scanned it.

"What does insurance have to do with that *pendejo*?"

"What is he using to extort you?"

"We're not having this conversation," she said. "Get out of my store."

"Sure, I'll hit the bricks. But you could help me shut him down. Why wouldn't you want to talk about that?"

"Out," she said, raising her voice.

The little bell above the front door tinkled as a woman stepped in from the street, and pulled off her sunglasses, and looked around. Mara called out a cheery greeting, then looked back to Slater, and pointed a finger at him, and mouthed "Out."

He watched as she stepped around the counter to talk to the customer, then he walked out to his car, past the messed-up rosebushes in the rat boxes.

"Idiots," he muttered.

Once he was behind the wheel of the Continental, he looked at the photo he'd taken, and punched the phone number into a search engine. It came back with a business listing: Chalo's Rims. That fit with the name Mara had written down: Chalo was one of the nicknames for Gonzalo.

Reading the customer reviews of the place, it

seemed like a legit business, but it sounded more like an auto repair shop than just a place for wheels. The address was on Whittier Boulevard. That was at least an hour from here this late in the day, but afterward it wasn't far to get to the city.

RUISING THE BOULEVARD, SLATER realized it had been a while since he'd been out here. The neighborhood looked like it had been spiffed up—not gentrified, exactly, but somehow easier on the eyes. Maybe there was less razor wire and graffiti. He parked at the curb in front of a tall iron-picket fence. Near the open gate a metal sign was attached to it that said CHALO'S RIMS.

The yard was chockablock with vehicles, like lots of car repair shops were, and as he walked among them toward the open garage bays, he saw the tailgate of a little white pickup painted with a *retablo*. The prominent Virgin Mary in the painting gave it away—something had gone down that evoked gratitude to the Virgin, to the point that the driver was motivated to commission an artwork.

Slater paused for a minute to look it over and decipher the story. In the center of the painting was a thick oak tree, and next to it was a little white truck with a crinkled front fender. The Virgin hovered in the air nearby, in the rendition of her from Mexico, where she was clad in blue with golden rays emanating all around. It seemed that the driver had survived crashing into that tree.

A guy stepped out of one of the garage bays, dressed in dark-green work duds. He had salt-and-pepper hair and a couple of days' stubble on his lined and swarthy face. Totally fuckable, Slater decided.

The guy said something in Spanish, and Slater spread his arms. "No comprendo, brother."

"I asked if you like the truck."

"I like the *retablo*. Somebody's grateful for a narrow escape."

He chuckled. "You should meet that guy. He's a terrible driver."

"You're Gonzalo."

His brow furrowed. "That's right. Come on in."

Slater followed him inside through the open bay door. An SUV was up on a hoist in the first bay, and a guy in coveralls stood working under the engine. Gonzalo led him to the side of the big space, into the office, with a wide window that looked into the shop. Inside, the linoleum floor was ancient and grimy, and paperwork was piled on file cabinets and a table next to the back wall. A messy desk had a couple of stackable guest chairs in front of it.

A woman sat behind the desk, eyeing him as Gonzalo led him in, her brow furrowed. Moon-faced, she wore her hair tightly pulled back, and heavy eye makeup. Her lipstick was dark red, clashing with her pastel-purple cardigan.

"This is Viviana," Gonzalo said. "She's the one who transmits the inspection reports."

She shot him a look. "I'm not the only one who does it."

"Have a seat," Gonzalo said. "Vivi can show you all the paperwork. I know there's nothing missing in our records."

He walked out, and as Slater dropped into one of the chairs across from her, Vivi leaned forward and folded her hands, revealing her carefully manicured nails.

"You really should be talking to Gonzalo," she said.

"You think?"

"It's his business." She shifted in her chair. "What months do you want to look at?"

"We'll get to that," Slater said. "First I have some general questions."

She frowned. "OK."

"How well do you know Gonzalo?"

Her eyes flicked to the window behind him, and she lowered her voice. "I've known him for years. Of course I don't know everything he does. All his business deals. I stick to the accounting and the paperwork."

"He runs other businesses?"

"You'd have to ask him."

"What's his connection to Mara Ortiz?" Slater said.

"I don't really know her."

"But you know why she was around."

Vivi took a breath. "Her and Gonzalo did some

business together. They shared a shipping container bringing stuff from Asia. Gonzalo's part was wheels and stuff for cars, but hers was just garbage."

"She imported actual garbage?"

"Trashy furniture. I saw some of it. Ugly white rattan." She shook her head. "You wouldn't even put it in your dog's house. It would make them too depressed."

"They just did the one container together? Did you hear about any other projects?"

"In the middle of that one they had a falling out." Vivi leaned toward him. "I don't know all the details, but there was a lot of screaming." She mimicked a high voice. "'I'll fix you, you crooked fuck.'"

"When did this happen?"

"Not long ago. In the fall."

"Are they still beefing?" Slater said.

"No idea. I haven't seen her around since then."

"How did Mara and Gonzalo meet?"

Vivi's eyes shifted behind him, and her eyebrows shot up. Slater turned to look. In the doorway stood Gonzalo with another guy, an Anglo-looking redhead wearing a yellow shirt with a pen clipped in the pocket, a lanyard with a card around his neck. He couldn't read it from here but it looked like an ID, with a headshot and a seal from some government agency. He needed to get one of those—it was a great cover. This woman had spilled a lot when she thought he was some official.

"This guy says he's the state inspector," Gonzalo said.

The guy frowned. "I am the state inspector."

"There's two of you?" Gonzalo demanded.

"Easy, baby," Slater said. "I never said I was anything."

"I don't understand why you'd impersonate a state official," the redhead said.

"Don't feel bad." Slater raised his eyebrows. "Lots of people are stupid."

Gonzalo's expression hardened. "Mother fucker."

The guy looked like he had street-brawling chops, and Slater quickly leaped out of his chair. Sure enough, Gonzalo lunged for him, but Slater was ready with a right hook, and struck his chin, snapping his head. Not discouraged, Gonzalo landed a blow on his cheek, then grabbed the front of his shirt. In the moment that he was exposed, Slater punched hard at his gut. Gonzalo groaned and bent forward.

Yanking himself out of his grip, Slater moved toward the office doorway. The redhead was a big guy, and he was flushed now, alarmed at the dustup. He stood blocking his exit.

"I'm calling the cops."

"Go for it," Slater said.

Stepping up to him, Slater slapped his face, a rapid kovac. As the guy raised his arms to push him off, Slater grabbed the edge of the door and slammed it hard into the side of his head. He yelped and stumbled backward into the shop, his face contorted, his hand on his ear.

"Idiot," Slater muttered, and hustled out the garage bay door to the yard, and out to the Continental.

Jumping behind the wheel, he quickly nosed into the traffic, then pulled over a few blocks away, breathing hard. Gonzalo had earned that gut-punch, but the desk jockey should have known better. Why did these birds make him do things like that? If the door had given that guy a cauliflower ear, it was his own damn fault.

On his phone he checked his trackers, and saw that Walter hadn't gone straight home after work tonight. The Barracuda had moved just a few blocks, and when he zoomed in on the map, he saw it was at the Baltimore. He must love driving that car—he could have walked there from his office in a few minutes, and the cost of parking at that hotel was absurd.

It was a big place, with ballrooms and meeting rooms. Walter could be meeting someone who was staying there, or maybe going to an event. It also had a bar. Maybe Walter went to drink after work. He could find out soon enough.

As he drove toward downtown, twilight was deepening, and he flicked on his headlights. He nosed the Continental into the public garage under Pershing Square, then strode across the street to the Baltimore. It was a century-old classic, with stonework and intricately decorated coffered ceilings and an obscene amount of mahogany on the walls.

Slater walked the long hallway where the event rooms were, but none of them looked to be in use. Next he went to the bar, similarly clad in mahogany, with elegant carved stone between the panels. And there was Walter, perched on a barstool, wearing a gray suit.

The place wasn't busy, with just a couple of the tables in use, and Walter was the only person sitting at the bar. Slater walked over and climbed onto a stool, leaving one empty between them. The guy glanced over at him as he sat. His tie was loose, his top button undone.

Slater pointed to the pint glass on the bar in front of him. "What is that?"

"Wheat beer," Walter said, his brow furrowing.

A bartender in a black vest and a bow tie, her hair neatly bundled back, stepped up, and Slater pointed to the pint. "Bring me one of those."

"You like the look of it that much?" Walter said as she stepped away.

Slater pointedly looked him up and down. "I know what I like."

His face reddened but he didn't look away. The guy obviously didn't recognize him from when he'd walked past him at the front desk of his law firm. But then he hadn't been looking at his face.

When the bartender set down his beer, Slater put a twenty on the bar top and said, "Thank you, Dolores."

"You know her?" Walter said. "You must come here a lot."

"I just read her name tag," he said, and took a sip of his beer.

"So it's a tactic to get better service."

He met Walter's eye. "Or she's a human being in this world with a name."

Walter looked at his beer. "I'm sure that sounded cynical."

"I guess you can't really dodge your entitlement."

He frowned. "I'm not entitled."

"Entitled people always say that."

"You're kind of a dick," Walter said, sitting up straighter.

"Relax, Suit." Slater tipped his glass toward him. "We're just talking here."

"I have a name too. It's not Suit."

He raised his eyebrows. "Do tell."

"It's Walter."

"Slater. You seem like a no-nonsense kind of guy, Walter."

"It's my job. I have to cut through a lot of BS. I'm a lawyer."

"What kind of law do you do?"

Slater listened to him talk, and asked some inane questions. He didn't have to work too hard to engage the guy—most people liked to talk about themselves.

When he was near the end of his beer, he twisted to face Walter, spreading his knees apart so the guy could check out his crotch.

Walter gestured to his glass. "Do you want another round?"

"I had a different idea. You should come to my place and show me what's under that suit."

His eyebrows shot up. "Wow. The direct approach."

"Too much?"

"Maybe not." He looked him over. "Why me?"

"The light in your eyes," Slater said, "and your unique charm."

Walter's eyes narrowed. "I don't sleep around a lot, but I know a line when I hear it."

He threw up a hand. "You're good looking, and easy to talk to. You deserve to have some fun."

"Where do you live?"

"Nearby. The second exit north on the 101."

"You're not crazy, are you?"

"I'm totally crazy," Slater said, "but I'm not

dangerous. At least not to you."

"Is there somewhere to park?"

He chuckled. "Sure. And there's another part to it—my boyfriend will be joining us. He's not dangerous either."

Walter groaned. "That sounds kind of sleazy."

"It depends on your perspective. You have to admit it also sounds extremely hot."

"I don't know." He lifted his nearly empty glass. "I have to work tomorrow."

"Walter, look at me." When he did, Slater held his eye. "I know what I'm doing, and I can rock your world."

He took a deep breath. "Is your boyfriend as hot as you?"

"Way, way hotter."

"You're not plug-and-play guys, are you? No crystal smack?"

It was actually a good sign that the guy didn't know the phrase was actually *party and play*, or that those were two different drugs. Slater raised his glass. "This is as crunk as I get."

"Not even jazz cabbage?"

"You mean weed? Is that what you call it in court when you're trying to keep your clients out of jail?"

He laughed. "I do contract law, not criminal defense."

"Well, I don't smoke weed."

"I'm parked downstairs."

"Give me your number," Slater said, and thumb-typed it into his phone as he recited it. "I sent you my address."

"You do live close," Walter said, tapping at his

phone. "Navigation says it's eight minutes' drive."

"If there's nowhere to park on the street, pull across my garage door."

They both got up, and walked out to the lobby.

"My car is at the valet," Walter said.

"I'm the other direction." He met his eye and jabbed a finger at him. "Do not bail on me."

Crossing to the parking garage, Slater climbed into the Continental, and once he was up on the street, called Pike.

"Are you at the house?"

"I just took my shoes off," Pike said.

"I've come up with an activity for the evening. I'm bringing a guy home."

"Seriously? Who?"

"His name is Walter. He's hot. You'll like him."

"I guess we can do that. I was going to watch the last part of that documentary."

"Choosing television over a hookup would be a terrible mistake," Slater said. "This will be way more fun."

"You're a very sexual person."

"You seem to keep up well enough."

Pike laughed, his tone deep. "When will you be here?"

"Eight minutes," he said, and ended the call.

NINE

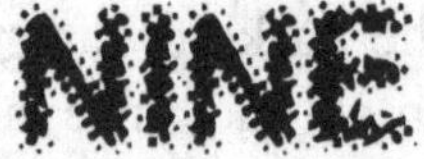

A S SLATER NOSED INTO his garage, and the door started to roll down, he saw the Barracuda roll by in the rearview. He stepped into the little foyer at the bottom of the stairs and went out the front door to the street. Walter had pulled to the curb behind Pike's janky old SUV. Walking over, he admired the Barracuda as Walter climbed out.

"What a magnificent beast," Slater said. "It gives me wood just looking at it."

Walter chuckled. "My paralegal says I'm over-compensating for something."

"It's a '73 or a '74?"

"Very good. A '74."

"I knew it was the third gen."

"It sounds like you know your stuff."

"I like beautiful things," Slater said.

"Other gearheads have told me I shouldn't use it as my everyday ride. But I can't imagine letting it languish in a garage six days a week. It needs to be seen."

"Hey, smoke 'em if you've got 'em." Slater stepped around to look at the grille.

"It looks better in daylight," Walter said, gazing at his phone. He held it out. "You can flip through."

There were a lot of photos of the Barracuda, he saw, swiping through them. Walter was often in the frame with the vehicle, sometimes in sunglasses and driving gloves, beaming at the camera.

"That's up the coast," Slater said. "And Yosemite … this looks like the Mojave."

"I have a chunk of land near Joshua Tree. Ten acres of heaven."

"You're a lucky man." He handed the phone back and gestured to the house.

As they approached it, Walter said, "Nice place. What do you do, exactly? You never said."

"It really is mine." He twisted his key to unlock the front door. "I know I don't look like the kind of guy who could afford an obnoxious postmodern box like this."

"I guess I made assumptions."

"That I was a gardener or a busboy, am I right? That happens a lot." He pushed the door open. "I'm an insurance investigator."

"What about your boyfriend?"

"He works for your Uncle Sam."

Slater started up the stairs, with Walter following, and went into the bedroom. Pike stepped out of the bathroom as they walked in. His hair was wet and he wore a towel around his waist. He flashed that thousand-watt smile and introduced himself.

Red-faced now, Walter said, "I guess this is really happening."

"Can I take off your suit?" Slater stepped close and slid his hands under the lapels, and pushed it back, letting the jacket drop to the floor.

Pike snatched it up and tossed it neatly on the back of the club chair. "He's going to want to wear that again."

Walter giggled like a kid. "You boys do this a lot?"

"Less often than we should," Slater said, and started to unbutton Walter's shirt.

Walter leaned in to kiss him, and started a little when Pike stepped up behind him, running his hands around his belly and under the shirt. Slater shoved the shirt back, and Pike took hold of the collar to pull it off, then tossed it neatly on the chair.

"Sweet tats," Pike said.

Thoroughly inked on both arms, Walter had a winding dragon on the left, and a darker tiki motif on the right. Slater caressed his bicep, looking over the artistry. He would have pegged this guy as too square for tats.

Grabbing Walter's belt, he started to unbuckle it. "So what's your sex thing?"

"You mean, what do I like to do?"

"What turns you on?"

"I want to watch you take off those jeans."

Slater chuckled. "That's easy."

He shoved Walter's pants down. The guy was bulging in his skivvies, already a little chubby, and Slater squeezed him through the stretchy black fabric, then pushed them down.

Pike had lost the towel, and sat on the bed, his back against the headboard. He jutted his chin to Walter. "Come here."

When Walter stepped over, Pike reached for his hand, and pulled him down, positioning him in front of him, facing the same way. He caressed his torso, and squeezed his cock, eliciting a gasp.

Slater pulled off his shirt and threw it toward the closet, then squatted to untie his boots. Rising again, he held Walter's gaze and yanked on the end of his belt.

"It won't come undone." He raised his eyebrows. "I'm going to need your help."

Stepping to the side of the bed, he jutted his crotch toward him. Walter reached up and gingerly unbuckled his belt.

"What about the fly?" Slater demanded. "Hop to it, son."

He chuckled and pulled open the buttons, popping them one by one. Slater pushed his jeans down, and stepped out of them, and squeezed his swelling cock.

"There's more," Walter said.

"More what?"

"More stuff that revs me up."

Slater gestured impatiently. "Spill it."

"It was really hot when you two were on either side of me." He turned his head to look sidelong at Pike. "I kind of like the feeling of your arms around me. The strength in them."

"You like to be cuddled," Pike said, "or you like to be restrained?"

"I haven't really figured it out yet. Something

about power. Being powerless."

"People with big jobs are like that sometimes," Pike said. "It inverts the daily experience of being the one who has to make all the decisions."

Slater put his hands on his hips. "Enough with the psychoanalysis, Dr. Jung. Should I break out the handcuffs?"

Walter's eyebrows shot up. "You have those?"

"I've got lots." He stepped around to the night-stand, and dug around, and pulled out a heavy pair. "These are really comfortable."

"This is crazy," Walter said.

"Your cock says otherwise," Pike said, and squeezed it.

Walter took a breath. "All right. Hook me up."

He handed the cuffs to Pike, and Pike flipped Walter onto his belly. He yelped but didn't struggle, and Pike grabbed his wrists, pulling them behind his back, and deftly clicked on the cuffs. Walter was red-faced when he pulled him up to sitting again.

"You did that so fast."

"I've had practice," Pike said.

"What happens now?"

"You shut the fuck up is what," Slater snapped.

Walter's eyes grew wide, and Slater sat next to him on the bed.

"Unless you want to have input. I'm role-playing here."

"It's actually good," Walter said. "You can be tough with me."

"Can I fuck you?" Pike said, massaging his chest.

"Don't ask him," Slater said. "Tell him." He waved an arm at Pike. "He's going to fuck you."

Pike reached for the bedside table, and grabbed the lube and a condom, and rolled it on. Shifting Walter onto his side, he massaged a lubed thumb into him. Stretching out in front of him, Slater squeezed Walter's swollen cock, then pressed his mouth onto his, probing it. The guy was good at this, responsive, and he could feel himself getting hard.

Pulling back, Walter groaned. As Pike pressed into him, his face contorted and reddened.

"Look at me," Slater said, and held his gaze for a moment as Pike started to pound him, his arms around Walter's torso.

He lubed up Walter's cock and squeezed it between his thighs, then pulled himself closer, letting the momentum of Pike's thrusts press Walter into him. He mouthed Walter's neck, and his ear, and his jaw. He could feel Pike building up to it, and soon he climaxed, pulling himself closer to Walter.

Once Pike had shifted back, Slater squeezed Walter's cock and explored his mouth again. Once Walter was hard enough, he straddled his hips and lowered himself onto him, wincing as he penetrated him. He rocked back and forth, and after a minute Walter grunted and came, his face contorted, his body shuddering. Slater caressed his chest as he caught his breath.

"Can I smoke you?" Walter said finally.

Slater shifted up and slapped his face with his woody, then let Walter take him into his mouth. The guy worked him hard. Pike wrapped an arm around Walter's belly and met Slater's eye. His lip curling into a sneer, Pike jutted his chin. Pike knew him so well, knew that it would send him, make him climax.

He pulled back from Walter, breathing hard and red-faced from the exertion, and lay with his eyes closed, enjoying the warmth and the stillness, the feeling of satiety.

"Maybe you can uncuff me," Walter said.

"In a minute," Slater mumbled. "Where are your car keys?"

He chuckled. "Don't even joke about that."

Slater sat up and scrabbled in the drawer for the key to the cuffs.

"What do you drive that's so hot Slater wants to steal it?" Pike said.

"A '74 Barracuda."

"Another classic car guy."

Slater leaned behind him and unlocked the cuffs, and pulled them off, and dropped them into the drawer.

"It's cherry," Walter said, massaging his wrists in turn. "It has the 360 V-8."

"I don't really know what that means. Slater's the car whack."

"Can we do that thing again?" Walter said. "Where I'm in the middle of the sandwich? It felt really good."

Pike chuckled. "Sure."

He flipped onto his side, with his back to Walter, and Walter shifted close to him. Slater moved behind him and shoved an arm under Walter's neck, wrapping his other arm around them both, resting his palm on Pike's chest. The guy was right—this was pretty amazing.

After a while Walter sat up and went for a shower, then Slater joined him, and then Pike stepped in as

Walter got out and grabbed a towel.

As he was stepping into his skivvies, Walter said, "Any chance you want to eat? I worked up an appetite."

Pike eyed Slater and raised his eyebrows.

Slater shrugged. "I could eat."

"I make decent pancakes," Pike said. "I even learned how to do them vegan."

"That suits me." Walter was buttoning his shirt. "I'm lactose intolerant."

Pike pulled on his sweatpants and a Henley before he walked out. Putting on a pair of Pike's baggy boxer shorts and a white T-shirt, Slater beckoned Walter to follow and trudged up the stairs to the kitchen.

Walter draped his suit jacket over a chair at the dining table, and they watched as Pike threw together the batter.

"You cook like my mother," Walter said, leaning back on the counter. "You're not measuring anything."

"I've done it often enough that I can eyeball it."

"When she makes pancakes, she serves them with ranch dressing."

"That's the most goyishe thing I've ever heard," Slater said.

He laughed. "You're both Jewish? I noticed Pike's star tattoo."

"My mother hates that I have tats," Pike said.

"My mother doesn't know that I have tats."

"Why not?"

"It would give her a coronary." Walter waved a hand. "One of the name partners at my firm uses that word, *goyishe*. He saw my car, and he said, 'Big cars are goyishe, but big jewelry is Jewish.'"

Slater folded his arms, watching them chat. This was the part that was unfamiliar, the socializing, the yapping. He'd never invested time in stuff like this before Pike because it seemed so pointless.

Eventually Pike loaded pancakes onto a couple of plates and took them to the dining table. As he set down a bottle of syrup, he said, "This feels a little awkward."

"What's awkward?" Slater frowned at him as he dropped into a chair.

Pike gestured with the lifter. "A colored woman such as myself making pancakes for two white folks. It feels like Jimmy Crow's South."

"You are so fucking weird," Slater said.

Pike laughed and stepped back into the kitchen.

Scooting his chair closer to the table, Walter called to him. "You know I'm not white, right?" Eyeing Slater, he furrowed his brow. "Neither are you."

Slater dug into a pancake with his fork. "I think your advanced sexual abilities damaged his psyche."

"Now I know you're messing with me." He called to Pike, "You're a pretty upbeat guy."

"I call it his persistent optimism," Slater said through a mouthful of food. "Like a cork in the water. It doesn't matter what happens to it. Push it down, move it around. It instantly bobs back to the surface."

"It's just the way I'm wired," Pike said, sitting down with them. "I can't really switch it off."

———•———

AFTER THEY'D EATEN, WALTER pushed his plate away and waved at the room. "There's so much empty space here. And the wood floor. You could hold ball-room events."

"You dance?" Pike said.

"I used to take classes."

"We just took a swing class." He stood up. "Come on."

"I'm not wearing the right shoes."

"We're just messing around." He beckoned for him to follow and walked to the other end of the room, next to the lounge furniture, and turned on the audio unit. "What kind of music should I play?"

Walter pulled off his socks and tucked them into his pants pocket. "Big band. Benny Goodman or Duke Ellington."

"That seems a little fast." Pike tapped at his phone.

"They're easy to follow. If you've taken classes, you'll be able to keep up."

An upbeat tune came on, with a lot of brass, and Walter walked over to Pike. The pair of them stood in the middle of the room facing each other.

"Foxtrot?" Pike said.

Walter put his hand on Pike's neck, and Pike held his waist, and they started moving to the music. Still sitting at the dining table, Slater leaned back, and laced his fingers behind his head, and watched them. It was incongruous, Pike in his sweats and Walter in suit pants and a dress shirt, but the way they moved was smooth and coordinated. These two made it look easy, even though he knew damn well it wasn't.

At one point Pike stumbled, and laughed, and they pulled apart.

"That was my fault," Walter said.

"You're better at this than I am."

They stood together again and started to move. It was mesmerizing to watch, as they were both good at it, but it made Slater feel odd—his stomach was queasy, and he could feel his heart pounding.

The next song was faster, and the pair of them switched to swing style, laughing as they played around with spin moves and under-arm turns. When the song ended they were both sweating.

Pike approached the dining table, a silly grin on his face. "Want to take a turn?"

"Compared to you two I'm a stumblebum on the dance floor," Slater said. "It makes me happy just to watch you. That's what this house is for." He waved his arm. "That's why this room is empty. To make space for you, so that you can laugh, so that I can hear you laugh. It makes my heart beat faster, and it makes my stomach hurt. In a good way."

Pike's face contorted, and he dropped to one knee, and pressed his mouth onto Slater's neck, wrapping his arms around him.

"We kind of did things backwards," Walter said. "Evangelicals say dancing is the devil's gateway to sex. Up in here the sex led to dancing."

Pike chuckled at that as he rose and sat on Slater's knee, draping his arm around his neck.

"Isn't that kind of the way the world works now?" Slater put his hand on Pike's back. "Things move faster, and not always in sequence. Like with clothing. Trends change so quickly that no single style can spread and become a whole thing."

"Interesting commentary from the man who has exactly one look, and it dates to the 1850s," Pike said.

Walter laughed. "It sounds like somebody's been

reading *Women's Wear Daily.*"

"My office is surrounded by the fashion industry," Slater said. "I hear things."

"I think I'm overheated." Walter flapped the front of his shirt, wet with sweat below his pecs. "Can we go out on your deck?"

Pike rose and started picking up the plates, and Slater led Walter out through the French doors, into the cold evening air.

"I can almost see my office from here." Walter braced his hands on the low wall that surrounded the deck.

Slater stood next to him. "You signed an IOU to a guy named Chad. I assume he's blackmailing you."

Standing erect again, he stared at him for a moment. "Are you working for him?"

"I'm working for one of his other victims. My plan is to shut Chad down."

Even in the low ambient light of the city, Slater could see that his chest was heaving.

"You got me here under false pretenses. Hitting on me in that bar. I knew it was too good to be real."

"You got free mind-blowing sex, complete with props," Slater said. "That was completely authentic. I wouldn't have hit on you if I didn't want to fuck you."

Walter didn't respond, but stood staring at him.

"If I'd mentioned my investigation up front, you wouldn't have even talked to me."

"You lied to me."

"I lie to everyone," Slater said. "Get over it. What's important is that our interests overlap. Chad is messing with you, and I want to mess with him."

"I can't believe you did that to me," he said, raising

his voice, then struck Slater's shoulder with the heel of his hand.

Turning to face him, Slater balled his fists. "Walter, believe me, you do not want to go there."

He hit him again, using more force this time. Slater slapped him hard, left and then right, a rapid kovac.

"Why do you make me do this to you?" Slater demanded. It took all his strength, all his willpower to take a step back, not to lunge at him, not to grab him by the throat.

Holding his palm to his cheek, Walter's eyes grew wide. He turned suddenly and strode inside, leaving the door open, and grabbed his jacket from the back of the chair at the dining table. Slater saw him jab a finger at Pike and shout something before he went to the stairs. As Slater stepped inside and crossed to the kitchen, he heard the front door slam.

Pike leaned back on the counter. "That went south in a hurry. He was beet red. What happened?"

"He's part of my case. The guy I'm after is blackmailing him. Walter didn't actually know that until a minute ago."

Pike folded his arms. "I can't believe you'd do that. How can you be objective about your targets when you're that intimate with them?"

"I thought I'd soften him up with a little action, feed him some pancakes. Then he'd be predisposed to leveling with me."

"I guess he doesn't like surprises."

He gestured helplessly. "I miscalculated."

"You know, I've seen that before," Pike said. "The freak-out, the overreaction. People who've been in combat. I'd say that guy has PTSD."

"Is that it, or is he just uptight?" Slater ran a hand through his hair. "Don't you just want to skull-fuck the guy, and make him chill out?"

Pike's eyes narrowed. "Interesting approach, petal. As an alternative, I'd maybe give him a little neck massage, offer him a beer, ask how his day was."

"You'd still wind up in the sack with him. How could you not? My way is better."

TEN

N THE MORNING SLATER got dressed and climbed the stairs. He found Pike in the kitchen, dressed for work, eating a bagel.

"Java?" Pike said.

"Hit me."

He poured him a mugful from the pot, and as he handed it to him, the doorbell rang.

"Are you expecting anyone?" Slater said, slurping at the joe.

"I'm not. I'll go."

He headed down the stairs and returned a minute later with a big arrangement of red roses in a glass vase.

"Can you believe this?" Pike said.

"Who's it from?"

"Let's have a look." He set the vase on the counter

and pulled off the card, reading it aloud: "Apologies for my inappropriate outburst. I hold you both in deep esteem. Warmest regards, Walter."

"Why would he do this?" Slater demanded.

"It's classic PTSD behavior. Freak out and blow up, then express remorse later."

"It's a lot of freaking roses."

"Two dozen," Pike said, and met his gaze. "That means we have to marry him now."

"It actually gives me an advantage. The fact that he's apologizing. I can push a little harder and get him to squawk."

"These need water." He set them in the sink and filled the vase. "Where should I put them?"

"Up to you," Slater said. "You're the one who danced with him. That means legally he's your fiancé."

Pike chuckled and moved the vase to the middle of the dining table.

"You packed a bag," Slater said, and gestured to the black duffel on the floor by the stairs. "Are you headed out of town?"

"I'm going to Bakersfield today. I might have to stay over. I'll be back if we can track down our biker."

"Are you going with Davis?"

"I am. Not that it matters. He's a colleague."

"He wants into your pants so bad," Slater said. "You know it, and I know it, and he definitely knows it."

"You're wrong about that."

He put his hands on his hips. "He needs to keep his grubby paws off the merchandise."

"Down here on planet Earth," Pike said, "in

consensus reality, he's straight and married and not interested in me."

"Two shots of tequila and any straight guy would be all over you." Slater waved at his body. "Look at you. You're a solid slab of man sex."

Pike stepped closer and embraced him. "You're so damn crazy," he said softly, and met his mouth, and lingered in it. Pulling him close, he ground his burgeoning woody into Slater's thigh. "I don't have time for this." He massaged Slater's biceps, and mouthed his neck, then wrapped his arms around his waist and pulled him tight. "Seriously, knock it off. I have to go."

"I'm getting mixed messages here," Slater said, and chuckled, running his hands over Pike's back.

With a hand in his hair, he nibbled at Slater's earlobe. "You're interfering with my investigation. That's a serious crime." Finally he pulled away, and adjusted his crotch, then scooped up his duffel. "I love you, forty-niner."

Slater spoke over the lump in his throat. "Forever." As Pike headed for the stairs, he called after him. "No monkey business with Davis, you big mook. Stay strong."

He heard the front door close, then found some berries in the icebox, and ate half a bagel, and finished his coffee. Digging out his phone, he checked on Chad. The idiot had gone downtown yesterday, then home to Pasadena. There were some terse texts with T, then an exchange with Liz. Chad wrote simply: "Thursday." Liz's response was, "I don't have time." Seconds later Chad shot back, "You don't have a choice." Her response to that was, "So sick of your bullshit. Sick of your ugly face." Chad responded, "Thursday."

That all jibed with what Liz had told him, that she was working for Chad under duress. Like she'd promised, she hadn't mentioned Slater, at least not by text. It made sense that if the guy was extorting her, she wouldn't have that kind of loyalty to him, to give him a head's up about someone poking around his operation.

When he checked on Walter's vehicle, the history log said that when he left here last night, he'd gone to his house in South Pas, then went to his office this morning. The circle for the vehicle's location was grayed out, but its last known location was the building where his law firm was. That made sense too— the tracker had lost connectivity in the depths of the underground garage, just like Slater's phone had.

Slater dialed Walter's number, and when he picked up, said, "Roses."

"Do you like them?"

"It's a lot of freaking flowers, man. Do you have time to see me this morning?"

"There's a coffee place on the corner near my office," Walter said.

Once Slater had backed into the street, he waited for the garage door to roll down, then headed to the nearby 101. It was one of the older freeways, and had short ramps, so he had to gun it to match the speed of the traffic, but the Continental was calm and confident in the task.

He found a meter up the block from Walter's office building, then walked to the coffee joint and stepped inside. The guy wasn't here yet, so he went to the counter and ordered an oat milk latte.

He saw Walter step in, and called to him, "What are you drinking?"

"An espresso."

Once he had the cups in hand, he sat with Walter at a table next to the wall.

"I wanted to apologize for my reaction last night," Walter said.

"I figured that out from the roses."

"I can't believe you hit me."

"I didn't hit you, Walter. I gave you a kovac. It's meant to focus attention, not cause any damage." He raised his eyebrows. "It was open-handed."

"I don't do criminal law, but I assume you say that because it would be a lesser assault charge."

"You started it, toots. That's what really matters."

Walter held up a palm. "I was surprised, that's all. It doesn't negate the delightful time we had with Pike." His expression sobered. "So how did you find out about the IOU?"

"I managed to get a look at some of Chad's files. You signed it, and it was on your firm's letterhead. From there it was easy to find you."

"That doesn't explain how you found me at the Baltimore."

"There's pictures of your Barracuda online," Slater said. "I followed it from your office. It's pretty distinctive."

"That feels invasive."

"I'm not the one who bought a fifty-year-old lime-green muscle car, and I'm not the one who posted selfies with it online."

"Fair enough." Walter watched him for a moment.

"Can you get it back for me?"

He shook his head. "I saw a copy of it, not the original."

"It would be great if you could put those two out of business."

"What was the shakedown?"

"Do you really need to know that?"

"Dude," Slater said. "Last night I had my dick down your throat. I can handle your raunchy stories."

Walter glanced sidelong at the woman sitting at the next table. She was ignoring them, absorbed in her phone. He sighed and lowered his voice.

"I was in a nightclub, and Tanner offered me molly."

"What does Tanner look like?"

"Blond, beefy. The jock type."

"He works for Chad?"

"I don't know who's the mastermind. I know they're working together."

Slater gestured with his cup. "What's the name of the club?"

"Electric."

"So you're in the club, and now you're rolling ecstasy."

"Is that the same as molly?"

He narrowed his eyes. "It is."

"I don't have a lot of experience with drugs," Walter said, "or hooking up. I'm a little sheltered."

"You knew exactly what you wanted last night. You managed to articulate it clearly."

"I figured that was a rare opportunity. The fact that you were tuned in enough to ask. Lots of guys are selfish about sex."

"It sounds like you're hooking up with the wrong guys."

"I really enjoyed that, by the way."

"Me too." Slater shifted in his chair. "So Tanner gave you molly."

"It makes you feel all loose, right, and being touched felt amazing. Once my inhibitions were down, he pulled me into a stall in the men's room, and I'm kissing him, and then Tanner puts a needle on my arm."

"He injected you with something?"

Walter shook his head. "He just held the syringe against my forearm. It was kind of pressing down into the skin, so in the photo it looked like I was injecting drugs."

"When did you see the photo?"

"It was right after. Like the next day. Chad was the one who sent it. He threatened to send it to my firm, and to my family. I'd lose my job if they saw me doing drugs. My parents would see their worst fears come true. They'd never believe it was a setup." He sighed. "It was pretty blatant."

"So you're paying him."

"What choice do I have?"

Slater slurped his latte. "Show me the photo."

He winced. "Is that really necessary?"

"I'm not judging you. I already know what's going on."

Pulling his phone out of his jacket, Walter tapped at it, then handed it over. The image was lurid, taken with a flash, at an angle from above. Walter had his shirt unbuttoned, his arm tied off with a length of red cord around the Polynesian tattoo on his bicep, a syringe against his forearm. It was hard to tell that the tip of the needle wasn't actually in his skin. A pale hand was wrapped around his forearm, with a couple of fingers holding the syringe against him. He could see part of the guy's torso, and his blue satin shirt, but not his face.

"Did you see who took this?"

"I assume it was Chad. He must have held the camera over the stall door. I know they're working together."

"It's pretty damn convincing. It totally looks like you're shooting up." Slater handed the phone back. "Why is your arm tied off?"

"I was so out of it. I didn't know why he did that. I thought it was some club thing people were doing."

"You could tell your law firm that it's a faked photo. Some generative AI bullshit."

"It seemed easier just to pay the guy than to break open that wasps' nest." Walter looked away. "I'm also not completely out with my family. I mean, they know. My sister knows. But I've never clearly explained it to my parents." He met Slater's gaze and furrowed his brow. "It's a cultural thing. They're old-school."

"Again, Walter, I'm not here to judge you. So Chad hit you up for more dough?"

"Over and over. One time I didn't have the cash, so he took my pinkie ring. It's a family piece. Gold with a jade stone." He scoffed. "I fantasize about murdering that fucker. I could bury his body out in the desert. The gangsters do it. Nobody would ever find him."

"That's what they call the blackmailer's ultimate reward. I can't say he hasn't earned it."

Walter glanced at his watch. "I should get back to the office."

They walked out together, and Slater headed to his car. Before he started the engine, he looked through Chad's texts again. He didn't remember seeing the name Tanner, but he often texted with somebody named T. The messages were so brief that they almost felt coded: "OK," and "Thx," and late last night, an eye-roll emoji with no context. This might be the guy.

A search for the phone number with the name Tanner brought up no useful results. Andy's place was right around the corner, and he started the engine, and drove over, and parked in the surface lot behind his building. Upstairs Andy pulled open the door.

"You should call first. I'm headed out soon."

"You're here, aren't you?"

Andy waved him in, and dropped into his desk chair, and swiveled to face him. "What do you need?"

"I have a cell number and a first name. I need whatever you can find."

"Text it to me. I'll do it right now, if you … want, before I go."

Standing with his feet planted apart, Slater tapped at his phone. "Are you headed over to spouse B's lair?"

"It's not really any of your business what I do."

"Not anymore," Slater said, looking up. "Not since you dumped me in the gutter like street trash."

He scoffed. "I'm going to the doctor. I've got this … intermittent cough. It's probably just an inevitable … consequence of the CP, but it's been bugging me." He turned to his computer. "Give me a minute."

Slater watched as he pulled on his gauntlets, a pair of black plastic sleeves wired to his computer as an input device. Somehow they compensated for his lack of fine motor control. While he waited he gazed out the window toward the square, and the buildings on the other side.

"His full name is Tanner Newkirk-Sloane," Andy said.

"Where did you find that?"

"Some stuff about a football team. The Voles. Wasn't that … on the phone you had me copy?"

"Totally. This fool has the same last name as the idiot with the phone. They have to be related."

"There's lots of hits about … Tanner on the web," Andy said, and jutted his chin at the screen. "This is him."

Slater stepped closer and peered at the image. It was a portrait of a guy in the purple Voles uniform with padding under it. He was seated and cradling a football in one arm.

"He plays on the team," Slater said.

"He's easy to look at. Maybe a little dumb."

As he clicked to other photos, there were several of him on the gridiron.

"The guy is hot." Slater leaned in. "That butt is pretty close to perfect."

"I guess. If you like them beefy."

"Is there anything about where he lives?"

"I could dig deeper, but here it … says Pasadena. No street address."

"Don't bother. He's around the same age as Chad, the idiot with the phone. I can see a family resemblance. I'll wager they're brothers. Chad still lives with his parents. I bet Tanner does too."

"So you have enough on the guy?" Andy said.

"It's all I need. That took you no time at all. I can't believe what you charge me for this."

"You can't do it yourself, can you? The time it takes isn't … the point. It's my skills, and my extensive resources. You owe me for the … last one too, by the way. Let's say six dollars total."

Slater scoffed. "You're a damn chiseler." He dug out his wad and peeled off six C-notes. "Why don't you live off that gunsel spouse of yours for a change and stop squeezing me so hard? I'm going to have to start eating cup noodles and selling loosies outside a tiendita."

Sliding off his gauntlets, Andy took the cash from his hand. "It's fair payment for the … work I do. And you claiming poverty is a laugh. I'm still … living off that fifty large you walked into out … in New Mexico."

"I busted my ass for that."

"So did I. Plus you got a … boyfriend out of the deal."

"Such a simplistic word," Slater said. "It's so much more than that. What Pike and I have is a multi-dimensional narrative complex."

"So I've heard." He raised his eyebrows. "I know you … love it, by the way. Handing over the cash, making it rain for … someone as gorgeous as me."

"No one could deny that you are a total smoke show." Slater watched him for a moment. "Bye, beautiful."

Walking out, he went down to the street and got in his car. Before he pulled out of the parking lot he checked Svetlana's tracking app for Bucky. Did he know about Tanner? Walter was being extorted in a similar way, and he knew Chad and Tanner both. The map showed that Bucky was in Thai Town. He tapped his number to call him, but he didn't pick up.

"Idiot," he muttered. He sent him a text:

Call me.

Thinking about it, Chad and Tanner were running the squeeze play together, and they lived at the same place. He pulled up a street view of Chad's address. A tall hedge obscured the house, but the gated driveway was visible. If he borrowed somebody's nondescript car, he could sit there and watch who was coming and going. Usually that kind of stakeout took hours and hours, and rich folks were way more likely to notice a vehicle that didn't belong, especially with a brown guy sitting in it. Some bored neighbor would get him pinched. Maybe there was a better way.

ELEVEN

PANNING AROUND THE STREET view of Chad's house, Slater found a well-positioned utility pole, almost directly opposite the house's driveway. That could work—he wouldn't have to sit on his ass in the cold for half the night. He didn't know where to get a bucket truck, but Gabe might. It was already late afternoon, and Gabe would likely be home. He was a painter, and those guys worked early in the day. Gabe had once told him the wind didn't come up until eleven, so morning was always the best time to paint building exteriors.

Scrolling through his contacts to find Gabe, he dialed his number.

"Hey, *cabrón*," he answered. "It's been a while."

"I need a couple of things," Slater said. "Maybe you can help me out."

"What do you need?"

"Are you at your place?"

"I'm driving through downtown LA, but I'll be home in a minute. You can come by." Gabe had that East LA dialect, where *LA* sounded like *el lay*.

Slater ended the call, and started the engine, and pulled into the traffic, heading north on Broadway to Lincoln Heights. The houses on Gabe's street were squeezed tight together, all with fences fronting the narrow sidewalks. Gabe's yard was easy to remember, with the flourishing deodar cedar in front, the only one on the block. He pulled to the curb in front of the tidy little house. The gate was open, and Gabe's familiar white work truck was in the driveway.

Walking up to the screen door, Slater pressed the bell. It wasn't really a screen, built from heavy security bars backed by steel mesh to let the air through. People usually painted them white to make it look less like the hoosegow. Gabe's wife opened the inner door and peered out at him through the mesh. Her name was Lupe, he remembered.

She smiled in recognition. "I'll get Gabe."

Interesting that she remembered he didn't speak Spanish, Slater thought, even though he looked like he should. She'd left the inner door open, and he could hear a kid's voice. They had a daughter or two, he remembered, and a toddler-age son.

Stepping down to the scrubby front yard, he looked over the cedar. These weren't native, but the local animals loved them, and they stabilized the soil. They weren't susceptible to pests either, and tended to live a long time. He put a hand on the bark. Gabe's was in admirable shape.

A minute later Gabe stepped outside, pulling both doors closed behind him. Wearing a work shirt and jeans, his black hair was slicked back, and he'd grown a mustache since Slater had last seen him.

"What do you need that you can't talk about on the phone?" Gabe said.

"Either a bucket truck with a lift, or some lineman's gear."

He laughed. "So you're going up a pole."

"That's the plan."

"I don't know anyone who has a bucket truck, or even uses one at work."

"What about a lineman?"

"You want to hire one?"

"I can do it myself," Slater said.

He raised his eyebrows. "Have you done it before?"

"How hard can it be?" He put his hands on his hips. "I've climbed trees before to trim them, and I can get that kind of equipment. The spikes for your boots. But poles are different. There's no branches to grab. Those lineman types have a safety belt and all that."

"Getting the gear will be a lot easier than hiring somebody. If you work for the cable company or the DWP it would be big trouble to get caught up a pole when you're off the job."

"So you know people?"

"I'll find out," Gabe said. "When do you need it?"

"As soon as possible. I'll pay to use the stuff, but don't let them gouge me." He waved a hand. "Maybe you can help me out too. Stay on the ground and be my lookout. Play dumb for any chumps who question what I'm doing."

Gabe nodded. "I got you, bro. It'll look more legit if we take my truck."

As he walked out to the Continental, daylight was fading to dusk. Once he was behind the wheel he checked on Bucky again. He was still in the same place in Thai Town. What the hell was he up to? Shopping for more crystals and tarot cards, dried sage in little sisal-bound bundles, maybe a Ouija board? Zooming in on the map, he saw that the dot was in a grocery store. The location history said he'd been there for nine hours.

That seemed extremely odd—nobody spent nine hours shopping for groceries. Real estate wasn't a nine-to-six job, but even if he was going to sell the building, no way would he spend that much time in it. Bucky must have left his phone there, the fricking idiot. That's why he wasn't responding. Nobody would go nine hours without retrieving their phone—he didn't know where he'd lost it.

Slater thought it through. He could retrieve it for him, and tell him that he'd found it in the driveway of his house. That way he wouldn't have to reveal that he had a tracker on the device. He scoffed. Other people's stupidity was so damn frustrating.

Starting the engine, he flicked on the headlights and navigated toward Thai Town. The navigation software sent him on the 5, which seemed counterintuitive, but it must be the best of the bad options. At this hour it was a sluggish river of brake lights.

When he got to the market he parked on a side street off Hollywood Boulevard, then walked around to the entrance. He had to squint at the sudden glare as he stepped into the bright fluorescent-lit interior.

Studying his phone screen, the tracking app showed the location for Bucky's phone as a green dot in the middle of the store. Slater walked toward it, turning down a long aisle, and stopped when the dot for his phone overlapped the one for Bucky's.

Waving the phone around, he waited for the dot to shift, like it sometimes did, as the software calculated its position more precisely and made adjustments. But it was already confident about it, and the dot didn't budge. It made no sense—he was in the middle of a grocery aisle, and there was nowhere for the phone to be hiding on the floor. It wasn't upstairs either—from outside he'd scoped out the building, and it was a one-story structure, with an old flat roof, from the middle of the last century.

Looking over the shelves nearest to the location dot, he reached behind some packages of noodles, then pulled them forward, but there was nothing behind them.

A guy with a buzzed haircut approached him. In his early twenties, he was wearing a green apron with the store's logo on the front.

"Are you looking for something specific?" he said.

Slater shoved the noodles back into place. "Does this building have a basement?"

His eyebrows shot up. "Why are you asking?"

That had sparked a reaction, a shift in his expression. The guy was worried now.

"Because I want to go down there," Slater said.

"You're not the cops?"

"Do I look like the cops?"

His eyes flicked up and down Slater's form. "It's one fifty to get started."

"I'll deal with that when I get down there."

"Pon won't let you do anything until you pay."

"It sounds like I need to talk to Pon. Where can I find her?"

He beckoned him to follow by tilting his head, and walked toward the side of the store, leading him to a doorway between two refrigerator cases. The heavy wooden door was marked EMPLOYEES ONLY, and had a little window in it, with wire mesh in the glass. Beyond the window it looked completely dark.

Above the handle was a keypad, and the clerk stood to block Slater's view of it with his body. There were a series of faint beeps as he punched in a code, then pulled open the door. The movement switched on a lone fluorescent tube, revealing a flight of stairs leading down. With his hand still on the door handle, the clerk waved for him to go down, and glanced around the store.

It wasn't well lit, just enough to see where he was stepping, and Slater started down. Behind him he heard the door close and latch. The air was thick with a musky smoky smell. It wasn't weed, he decided, or incense. Something organic. It smelled a lot like burning yard trimmings.

At the bottom the lighting was low, and he found himself in front of a small counter, like at a restaurant. With the drop ceiling and the grimy ceramic tile floor, that might be what this place had been in a former incarnation, a banquet hall or a diner. Facing the counter a walkway led deeper inside, lined on both sides by floor-length tan curtains.

A guy stood near the counter, clad in a dark suit and with buzz-cut hair, his face lit by the blue glow of his phone screen. Slater knew the type—this was the heavy, security for whatever was going on down here. He didn't looked to be armed, with no telltale bulge under his suit. The guy was more flabby than he was muscled, and he looked sweaty, but he was still fuckable.

The guard glanced up at him, and didn't say anything, instead looking back to his screen. A moment later a woman stepped out of a doorway behind the counter. In her fifties, maybe, she was slight, and dressed in black, her hair cut in a wedge.

"Are you Pon?" Slater said.

"It's one fifty to start."

"Can you show me what I'm paying for?"

She frowned but reached below the counter, then set a lump of black stuff on it. The size of a quarter, it looked sticky. He wanted to probe it with a finger but he knew she'd probably smack him. Was it hash? Then it struck him—opium. This was raw opium latex.

Pon produced a long-stemmed pipe, and set it on the countertop, and met his eye. "Do you want a bed or not? I don't have all day."

He glanced at the map on his screen. Bucky's phone was just a few yards away. "I'm going to see what they look like first." Not waiting for a response, he turned and walked toward the location of the dot.

"Hey," Pon called after him, her tone sharp.

He knew the guard would be at his heels, and he quickly pulled a curtain aside. It felt thick, like raw canvas, and revealed a small space surrounded by more curtains. There was only room enough for a grubby narrow mattress. This one was currently unoccupied.

Slater moved to the next one, but before he could grab the curtain, he felt a hand on his shoulder, and it bodily yanked him back.

"Not so fast," the guard growled.

Before the guy had even got him turned around, Slater struck, a fast right to the side of his jaw. The guard yelped as his head snapped sideways. Slater ducked the guy's arm as he swung wildly at him, then landed a punch on the other side of his face, snapping his head again. The guard stumbled backward and sank to his knees, then slumped to one side, bracing himself with his hand on the floor.

The guy was dazed, Slater decided, watching him. He'd be out of commission for at least a minute or two. Yanking back the curtain of the next bed, he found Bucky lying there. He was on his side, wearing sweatpants and a hoodie, with one of the long pipes next to him on the skanky mattress.

Slater dropped to one knee and pressed two fingers to his neck. He had a pulse. Grabbing his shoulders, he gave him a shake. Bucky groaned but didn't open his eyes. Next he slapped him hard, left and then right, a firm kovac.

Pon was standing next to him now. "You can't harass my clients like that," she hissed.

"I'm taking him out of here."

"You knocked out my guy."

"He's down, not out. He'll come around." Slater met her gaze. "He's coming with me. It's not negotiable. Do not get in my way."

She frowned. "Just wait a minute."

Pon walked back toward the front counter, not hesitating as she stepped over the slumped form of the guard. Turning back to Bucky, he held a palm to his forehead for a moment. He felt warm enough.

A moment later Pon returned with a boxy little device in hand. He'd half expected her to come back with a six-gun, but then brandishing a weapon would be bad for business, and greasing him would definitely get her shut down. Slater had seen these before. He kept one in his glove box. It was an auto-injector for the drug that counteracted opioids.

"He overdid it," she said. "It's not going to kill him. He just needs to sleep it off. But this will speed things up."

Pon crouched next to him and yanked up Bucky's shirt sleeve, then slammed the device into his bicep. The thing beeped a couple of times, then she pulled it away and stood up.

A moment later Bucky opened his eyes, and frowned as he focused on Slater.

"It's amazing how fast that stuff works," he said, and slapped Bucky again.

"Stop that," Bucky said, swatting his hand away.

"Get up," Slater snapped.

He slowly sat up. "My head hurts."

"On your feet." He grabbed his arm and pulled him to standing. "Where's your car?"

"I took a rideshare. I can't really drive after coming here."

Slater eyed Pon. "Does he come here a lot?"

"Once in a while." She folded her arms. "Are you going to make trouble for me?"

"Why would I do that? You brought him out of it. Plus you're actually protecting the junkies." He waved at the curtained walkway. "Nobody's going to die here, like they do when they get fetty on the street."

Pon nodded and took a breath, then gestured to the far end of the space. "Take the back stairs."

The guard groaned, and Slater saw that he was starting to get up. With one arm around Bucky's waist, he eyed Pon again.

"That guy is no security guard. He has no idea how to brawl. I'm half his size and I knocked him down with two punches."

"Thank you for the editorial," she said flatly.

He walked with Bucky toward the stairs and followed him up. The guy was stable enough on his feet to trudge up the steps without help. At the top was a fire door with a crash bar, and when Bucky hesitated in front of it, Slater shoved him into it, snapping the door open. They emerged in the parking lot behind the building, in the sudden cool evening air. Bucky took a sharp breath and shrugged off Slater's hand.

"This way." Slater led him to the Continental and opened the passenger door for him.

When Bucky sat down, he closed his eyes and rested his head on the back of the seat. He rolled his head to the side to look at Slater. "Buzzkill."

Ignoring that, Slater fired up the engine and pulled into the street. There were low clouds drifting in the night sky, he saw, and it wasn't just the marine layer. These had texture, like actual weather. They rode in silence until Bucky sat up and heaved a sigh.

"You seem to have your life together," Slater said. "Why can't you find a less stupid way to get turnt?"

"It makes all the nonsense fade away. Have you ever tried it? It's truly amazing. I don't really hallucinate but I get these vivid waking dreams."

"How fascinating," Slater said flatly. "Did you smoke that stuff before you lost your memory on the airplane?"

"Maybe. It's an organic high, not like oxy or purple drank. I never lost my memory before. I can't imagine a daydream would have made me go to Albuquerque."

"Maybe you should look for some essential oil fragrances that counteract opioids. Some pretty seashells might do the trick. Or get your aura power-washed."

"I know you're not being serious."

"I know a guy who's in NA," Slater said. "Do you want to talk to him?"

Bucky turned to him and smiled sweetly. "No thanks."

"In twelve-step the first thing you have to do is admit you have a problem. Maybe that's what you need to do."

"You're a twelve-stepper?"

"Lots of people around me wish I was. My boyfriend made me read the books."

"So it's good enough for me, but not for you," Bucky said. "You're just fine."

"I never said I didn't have problems. But as an objective observer, Bucky, I can assure you that you are an emotional wreck."

As he rolled up Bucky's street, a few sparse raindrops dappled the windshield. Slater killed the engine and climbed out to walk him inside. Bucky dug out his keys and opened the front door, then went over and collapsed onto the sofa.

"How did you find me, anyway?"

Slater stood facing him. "I followed your intense psychic energy. Your aura was lit up like those spotlights they use at movie premieres." He waved his index fingers in the air.

"Bullshit." He lifted his hand from the sofa and let it flop down. "Try again."

"The woman who runs the place was worried about you. You'd been there too long. She found my number on you."

"That seems odd. They usually don't care how long I stay, as long as I pay up."

Slater waved it away. "So Chad has accomplices."

He scowled. "That fucker. And you wonder why I smoke the dream stick."

"Did you ever meet a woman named Liz with him, or a man named Tanner?"

"I only ever talked to Chad. I didn't know he had a crew."

"Was he ever with anyone else at the Blue Dragon?"

"Never." Bucky raised his eyebrows. "He holds court at one of the booths. He's always by himself. Just what have you found out?"

"I'm still working on it." He put his hands on his hips. "You know you're not a junkie, right? You need to stop acting like one."

"Stop judging me. And don't tell me what to do."

Slater scoffed and walked out.

It was raining a little harder, still not enough to get wet between the front door and the car, but he turned on the wipers for the drive to his house.

Once he'd pulled the Continental into the garage, he walked up the stairs and through the kitchen, glancing at the big bouquet on the dining table. That was a lot of freaking roses. On the sofa he pulled off his boots, and set them on the artificial grass, then stretched out and folded his arm over his eyes. Food, sex, and booze, in that order.

His phone buzzed in his jeans, and he dug it out. The caller ID said REDDY KILOWATT.

"You're still in B-field," he said as he picked up.

"Davis calls it Bako. We're staying overnight."

"That little schvantz better have his own room."

"He does. And he's a decent guy. You need to give him a break."

"Like Odysseus did for the hundred guys sniffing around Penelope?" Slater said. "Would you murder-tize a hundred guys if they were macking on me?"

"I might look for an alternate resolution. Those guys were brutal. And I'm not going to ask you about what you'd do to a hundred guys macking on me," Pike said. "I already know the answer."

Slater asked him about his day, and told him about the opium den. Eventually Pike said he had to crash.

"Use the security lock on your door," Slater said. "Davis will definitely try to get in when you're asleep. When your defenses are down."

"You sound punchy. Maybe you got an opium contact high. You should get some sleep."

"When you get into bed, I want you to imagine me going down on you. Your woody deep in my throat."

"Stop that," Pike said softly.

"I'm looking up at you with puppy-dog eyes, and you run your hands into my hair."

"Damn it." He huffed. "I'm hanging up now."

"Lock your door," he said intently.

The sex rules said he could get with other guys when Pike was out of town, and he opened the hookup app, and spent a minute swiping through naked torsos and dick pics and other body parts. It was hard to parse which guys were homeless and which weren't. Homeless people needed sex too, but they were more work, more prone to steal, more likely to do something weird.

He was too tired for this, he decided. Maybe he could take a night off. Once he killed the app he forced himself up off the sofa, and went to the kitchen cabinet, and poured his ration.

The paucity of it was frustrating. If he couldn't do a hookup, maybe he could bend the booze rules a little. From the fifth he poured another healthy inch into the tumbler. Food, he remembered. He should probably eat something. Instead he walked over to the French doors, and stood looking out at the lights of the city. There was a coating of wet on everything now, and more of it was coming down. Even in the rain he could feel the metropolis out there, the weight of it, the never-ending dull roar of activity.

Fricking opium. Bucky and his vivid waking dreams. He slurped at his glass, relishing the heady burn. At least this stuff didn't amplify that kind of bogus noise. The effect was the opposite—it tamped down all the bullshit.

TWELVE

<hr>

MUTED GRAY DAYLIGHT WAS in the windows when he woke, and his head ached. He must have gone back for more bourbon. Sitting up, his head pounded, and he felt nauseous. Once he'd steadied himself with a few deep breaths, he stood up, and went to the bathroom, and eyed himself in the mirror. He looked haggard and washed out. Leaning in, he could see his eyes were bloodshot.

"Booze hag," he said through his teeth.

After he'd popped some ibuprofen and showered, he went upstairs. He could see that the deck outside was still wet, the sky gray, but it wasn't raining anymore. He stood and stared absently for a minute at the vase full of roses, breathing deeply to try to quell the achiness, then looked at his phone. Gabe had texted earlier:

I found a lineman. You can get the stuff later today. Are you around?

He thumb-typed a reply:

Tell them to bring it. Can we meet at your place?

While he was sipping coffee, trying to get up to speed, his phone buzzed with Gabe's reply:

Be here at 2.

All he wanted to do right now was crawl back into bed, but he had stuff to do. He texted Svetlana:

Can I come by?

Her reply buzzed his phone a minute later:

I am always here for you.

Taking a few breaths, he headed down to the garage, and did a neck roll to get the blood pumping before he backed into the street, the asphalt still wet from the rain.

This headache was why booze was legal and opium wasn't. He'd tied one on last night and he was still going to work. Bucky was probably going to sleep for three days. Dope was just bad for productivity. Booze had an immediate built-in punishment. It kept all this running, the airplanes and the lawyers and the florists.

Slater drove to Glendale and parked in front of Svetlana's building. Once he was through the scanner, and the inner door lock snapped open, he stepped into the workshop to find a woman he'd never seen before standing nearby, waiting for him.

In her twenties, she had her blond hair up in a messy bundle behind her head. She was wearing a crop top, even though it was winter outside. But it was warm enough in here for it.

The other unfamiliar element was a potted *Aglaonema* on the workbench, its wide leaves striated with silver. It looked lush and healthy, like it had just come from a shop.

"Sveta will come out soon." The woman gestured to the door that led to another part of the building. Her Slavic accent was thicker than Svetlana's.

"OK," he said, but she didn't step away, and stood there studying him.

"You are the one who helped Garik become gay, aren't you."

"I'm pretty sure he was already gay," Slater said. "I just took him out a few times."

"He has embraced it. He's a much happier person."

Russian and *happy* didn't really resonate, but he nodded anyway. "I'm glad to hear that."

"Garik has more boyfriends in one month than I have in a year."

He chuckled. "Good for him."

"You know he calls Sveta his aunt, but it's not a biological relationship."

Slater gestured to the potted plant on the workbench. "What's this?"

"The shopkeeper called it Chinese evergreen."

"I've never seen plants in here before."

"It's my intention to lighten up the place. Perhaps add some oxygen to this dark room. But I'm not sure how much to water it."

He stepped over and pressed a couple of fingers

into the soil. "It doesn't need water now. Let the soil dry out before you water it again. At least a week."

Her eyebrows shot up. "So rarely?"

"It needs tough love, not to be treated like a baby."

The electric lock on the inner door snapped, and Svetlana stepped in. She was wearing a blouse with a print of orange and purple hibiscus flowers. At her appearance the younger woman stepped away and wandered toward the other end of the workshop.

"I've seen you twice in one week," Svetlana said. "I'm a lucky woman." Her brow furrowed as she studied his face. "You have either been fist-fighting or overdrinking. *Pakmiriya.*"

"It's the bottle. I was on my own last night."

"Nights are long. Especially when it's raining. I know this."

He shifted on his feet. "So I want to put a camera high on a utility pole."

"For constant monitoring, or motion activated?"

"I just need to see vehicles entering and exiting a driveway."

"So motion activated with video clips. Also it needs to be zoomed in, I'm thinking, to record the number plates."

"That would be great."

"I have a camera that can do this," she said. "It will also list the numbers from the plates for you. How long must the battery last?"

"At least a few days. Maybe a week."

"I can connect a small solar panel. That way it can work forever."

"How small?" Slater said. "I don't want it to be noticed."

She held her hands up, less than a foot apart. "Like this."

"That'll work. I'm going to put it pretty high. Both components have to have mounting hardware."

"This pole is made of wood, or steel, or concrete?"

"It's wood."

She nodded. "I will need a few hours to construct the system. I'll text you when it's ready for you."

"Do you want me to pay you now?"

"Cash on delivery, my friend." Svetlana waved to dismiss it. "And drink pickle juice."

He narrowed his eyes. "Why?"

"For your alcohol headache."

"Got it."

Once he was out in his car, he sat behind the wheel for a minute to catch his breath. Why did he do this to himself? Pickle juice wasn't going to fix it. Even thinking about that made him nauseous.

Eventually he started the engine, and pulled into the street, and headed to the 5. It was just a few minutes' drive to Gabe's neighborhood.

Once he'd parked the Continental up the block from Gabe's house, he climbed out and stretched before he walked back. The sidewalk and the concrete in the driveway were already drying out. It was still overcast, but it hadn't rained since he'd been awake.

Gabe's truck was pulled all the way up the driveway, and Gabe must have spotted him, as he stepped out the door as Slater walked up.

"You look like you have the flu," Gabe said.

"Someone put too much bourbon in my glass."

"And you want to climb up utility poles."

"It doesn't have to be today."

"The lineman is going to give you some training, and that's definitely going to happen today."

"Great." Slater groaned. "What if it rains?"

"There's no more rain today."

The back end of a red pickup appeared at the gate, and backed into the driveway.

"Here she is," Gabe said, and leaning closer, lowered his voice. "She's a *pocho*."

He knew that word meant Americanized Mexicans, but it wasn't like Gabe needed to keep that on the down-low with him. Slater was even more disconnected from his Latin roots.

A woman stepped out of the cab. In her thirties, maybe, her dark hair was tied back, and she wore jeans and a plaid work shirt. She flashed a smile as she approached them, and Gabe introduced her as Rosa.

"You're the one climbing the poles?" she said to Slater.

"Just one pole."

"Gabe says you've never done it before. I feel a little queasy loaning you equipment for something you don't know how to do."

"I'm thinking a handful of lettuce will settle your stomach. What do I owe you?"

"Would three hundred work?"

"Done." Slater pulled out his wad, and peeled off the bills, and handed them over.

Rosa tucked them into her hip pocket, then stepped over to the pickup and unlocked the box behind the cab. She pulled out a pile of stuff, belts and carabiners and leather straps. It looked like old-school bondage gear. She piled it all in the driveway.

"Do you need gloves?" she said.

"I have my own."

She pulled a white helmet with a flared rim from the box. "You have to wear a hard hat. Do you have one of these?"

"I'm not going to be up there for long."

"It's not just for safety," Rosa said, and handed it to him. "It's so you'll look like you belong up there."

"Good thinking." Slater tried it on, and adjusted the inner band to get it to fit his head. "There's no logo on this. Do you work for the DWP?"

"I wish. Their benefits are stunning. I work for a small company that puts up fiber-optic lines."

"How does all this stuff work?" Gabe said, waving at the gear.

Rosa put her hands on her hips. "You know, I went to school for months to learn how to climb. I have a piece of paper that says I'm allowed to do it."

"Is it that complicated? I've been up trees before to trim branches and palm fronds." Slater gestured to the cedar in the yard. "I could climb that in a hot minute."

"Poles are probably easier than pine trees."

"That's a cedar."

"Whatever it is, the hooks are probably similar." She picked up a J-shaped piece of metal with a spike on the outside and straps dangling from it.

"Tree trimmers call those climbers," Slater said.

Rosa crouched and stepped her boot into it. "The Velcro goes around your calf, then the strap around your ankle. Make sure it's high on your heel."

Grabbing the other one, Slater strapped it on as Rosa watched.

"That looks right," she said. "The main thing is

the belt." She picked up the heavy leather strap. It had a series of loops and pouches on it. Pulling it on, she showed him how to buckle it, then grabbed the other big strap, and clipped it onto the belt with carabiners. "This is called the squeeze. It's the part that goes around the pole and supports your weight." She demonstrated by detaching one end and looping it in the air.

"We can try it on that one," Gabe said, and gestured to the utility pole just outside his front fence. It had electric lines at the top and thick insulated cables lower down.

"Won't your neighbors be suspicious about what you're doing?" Rosa said.

"This is a mind-your-business kind of neighborhood. Slater will wear the hard hat. No one will even look twice."

She took off the belt and handed it to Slater, watching closely as he fastened it around his hips. Finally she nodded approval, then pulled the hook off her boot and handed it over. Once he'd strapped it on, she checked that it was secure by tugging on it.

"Let's see what you've got," she said, and waved to the pole.

Slater pulled on the hardhat, and they trooped past her truck, out to the sidewalk. The pole was right at the edge of the concrete.

"You're supposed to bang on the pole first with a hammer to see if it's rotted or not."

"You do that with trees too," Slater said. "We call it sounding."

Gabe waved a hand. "How often do you find unsafe poles?"

"In the city it's rare," she said, "but out in the country it happens sometimes."

Slater stood next to the pole and unhooked one end of the squeeze, and reached around the pole with it, and connected it again with the carabiner.

"It looks a little loose," Rosa said, and showed him how to adjust it. "When you step, step hard, with your toes pointed out."

He lifted his foot and stepped firmly onto the pole, pushing himself up. The hook gave him solid footing. He took another step.

"Take your squeeze with you," she said.

He pulled it upward, and took another step, then leaned away from the pole, into the belt.

"When you lean back," she said, "lock your knees. It gives you more stability."

Moving up a few more steps, he experimented with the squeeze, tightening it a little, then leaning back. It was weird to look down. It didn't feel like he'd done any work, and it didn't feel at all precarious, but he was at least a dozen feet off the ground.

Rosa called up to him. "If you want to rotate around the pole, step a couple inches higher and push into it. you'll twist the opposite direction."

When he tried that, it felt instinctive, not even something he had to learn. "I can definitely do this."

Down below a teenage girl in jeans and a dark jacket walked up to Gabe and slapped him on the arm. Gabe leaned in and gave her a hug. That must be his daughter. She looked up at Slater, her brow furrowed.

Next he tried descending, lifting his foot and stepping lower. The pole was definitely easier than any tree he'd been on. The surface was uniform and there was no loose bark. With every step it felt like he had solid footing.

The daughter was gone when he looked down again, but Lupe was on the sidewalk, approaching them, holding hands with a little boy. The kid's dark hair was perfectly coiffed, making him look nattier than most adults. He'd been a baby the last time Slater had seen him. Rosa was wearing a dark suit jacket with a nametag, dressed for some customer service job. Faces upturned, they watched Slater experimenting with the climbing. The next time he looked, he saw Lupe and the kid walking up the driveway to the house.

"You're doing fine," Rosa said. "Do you want to practice losing your footing?"

"I don't plan on doing that."

"Well, if you do, the squeeze will hold you up. You just need to step on the pole again."

Slater started to descend, and soon he was standing on the concrete. "When do you need the gear back?"

"Whenever. It's extra from the shop. You can leave it with Gabe."

"What do I owe you for the lesson?"

She chuckled. "It's included in the rental fee. But thanks for offering." Her expression sobered. "If you get caught, you never heard of me."

"I'm not going to get caught."

"It's unlikely. Nobody pays any attention. I think people assume that if you're crazy enough to be climbing a pole, you must have a legitimate reason."

They walked back into Gabe's yard, and Rosa

pulled open the driver's door of her truck, waving as she got in and fired up the engine.

"So when are we doing this?" Gabe said.

"Do you have time tomorrow?"

"Let's start early. That's when all the work gets done."

Slater unbuckled the belt. "Can we put this stuff in your truck?"

He walked over and unlocked one of the outer compartments, and they tucked the belt and the squeeze inside, then the hard hat.

Gabe pointed to his feet. "Are you going to drive around with the hooks on?"

"I forgot. I guess they're pretty comfortable." He crouched to unfasten them, and Gabe loaded them into the compartment, then locked it.

"I'll be here early," Slater said.

"Before you go, I have a proposition for you. Amelia is having her quinceañera on Sunday."

"Your daughter. I saw her earlier. Mazel tov."

"We were wondering if you wanted to be the godfather of the cake," Gabe said. "We already got a godfather of the dress."

"What does that mean, exactly?"

"You buy a cake and come to the party."

He hated this stuff, the social bullshit, the obligations. But he needed Gabe as a resource.

"Sure, I can be godfather of the cake," Slater said. "Where do I get it?"

"Great." Gabe beamed and clapped him on the shoulder. "I'll get Lupe to call you. She'll know what she wants."

Walking out to the street, he had to chuckle.

Since Pike had come into his life he'd been turning into a square. He'd got himself mired in a mortgage, and had a ring on his finger, and now he was the godfather of the cake.

As he climbed into the Continental, he saw that Svetlana had texted a while ago:

Your order is ready.

Before he went over there, he needed to eat something. This neighborhood had good food, he knew, and as he cruised the boulevard he spotted a taco truck. Pulling over, he got a tamale without meat in it, and stood over the gutter to eat it. Once he'd dumped the corn husks in the trash, he headed back to his car.

He felt better, he realized, merging onto the freeway. His head wasn't throbbing anymore. It was a good sign that the food had stayed down.

At Svetlana's place he waited in the antechamber to be scanned, then stepped inside. Sitting on her workbench amid the jumble of components and circuit boards and wire was a shiny black solar panel, maybe ten inches square.

Svetlana swiveled on her stool and waved him closer.

"The solar panel has a mounting bracket, and wood screws already attached." She showed him the bracket, and the one on the camera as well. "Just twist the screws into the wood. The camera can be adjusted to point in the right direction."

The device was a brown box with a recessed lens, smaller than his phone. It was attached to the mounting bracket with a stiff ball joint.

"It doesn't look like a camera," Slater said.

"That is desirable, isn't it? The color will blend in with the utility pole."

"Totally. How much is it zoomed in?"

"Zoom is adjustable by my software. You can see the image on your phone and control it there, to make sure you're seeing the right place." She swiveled to her computer. "Look at this."

He had to step behind her shoulder to see through the privacy filter on the screen. Svetlana showed him which controls would adjust the zoom.

"What do I owe you?"

"No additional software charges. A very special price for you for the hardware, seven dollars."

Slater dug out his wad, and peeled off the C-notes, and handed them over. She briefly riffled through to count the bills, then tucked them into her bra.

"You always pay me what I ask," she said. "In Russia this would make you look weak."

"I respect your expertise. I'm not going to lowball you."

Svetlana reached under the counter and produced a brown paper supermarket bag, and flapped it open, and loaded the solar panel and the camera into it.

"I can respect American culture," she said. "I have to now. I have obtained my citizenship."

"Hey, congratulations. I know that's not always easy."

She shrugged and handed him the bag. "It's like what you said about the fire department and the emergency exits. I did it mostly so that they will leave me alone."

"That's an excellent reason to do anything."

Outside, he put the bag into the trunk of the Continental, then climbed in behind the wheel. He hadn't checked on idiot Chad today. Looking through the new activity on the guy's phone, there were some perfunctory texts, and the location history showed he'd gone to the Blue Dragon again. Nothing he'd done seemed informative.

Tucking his phone into its dash mount, he headed for the freeway. It was congested this late in the day, and the navigation app sent him off into Elysian Park and past the police academy to get to his neighborhood. As the garage door rolled up, he saw Pike's rig parked out front. That made his heart swell, knowing that beautiful man was upstairs.

He found Pike on the sofa, dozing, still wearing work clothes, his shirt open a few buttons. As Slater knelt in front of him and caressed his belly, he leaned in to kiss him. Studying his face, Pike's brow furrowed.

"Rough day?"

"It's just a katzenjammer."

"Ouch. Good thing you drink the cheap stuff."

He buried his face in Pike's belly, and relished the feeling of his fingers running through his hair. Eventually Slater pulled up.

"We're seeing Doris tonight."

"You say that like you're not sure," Pike said.

"My brain tends to suppress bad news."

"She and her girlfriend are at some event downtown. They wanted to have dinner after."

"At least it's not that deadbeat Albert. What friend?"

"I guess we'll find out when we get there."

"Did they pick a place?"

"It's all figured out," Pike said. "All you have to do is show up."

"You say that like it's easy."

"The place is a bit tony. You can't wear jeans."

"And there it is." Slater threw up a hand. "Of course they'd pick a place where I have to look like a damn hotel concierge, or a bank teller, or a salesman at a car dealership."

Pike chuckled as he sat up. "You're just going to have to power through it."

He led the way down to the bedroom, and Slater changed into a pair of black trousers, and pulled on the stupid black derbies that went with them. They were so light that he felt like he was walking around naked.

The shirt Pike pulled on was dark gray with a bit of sheen to it, and he stood in front of the floor mirror to button it. Stepping behind him, Slater reached around to caress his chest.

"You look so fucking hot in this."

"Do not tear it off me."

He slid his hands under his belt buckle. "Are you sure? Maybe we can just stay here and I can fuck you with that shirt on."

"Soon, horndog." Pike turned and cradled his head, and met his mouth. "I've been on the road all afternoon. You're driving."

THIRTEEN

HE RESTAURANT DORIS HAD picked was an Italian joint with big windows onto a busy downtown street. The place was crowded and noisy with conversation and the clatter of dishes. When they spotted Doris, the woman at the table with her was stout, with butched brown hair, wearing a gold leopard print blouse.

"I know her," Slater said as they walked over to the table. "I forget the name, but she had a messed-up *Liquidambar* in her front yard."

"What's that?"

"A tree. From the Southeast. They shouldn't really be here."

Doris beamed as she caught sight of them approaching. Petite, she had some gray in her dark hair, today wearing a royal-blue suit jacket over a dark blouse.

"I love that jacket," Pike said as they stepped up.

Slater eyed him sidelong. He really knew how to lay on the sweet talk. He leaned in to kiss Doris, then sat opposite.

"You boys look so handsome," Doris said. "You remember Daphne."

Pike gripped her hand and introduced himself.

He should have remembered that name, Slater realized. Daphnes were Eurasian bushes that looked like laurels but were totally toxic, from roots to berries, like this woman.

As Pike sat down, Doris eyed Slater. "You look rough. That explains the phone call."

"What call?"

"You called me in the middle of the night."

"I doubt that. You should check the time stamp— a.m. is actually different from p.m."

"You just don't remember."

Slater frowned. He had no memory of doing that, couldn't conjure it. But it had happened before. "I might have picked up a virus. Things get hazy late at night."

"Things get hazy when you're shickered," Doris said.

"What did I say?"

"No idea. My phone was on 'do not disturb.' I saw the notification when I got up."

"I'm glad you turn it off," Pike said. "I was worried it was too late when I called you last night. You sounded sleepy."

"I was actually in bed. You're on my allowed contacts list."

"And I'm not?" Slater demanded. "I'm your damn flesh and blood."

"You're also the one who gets liquored up and calls in the middle of the night."

He groaned and closed his eyes for a moment.

"I remember this in high school too," Daphne said. "You were a perpetual source of heartache for your mother."

Slater shot her a look. "Yeah, well, once a ruffian, always a ruffian, am I right?"

"That's all in the past," Doris said. "Slater's not a ruffian."

Daphne gave him the once-over. "If you say so."

"How was your trip to the Central Valley?" Doris said, shifting in her chair and eyeing Pike.

"It was a lot of time on the road. We talked to lots and lots of bikers."

"Motorcycle gangs? That's exciting."

"We're supposed to call them clubs. I might actually have to grow my hair out."

"So that you can go undercover with them?"

"Not to be fully embedded. Just to take meetings."

"Do I get a vote on this?" Slater said. "I'm not sure I'm ready to be shacked up with a biker."

The server stepped up and asked about drinks. Slater ordered a tonic water, and the others agreed to share a bottle of red.

When the woman stepped away, Daphne gestured to Slater and Pike. "I like your whole cops-and-robbers thing." Eyeing Pike, she added, "I bet you keep him in line."

"That would be like trying to bottle up a cyclone, Daphne," Pike said.

She tittered at that, and Slater scowled, and folded his arms.

"Did Slater tell you he's godfather of the cake for a quinceañera?" Pike said.

"I know that's a thing now," Doris said. "A way to distribute the burden of a big event."

"Better the cake than the dress. It's a lot cheaper," Daphne said.

Doris eyed Slater. "Whose quince?"

"The daughter of a guy who works for me sometimes. He's a painter. I rent his truck."

"When's the party?"

"I think it's Sunday."

"You'd better find out. You have to go. You're a godfather."

"Are you kidding me? I thought I could participate remotely. By providing the cake."

"Talk to your painter friend," Doris said. "I'm sure you're expected. You have to take a gift too. Besides the cake."

"This just gets better. What kind of gift?"

"Cash," Daphne said. "At least fifty bucks."

"Fifty if you're a friend of the family," Doris said. "But you're a godfather. That means they think you're rich. You have to give her a couple hundred."

"How did my life get this complicated?" Slater threw up his hands. "I don't get it."

Pike reached over and briefly rubbed his back. "No one is an island."

"It's part of living in this world," Doris said. "Everyone has relationships. You have to tend to them."

"You sound like one of those shrinks you sent me to."

The server arrived with their drinks, and Daphne took the wine bottle and poured.

"What happened with that *Liquidambar* in your yard?" Slater said, and sipped his tonic water.

"I had it cut down, thanks to you," she said, and frowned at him. "A hundred years of history and then twenty minutes of chainsaw work and it's just gone. It broke my heart."

"You know I didn't actually kill the tree, right?" Slater said. "Nature did that. I just told you to take it down before it fell on your damn house."

"It was sad to have to destroy something with so much history," Doris said.

"Again, not my fault."

"Well, there's nothing I can do about it now." Daphne waved a hand. "So how did you two meet?"

"Pike dropped in to my art studio to ask for career advice," Slater said. "I thought he had a strange fire in his eyes. Things blew up from there."

Daphne's eyes narrowed. "What art studio?"

Pike laughed. "That's how Frida Kahlo met Diego Rivera."

"Somebody's been watching PBS," Doris said.

"We met on one of my cases," Pike said, and reached for his wineglass.

"It was actually my case," Slater said. "This guy horned in on it, and then he tased me."

Pike gestured with his glass. "I had to. That's why he calls me Reddy Kilowatt."

"The man with the million volts in his pants," Slater said, and jabbed the air with two fingers. "Zap."

"What's your pet name for Slater?" Daphne said.

"Forty-niner is one," Pike said, "because he's a

classic California boy. Slater calls me *'mi vida'* sometimes."

"Interesting," Doris said. "That's what your father
called me."

Slater set down his tonic water. "Seriously? That
seems a little creepy."

"I don't think so." Doris smiled. "You never picked
up Spanish. It came from somewhere. The depths of
your subconscious memories."

"Where's your family, Pike?" Daphne said.

"Albuquerque."

"Is there any chance you two will wind up moving out that way?"

"I'm pretty happy here, now that I've settled in,"
Pike said. "I kept my house there but I rented it out.
Plus I don't think that city would suit Slater very well."

"Not enough work?"

"We were driving in the Coachella Valley a while
ago," Pike said, leaning back in his chair. "In a small
town along the back highway. We passed somebody's
yard where they'd set up one of those white tents to
keep the sun off a kid's birthday party. Slater said,
'Check it out—somebody got murdered.'"

"To be fair," Slater said, "the homicide cops put
up those same tents."

Pike laughed. "There were little kids running
around, and a piñata hanging in the yard."

"I thought those rugrats were the perps."

"I guess you can't take LA out of the boy," Doris
said.

Pike met her gaze. "My mother is going to visit
us soon. I hope you'll meet her."

"Of course I will. I was so relieved to hear your

mother is Reform. I feel like I can be more relaxed. She won't judge me for not helping repopulate *ha'aretz*."

"Esther is pretty casual," Slater said.

Pike eyed him. "I thought she stressed you out."

"Not because of anything she does. It's because she's your mother. I really don't want her to hate me." He eyed Daphne. "Or be a perpetual source of heartache."

———◆———

AFTER THEY'D EATEN, AND parted from Doris and her friend, Slater and Pike walked back toward the Continental.

"You know I'm going to demolish you later, right?" Slater said.

"Right on. Before that, though, it's still early, and we're already downtown. I thought we might hit up a pre-demolition event."

"You want to go to that place with the floor show?"

Pike dug out his phone, and tapped at it, and showed him the screen. At the top was a portrait of a woman with a broad Afro and big hoop earrings. Slater scrolled down to see the text.

"'Taytay channels Bessie Smith,'" he read aloud. "She's a psychic?"

"Not literally. It's just a performance in a little blues club. There won't be any crystal balls or trance states."

He scrolled down the page. "The place is on East Seventh. That's not far."

"Are you sure you're up for it?" Pike said. "I know you're hung over."

Slater handed the phone back and squeezed him around the shoulder. "I want to do what you want to do."

Once he'd found a meter, a couple of blocks from the club, they climbed out of the Continental and walked. On a side street Slater paused under a tree planted along the sidewalk and looked up into it.

"It's a ginkgo," he told Pike. "I didn't know these were street trees around here."

"How can you tell what it is? There's no leaves."

"It's really distinctive. See the spurs along the branches?"

Pike looked up into the tree. "What do the leaves look like?"

A lone leaf still clung to a low branch, and Slater reached up to grab it. It had faded from the bright yellow of autumn to muted tan, but the fan shape was intact. He handed it to Pike.

"These haven't changed since the dinosaurs were stomping around. The leaves looked exactly like this before any mammals even existed. It's basically a living fossil."

"That's a trip," Pike said, studying the leaf. He met his gaze. "I love that you know this stuff."

The club was in a low-slung building with a mural on the side that faced the street, an image of a guy in sunglasses blowing a saxophone, painted in moody dark colors. Inside, the bar was dimly lit, with red flocked wallpaper and dark wood tables and chairs. The place looked crowded.

"Did you book a table?" the host asked them after they'd paid the cover.

Pike dug in his pants pocket, and palmed a bill,

and slipped it to him. "My name might not be on the list, but here's one of my cards."

Slater couldn't see the denomination, just a flash of green as it disappeared into the guy's front pocket.

"Come with me," he said, and sat them at a little table in the middle of the room, with two adjacent chairs facing the stage.

"You're smooth, daddy-o," Slater said when they sat down. "How much did you tip him?"

"Just twenty."

"I don't think you would have done that when you first moved here."

"Brewster says it's about scarcity," Pike said. "There's just so many people in LA. It feels decadent to me, like Vegas. But whatever works."

Leaning in, Slater mouthed his neck. "You're whatever works."

A server appeared, a woman in her twenties with a tight black skirt and a white blouse with a few buttons open. Pike ordered a Corona.

"Soda water for me," Slater said.

As she stepped away, Pike said, "You can see her brassiere."

He chuckled. "Is that a concern for some reason?"

"Not at all. I think it's a fashion thing."

Slater looked at him sidelong. The guy was dead serious, blithely looking around at the people at the other tables, watching the band as they got set up on the stage. He was so damn obtuse sometimes. But Slater loved that, loved his quirks, loved all of him. His idiosyncrasies just made him hotter.

Soon after their drinks came, Taytay appeared on the stage. Her hair was different now than on the concert bill—more restrained, styled in fluffy curls. Curvy, she was wearing a midnight-blue crushed-velvet gown, and something in her heavy eye makeup that sparkled in the brilliance of the spotlight.

The crowd clapped at her appearance, and once they'd quieted down, she got into it. The woman had a great set of pipes, filling the room, easily outshining the piano and the bass and the drums. Slater didn't really know Bessie Smith's music, but Taytay made it vivid, made the emotion in it feel present and real.

The third song was about the fickle friends who abandoned her when she wasn't flush with cash anymore. She belted the last lines:

> No man can use you when you're down and out
> I mean, when you're down and out.

After they'd applauded, she said, "The band and I are going to take a little break. We'll be back in a minute."

Pike clapped and hooted, his eyes bright, a big goofy smile on his face. He was loving this, loved being out and doing stuff. LA suited him in that way—there was always something to do. It gave Slater a lump in his throat just looking at the guy.

"Would you dump me if I went broke like her?" Slater said. "Would you tell me 'Hey, I'll buy you lunch,' but then drive me over to a tent encampment under the freeway, and push me out onto the asphalt with both feet, and yell 'Spread out, sucker,' and then punch the gas and peel out, and leave me tits-up on the streets?"

Pike laughed. "You're the one with the house. It's way more likely you'd do that to me. I'd come home to find my stuff piled on the sidewalk."

"I'd never do that," Slater said intently. He grabbed the back of his neck and squeezed. "Get real. What is wrong with you? How could you even think that?"

"Even if I grew my hair out so I could talk to bikers?"

"That's more about the bathroom getting cluttered up with grooming products, and cleaning long hair out of the shower drain." He held his gaze. "You can do whatever you want. You know that. Grow your hair out, dye it pink. Just don't buy a motorcycle."

Eventually Taytay had run through her set, and the crowd clapped long enough to bring her back for a brief encore. Afterward they walked out to the street and found the Continental.

"I almost walked past it," Pike said. "I was looking for the Thunderbird."

"Yeah, that still happens. I miss it too."

When they got upstairs to the bedroom, he stood in front of Pike and grabbed the sides of his belt. "Are you ready to put out, Jazbo?"

Pike raised his eyebrows and shoved his arms under Slater's, pushing them off. He stood up straighter and puffed out his chest. "There'll be no doings here before you pay. No fancy prancing till the break of day."

"Channeling Bessie Smith must be contagious," Slater said, and pulled him in, and roughly pressed their mouths together. Running his hands over his back through the sheer gray shirt, he leaned into him and mouthed his neck.

"There was talk of a demolition operation," Pike said finally, pulling back.

"I'll fuck you, punk, and you'll stay fucked."

He used a wrestling move to throw him off balance, hooking his leg around Pike's, and Pike tumbled back onto the bed, laughing, his eyes bright. Slater quickly ditched the dress pants and the derbies, and yanked off his shirt, and climbed up to straddle him, massaging his chest through the shiny fabric, grinding his cock into his thigh. Unbuttoning the shirt, he let Pike sit up and take it off, then yanked off his trousers.

They were both naked now, and Slater grabbed the lube, and reached between his legs, and worked his way into him. Wincing, Pike tilted his head back, and Slater shifted closer, pushing his knees apart, and pressed into him. He started slowly as Pike groaned, then built up the pace.

Breathing hard, Pike met his eye. "Is that all you got?"

Slater pounded him harder, and gritted his teeth. Pike grabbed the back of his neck, pulling him closer, his lip curling into a sneer. He knew what that would do to him, knew that it would set him off. As he came he yelled out with a guttural roar.

When he pulled back to catch his breath, Pike wrapped an arm around his neck, and mashed their mouths together.

"What do you want me to do?" Slater said.

"Should I skull-fuck you?"

"You can try."

"It sounds so unhinged." Pike massaged his chest. "Can I do you?"

He squeezed his cock. "I'd say you're ready."

Pike shifted closer, positioning himself between

his thighs, and soon penetrated him. Leaning close, he met Slater's mouth. When he pulled back, Slater slapped him.

"Damn it," he snapped, a flash of anger in his eyes.

He started to pound him, and Slater slapped him again. Pike grabbed his arms to hold them down.

"Fucking hooligan," Pike growled.

Slater could feel the tension building in his body, and Pike came, straining into him, his face contorted, and collapsed onto him.

After a while he rolled onto his back. Slater stretched out and started to drift off.

"Why would I do that?" Pike said, still breathing hard.

"Do what?" he mumbled.

"Why would I dump you under the freeway when you make me feel like this?"

FOURTEEN

I N THE MORNING HE got up before Pike, well before sunrise, and pulled on a heavy shirt he wore to do yard work. Upstairs he tried to make coffee, fumbling with the machine. Pike usually did this before he even got up. Eventually he managed to get the java flowing, and pulled out the pot to pour a mug, a few stray drops hissing on the hot plate as they fell.

Downstairs in the garage he grabbed a pair of heavy gloves from the tool bench, and snapped a battery into his impact driver, then opened the trunk of the Continental to check the screws on the mounting brackets Svetlana had attached to the camera and the solar panel. Of course they were Torx. She did everything pro. He tightened a Torx bit into the chuck on the impact driver and put it in the trunk.

Even at this hour, with the sky still gray before

the looming dawn, the navigation routed him on surface streets, completely avoiding the freeways. When he pulled up in front of Gabe's place, he retrieved the stuff from the trunk, then walked into the driveway.

Gabe was out already, messing with something in the back of his truck. He was dressed for work, in jeans and a plaid shirt. They loaded Svetlana's gear and the impact driver into a compartment and locked it.

"You'll need that alternate ID I got you," Slater said. "Just in case we get questioned."

"Good idea." He gestured to the cab of the truck. "It's unlocked."

As Gabe walked over to the house, Slater pulled out his own fake ID card, and climbed in the passenger side, and put the rest of his cards in the glove box of the truck. It wouldn't work if he got hauled in and charged with something, but it would fool a beat cop doing a cursory check.

When Gabe returned, he backed the truck out of the driveway, and followed Slater's directions to Pasadena. The clouds had dissipated since yesterday, and once the sun was up, it started to feel warmer.

Slater pointed out the pole across from Chad's driveway, and Gabe pulled onto the earthen roadside just past it.

"Why don't rich people have sidewalks?" Gabe said.

"Maybe they don't need them. They can drive everywhere."

"Don't the kids have to walk to school?"

"Chauffeurs and rideshares," Slater said, and climbed out.

As they walked up to it, the pole looked solid, and not weathered at all, but the lower part was half buried in a ficus hedge.

"Can you climb it with all the greenery?" Gabe said.

"I should have come and looked at this beforehand."

He put a hand into the hedge to assess the density of it. It was a *benjamina*. The laterals were thin and pliable, and the front face had recently been trimmed.

"I'll be able to get through this without doing any damage," Slater said.

"Let's get your stuff."

He unlocked the box on the side of the truck, and Slater put on the white hardhat, then strapped on the hooks, and the belt.

"You'll need your drill," Gabe said, and pulled it out of a different compartment, along with the grocery bag with the camera in it.

Slater hung the tool from one of the loops on the belt, and put the camera into a pouch. But the solar panel was too big.

"Can you tuck this under the belt without busting it?" Slater said.

He felt Gabe positioning it next to his back.

"It's not going to fall out," Gabe said finally.

Stepping up to the pole, he looped the squeeze around it, reaching through the ficus foliage, then connected it to the belt with the carabiner. As he started to climb, one firm step at a time, the hooks confidently bit into the wood every time, even through the greenery. The squeeze wouldn't let him move higher unless he pulled it up with each step.

Soon he was above the top of the hedge, almost as high as the lowest set of wires, thick and wrapped in black, for cable TV or internet or both. It felt like he was a lot higher than yesterday at Gabe's. Looking down at the street made his heart pound, so he avoided that.

He could see more of Chad's house now. It was a bland twentieth-century mansion, from when Pasadena was a winter escape for wealthy Easterners. The house was set back from the street, with lots of gravel in the space from the driveway to the garage that sat off to one side, but there wasn't any grass—the outdoor space must be in back. A dark sedan was the only vehicle parked by the garage, but it had four bays, so there could be several other vehicles.

Slater pulled out the little camera box, and the impact driver made quick work of attaching it to the pole. He adjusted its ball joint to point it in the general direction of Chad's driveway. As he reached for the solar panel in the small of his back, he forgot about his footing, and bent his knees, inadvertently lifting one foot. Instantly thrown off balance, he pitched toward the pole. The squeeze saved him from falling, but he rammed his crotch into the pole, a solid blow to the balls.

"Fuck," he roared.

"Careful, man," Gabe called up to him.

It was easy enough to regain his footing, and he locked his knees, but he had to take a minute to breathe deeply, waiting for the pain to subside. How fucking stupid was that, to dick-punch himself?

Eventually he twisted sideways, and reached for the solar panel, and yanked it out of the belt. He knew the street ran north-south, and he looked around to confirm which direction the sun was in. With the impact driver he mounted the panel on the south side of the pole, and angled it upward, then connected the little wire from the panel to the camera box.

Now he had to aim the camera. Pulling off his gloves, he tucked them into the belt, then dug out his phone. Svetlana's app showed a new device, labeled "солн.," and he tapped on it. Her interface was always a mishmash of broken English and Cyrillic. That made him think she got the actual coding done in the old country.

The camera was already working, as the app displayed a video image of trees and roofs. That was the top of Chad's house. Grabbing the camera, he adjusted it to aim downward, and to the side, where the driveway was. The image on the phone didn't change right away, and he watched it for several seconds until it finally shifted.

That had to be about Svetlana's tech setup. He knew the signal went from the camera over the cell network, but then he had no idea where—her servers at her workshop, or maybe in the motherland, or some shady-as-fuck third jurisdiction, and it took a while to bounce back to his phone.

The gate across the driveway was in the frame now, but he needed to zoom in. He touched the control she'd shown him and waited for the image to respond. Eventually he had the gate well framed, and adjusted the settings to record clips when there was motion. He double-checked that the mounts were solidly attached to the wood by tugging on them, then started to make his way down the pole.

Below he saw a pickup had pulled over in front of Gabe's truck. On the tailgate it said WATER AND POWER. Walking back toward the pole was a guy in a uniform shirt and jeans, wearing those fuck-me logger boots, with graying hair, a neat little mustache, and wraparound sunglasses. He was looking up at Slater. What were the freaking odds? This was a quiet backstreet, and they'd only been here a few minutes.

Gabe stepped up to intercept the guy, speaking rapidly in Spanish. That would only work to obfuscate things if the guy didn't speak the language. But it was a smart move—he looked pretty Anglo.

As Slater stepped onto the ground, Gabe was still waving his arms and talking.

The guy eyed Slater. "Do you speak English?"

He pushed the helmet back on his head, and looked the guy in the eye, and affected an accent. "A little."

"What are you doing up there?"

"We're contracting with the fiber-optic company."

His brow furrowed. "There's no fiber going in here."

"It's testing for the fiber," Slater said. "To see if there's interference."

He gestured up the pole. "Did you put up that solar panel?"

"It's for the testing. The radio box needs power."

"Are you sure you're in the right place? This isn't a distribution line. It's for transmission."

That actually made sense, Slater realized. The wires were a lot higher up than on Gabe's street. He threw up his hands. "I just do the work I'm told."

The guy looked up the pole again. "It doesn't really

make sense. Do you have paperwork? A work order?"

"The fiber-optic company has all the papers," Slater said. "You have to talk to Miss Jennifer. You want me to find her phone number?"

He scoffed. "Don't bother. How many installs are you doing?"

"Only this one in Pasadena. Two more today in Atwater, then one in Frogtown."

"Christ," he muttered, and walked back toward his truck.

Slater stooped to unstrap the hooks from his boots, and as he rose again saw the truck pull out and drive off.

"When you talk like that," Gabe said, "you sound like my cousins from Zacatecas."

"I figured if he thought we were day laborers, he wouldn't keep pushing."

"Miss Jennifer would be disappointed in you. She loves us like full-time employees."

Slater chuckled at that, and they loaded the gear into the truck, and climbed in. Once he'd started the engine, Gabe pulled a U-turn and headed back toward civilization.

When he checked the app, the camera hadn't recorded any clips yet, but he found he could view a live feed of the gate anytime. He checked on Chad's phone and its location history. The idiot had gone to his house, and the Blue Dragon, and somewhere else in Hollywood last night. Zooming in on the map, he saw that he'd been at Electric, the nightclub Walter had mentioned.

That's what Chad meant when he texted Liz "Thursday"—he'd wanted her to work baiting straight guys last night for his extortion racket. The history showed Chad had gone home after bar hours, then today he'd gone east, somewhere on Whittier Boulevard. Slater zoomed in on his current location. He was at that repair shop, Chalo's Rims.

The office clerk had told him Gonzalo was in business with Mara, the woman from the eyewear boutique, but nothing had been said about lowlife Chad. And now Chad was out there.

When they got back to Gabe's place, they both climbed out, and Slater retrieved his impact driver from the box in back.

"You can get all this gear back to Rosa?" he said.

"That's the deal."

"What do I owe you?"

Gabe cocked his head. "Well, there's my time, yesterday and today, and gas. Then there was playing clueless migrant for the power company. And I don't think Miss Jennifer is going to pay me. Maybe five?"

"Done." Slater pulled out his wad and peeled off the C-notes.

"Sweet dollar, dollar bill, y'all," Gabe said as he took hold of them.

Slater had to grin. "I never pictured you as Wu-Tang fam."

"I was young once."

"You're not exactly an old man now." He jabbed a finger at him. "Tell Lupe to call me about that damn cake."

Walking out to the street, he ditched the impact driver in the trunk of the Continental, then got behind the wheel and headed for Whittier Boulevard. Gonzalo might try to deck him again, but he'd be curious too, and worried about who Slater was working for, and what his motives were. That meant he'd be predisposed to talk before he came at him.

As he rolled past the repair shop, he saw that the bay doors were down now, even though it was still early in the day. It was Friday—no way would the place be closed. He parked around the corner and walked back.

The yard was still jammed with cars, but the sweet little pickup with the *retablo* was gone now. The door beside the garage bays looked closed, but as he stepped up to it he saw it was actually hanging a few inches ajar. He pulled it open and stepped inside.

There were vehicles in each of the bays, but nobody working on them, and the place was silent. He paused to look around. The back of his neck felt prickly. Something here was definitely off.

On the floor in front of the office doorway was loosely scattered paperwork, like someone had dropped a file folder. He stepped closer and looked into the office. It had been messy before, but now the top drawer of a file cabinet hung open, and the middle drawer of the adjacent one. A messy mound of documents was dumped in front of them, and more was strewn around on the linoleum, and on top of the desk, and on the chairs in front of it. The blotter and the desk phone were on the floor. The place had been ransacked.

As he walked inside he saw a pair of work boots sticking out from behind the desk. It wasn't Gonzalo, he realized, stepping closer. This guy was younger than him, wearing dark-blue coveralls, with stubble and a black ponytail. Flat on his back, his mouth hung open, his arms sprawled at his sides.

Slater crouched and pressed a couple of fingers to his neck. The guy was still alive. Just out cold. He pulled his arms to his torso and rolled him onto his side, then pulled one knee up across the other, shifting him into the crash position. The guy didn't stir.

As he stood up he glanced around the room. This didn't concern him—he needed to vamoose. He strode out toward the yard and paused at the front door, thinking about it. Besides the longhair, the only thing he'd touched was the handle. He took a second to wipe it off with his shirtsleeve.

There were a couple of cameras inside, but with any luck whoever watched the video would see he'd only been here a minute, sometime after the ransack, and they wouldn't come after him.

As he hustled out to the sidewalk he heard sirens in the distance. They were definitely getting closer. At the end of the block he paused to watch. A prowl car pulled onto the sidewalk, across the repair shop's gate, and two uniforms climbed out. It didn't look like they were in a hurry, but they'd been rolling priority, and they'd blocked access to the place. They'd find the longhair—Slater didn't need to call anybody.

Climbing into the Continental, he took a breath and checked the tracker on Chad's phone. The guy had left here almost an hour ago. The ransack must have happened since then—Chad seemed too spineless, not really the type to barge in and toss somebody's office during business hours. But what the hell had he been doing here? He twisted the key in the ignition and headed toward Silver Lake.

FIFTEEN

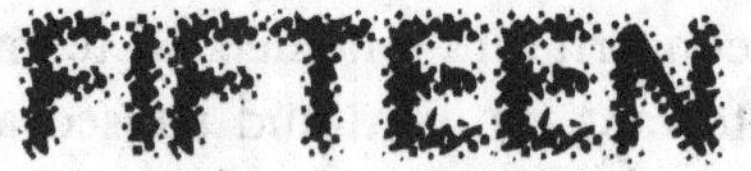

AN OBNOXIOUS SILVER G-CLASS was parked in Bucky's driveway. Obviously the guy had terrible taste in cars. Slater parked next to it and walked over to ring the bell.

When the door opened, inside was a hulking big guy, wearing dark sunglasses and an oversize white T-shirt, with gold chains around his neck.

"How you doing?" he said, then turned and called into the house, "Your plumber's here." He waved Slater aside. "I'm on my way out, amigo."

Slater scoffed, inhaling a whiff of his patchouli cologne as he went by, and walked in. Bucky was in the kitchen, wearing a shiny gold-patterned bathrobe, a coffee mug in hand. When he spotted Slater, his eyebrows shot up.

"I thought he was joking."

"Are you sober right now?" Slater demanded.

"Not that it's any of your business, but yes, I am."

"Are you actually waiting for a plumber?"

"I'm not."

"So the big guy was just throwing shade."

"L-Rat has a sophisticated sense of humor," Bucky said. "He specializes in smack talk."

"I'd say L-Rat is a dick."

He chuckled. "You should see his dick."

"You're sleeping with him?"

"You sound incredulous, Slater."

He put his hands on his hips. "I guess the dick wants what the dick wants."

"Despite his portly frame, he's quite virile."

"I believe you," Slater said. "I'd fuck him. I can't quite figure out why you would. You're a fancy lad."

"So many labels. You also called me a junkie."

"It seemed reasonable at the time." Slater raised his voice. "I found you passed out in an opium den."

Bucky looked away. "I'm trying to stop doing that."

"Listen, do you know a repair shop on Whittier Boulevard called Chalo's Rims? A guy named Gonzalo runs the place."

"I don't know it. I get my car serviced in Glendale. How is the case going?"

"I've tracked down two of Chad's accomplices. I'm trying to come up with a way to put them out of business."

"That's encouraging. It's been almost a week. Do you need more money?"

He hadn't even thought of that, but said, "I'm glad you brought it up."

"Another two grand?"

Slater nodded. "That'll do. I've also incurred some expenses."

"Shall I add another two?" he said. "Three?"

"Twenty-seven hundred." It was a wild guess at what he'd spent on this case, but Bucky didn't seem like the kind of guy who'd ask for receipts.

As Bucky strode into the back of the house, he stepped over to the side table under the big TV. Displayed on it was an egg-shaped rock, broken into two uneven parts. On the outside it looked gray and ordinary, but inside it was full of dramatic jagged purple crystals.

"You like the amethyst?" Bucky said when he came back.

"It's interesting. Does it keep your aura from getting stale?"

He handed him a sheaf of bills and smiled. "You're making fun of me."

"You keep a lot of cash around." Slater folded the bills in half, not counting them, and tucked them into his jeans.

"It's a Black thing."

He frowned. "How is that a Black thing?"

"You never know when you're going to get railroaded, or cut off, or displaced. They call it minority stress."

Slater did it himself, kept cash where it was always accessible, but it wasn't about stress.

Caressing the back of his neck under his bathrobe, Bucky met his gaze. "Are you in a rush to get somewhere? I could pour you a drink."

"Didn't you just fuck L-Rat?"

"That man is a total bottom, if you can believe that."

"I have no problem believing that." He raised his eyebrows. "Like, at all."

"You have something different to offer. A firm hand and a firm baloney pony."

"There's a rule in my business," Slater said. "I have to keep my dick out of my cases."

"That didn't stop you last time."

"Yeah, there's that." Pursing his lips, he thought about it. "Technically I wasn't working for you yet." He turned and walked out.

The G-Class was gone from the driveway now. That meant it was L-Rat's ride. Good thing he hadn't put that vehicle tracker on it. Bucky's wheels must be in that garage, and it would be locked. No way could he get access to it without Bucky noticing. Slater pulled onto the street and headed toward the boulevard. Glancing at his phone, he dialed Walter, glad that he picked up.

"Is this important?" Walter said. "I'm working."

"Put your dick away, and wipe the drool off your chin, and listen up." Slater asked him about Gonzalo and the repair shop.

"I've never heard of it. I don't even know where that is."

"All right. Go on now, get back to work." Not waiting for a reply, he ended the call.

Once he'd parked in the surface lot opposite his office, he hustled across the street in a break in the traffic. The lobby was devoid of day laborers, the little sticky notes on the wall with job offers all gone this late in the day. Upstairs the lights were off, and he eyed the little skeleton statue on the front desk as he stepped in.

"How you doing, Rey?"

Dropping into his desk chair, he looked at his phone to see what all the alerts were about. There were several from the camera named солн., the one he'd just put on the pole across from Chad's place. On his computer he pulled up the footage.

The first clip was a sparkly blue sedan with a scoop for a turbocharger in front and a spoiler in back. He knew it was a Subaru, but not the model. He checked the time stamp on the video, then pulled up the location history for the tracker on Chad.

That trash bag's phone had left at the same time, with the green line for his movements leading away from the mansion. So that was Chad's vehicle. He watched the clip again, but couldn't make out the driver with the glare of the sun and the tinted glass. A box at the side of the video frame had a short string of characters in it. It took him a second to realize that was the Subaru's plate number. Svetlana said she'd built a plate reader into her software.

He didn't need to run the plate, as he knew who was driving it, but knowing the tag number made it easier to recognize. For stakeouts the technique was to memorize the three letters in the middle using a mnemonic. That way he didn't have to look it up again to make sure he'd spotted the right vehicle. For Chad's plate the letters were ERD. Thinking about it, that was easy to remember: *extortion racket dick-smack.*

The next clip was from a few hours later, and showed the dark sedan he'd seen parked there pull out of the driveway. The hood bore the familiar badge of a Bimmer, and as the vehicle turned he got a brief glimpse of the driver. A woman with big sunglasses and long hair. Maybe that was Mom.

A video clip from a few minutes later showed a bright-red muscle car pull out of the driveway. It looked like a Camaro. As the vehicle turned into the street, he saw that the driver's window was down, and caught a glimpse of blond hair. Walter said Tanner was blond. This was Tanner's ride.

The plate number popped up next to the video frame, and it had the letter sequence LFH. He thought about it and soon came up with *loser fucking himbo.* No, even better: *loser football himbo.* That was easy to remember.

He locked his computer and went out to the elevator. On the ride down to the street he recited the phrases to remember the letters from the plates, trying to make them stick. Climbing into the Continental, he drove west, out to the Fairfax District, and pulled up on Mara's shop. Once he'd parked and plinked some quarters into the meter, he stepped past the rat-gnawed planter boxes and into the store, jostling the little bell over the door.

Mara was at the counter, talking to a woman with a lot of blond hair. Her face clouded when she spotted him. Slater stepped over to the racks of eyewear on the wall and pulled off a pair of frames. The little tag said $850. No wonder there was nobody in here.

A lanky guy with a tight Afro, in his twenties, with pleasing pecs visible under his tight dress shirt, stepped out from the back. He frowned as he approached Slater. "These are women's frames."

"What are you, the gender police?" Slater said.

"If you're not shopping, I'm afraid you'll have to leave."

The blond walked out, a little paper bag dangling from one hand, ignoring them. Once the door closed behind her, Slater called to Mara.

"Your lackey thinks I'm here to steal."

The guy stepped between them. "What did I just say?"

Slater slapped him hard, left and then right, a rapid kovac. The guy shoved him off, then held his palm to his cheek.

"What the hell?"

"What did I tell you last time you were here?" Mara said.

"Before you eighty-six me again, can you listen to me for a minute?"

"I'm calling the cops," the guy growled.

"Sure," Slater said, and eyed Mara. "I'd be happy to explain exactly why I'm here. I don't think they've heard about Chad yet."

"Michael, cool it," Mara said. "No cops." And to Slater, "What do you want?"

He stepped toward the counter, ignoring the clerk and his murderous glare. "I was at Gonzalo's place today."

She folded her arms. "What place?"

"You know damn well what I'm talking about. Chalo's Rims."

Her eyes followed the clerk as he stepped into the back, then met Slater's. "So what?"

"The place had been tossed. There was a guy on the floor out cold. What do you know about it?"

"Nothing," she snapped, and then closed her eyes

for a moment. "Was it Gonzalo on the floor?"

"Somebody I'd never seen before. He looked kind of ratty and beat-up. Black ponytail, wearing coveralls. I'm thinking he works there. The cops showed up as I was leaving."

"That's an interesting story, but it has nothing to do with me."

"What's the connection between Chad and Gonzalo?"

She threw up her hands. "How the hell is it that you know all these people, and I've never seen you before?"

"I'm an investigator. I know what I'm doing."

"Is it standard investigative procedure to rough up retail employees?"

"Only when they insist on serving up stupidity."

Mara chuckled, and her tone softened. "I won't say that wasn't vicariously pleasing. I've wanted to do that a dozen times today alone."

"You're welcome. How does Chad know Gonzalo?"

"Why would I tell you anything?"

"Well, talking to me doesn't cost you a dime. I'm being pretty tits-out about what I'm doing. And I just might be the guy who can get Chad off your back."

"Who are you working for?"

"One of Chad's other blackmail marks."

"What's her name?"

"Why does that matter?" Slater said. "Do you know any of his other victims?"

She huffed. "Chad and Gonzalo aren't connected. They're two separate and distinct nightmares in my life."

"Bullshit. Chad went to Chalo's Rims this morning, and when I got there the place had been ransacked."

"How do you know all this?"

He waved impatiently. "It's my job."

"I have no idea why Chad would go there. Maybe he needs rims."

It was hard to tell whether she was telling the truth. He couldn't see any glaring signs of obfuscation.

"OK," he said evenly.

She glanced toward the back room, then lowered her voice. "Gonzalo is bad news. Did you know that? He works with a syndicate. If his place got trashed, I'd say he must have pissed them off."

"What does he do for them?"

"Launders their money, I think. Maybe other stuff. I don't know the details."

"Is Chad involved with the syndicate?"

"I doubt it," Mara said. "He's a small-timer, and not very bright."

"You never introduced them?"

"Why would I do that?"

"What else do you know about Chad?" Slater said.

"Nothing. I met him at a nightclub."

"Electric."

She frowned. "That's the place. He set me up for a photo that made me look like a doper. Then he started bleeding me."

"Did he give you molly beforehand?"

"He did." She looked away. "And I took it, being a freaking moron."

"Can I see the photo?"

"Hell, no."

"Where did you meet him to make the payoff?"

"Payoffs, plural. I'm on the installment plan. A dive bar in Hollywood."

"The Blue Dragon."

Mara waved a hand. "You seem to know it all already."

"Was there ever anyone else with him? Any of his crew?"

"I didn't know he had one."

Slater put his hands on his hips. "Listen—you're not a moron. Chad is an abusive grifter. It's not your fault that you got caught up in it."

"It doesn't feel like that. It feels like I dug myself into a hole, and I can't get out of it. I seriously screwed up my life."

"Everybody screws up. Stay mad at that lowlife, not at yourself."

"Do you bill by the hour for the shrink work?" she said.

He threw up his hands and then turned to walk out.

SIXTEEN

᠆᠆᠆᠆᠆᠆᠆᠆᠆᠆

WHEN HE CLIMBED INTO his car, Slater saw that he'd missed a call, from a 323 number. There was a voice mail, from Lupe, and he called her back.

"*Hola*, godfather Slater," she said when she picked up.

"So what do I need to know about the cake?"

"I'll tell you the name and the size. You have to go to the bakery and order it. They can deliver it to the party."

"Can you call it in," Slater said, "and I can just pay them?"

"I can't do that. You have to go there. Have you got a pen?"

He knew damn well she could call, but he couldn't blame her—she didn't know him, didn't trust that he wouldn't bail and leave her stuck with the expense. As she explained it, he spent a minute thumb-typing a note with the details.

"I'll text you the party invitation later," Lupe said, and ended the call.

As he started the engine, he took a breath. That bakery was in Pasadena. It was going to take a while to get there. First, though, while he was way out here, he had a stop to make. His tenant in the ADU behind the garage, Grace, liked the rugelach from the deli on Fairfax, and he drove around the corner, and parked in the little lot, and picked up a box of them for her.

Eventually he rolled up on the bakery Lupe had sent him to, and parked at a meter out front, and looked it over. The place felt upscale. What was this going to cost him?

Outside the shop a string of scrubby weeds was growing where the sidewalk met the building's facade. Slater pulled the door open and saw a woman behind the counter. Curvy, she was wearing a white uniform and a hairnet.

"I need to show you something out here," he called to her. "On your storefront."

She frowned at him. "Like what?"

"Come out and I'll show you."

He let the door swing closed, and watched as she stepped around the counter. As she came outside, she gave him the once-over. Slater pointed to the line of green growth in the crack.

"How much effort would it be to get rid of these?"

"The weeds?"

"Get somebody with a string trimmer. It's half a minute's work."

Her brow furrowed. "Thanks for your concern."

As she went inside, Slater followed, and stepped up to the counter, where the woman stood facing him. He looked over the colorful riot of cakes in the glass case below.

"A lot of these have fondant icing," he said.

"One of our specialties."

"I'm sorry to hear that. The stuff is nasty. It sticks to your teeth and tastes like spackle."

She raised her voice. "What can I help you with today?"

Pulling out his phone, he recited the details Lupe had given him. "You have to deliver it," he added, and gave her the address.

She asked for his contact info, and he gave her Lupe's name and number. Stepping over to the register, she tapped at it, then said, "That'll be four twenty-five plus tax."

Slater had to suppress a smile. He was getting off easy—he hadn't planned to squawk unless it was over a grand. Digging out his wad, he peeled off the bills.

"So it's all set?"

"We'll call you if there are any issues," she said.

"There'd better not be. If I don't see that cake at the party, I'll be back." He jabbed a finger at her. "And I'll be looking for you."

Not waiting for a reply, he walked out, and climbed into his car. His phone had buzzed a minute ago, and he dug it out of his jeans to check. It was an alert from the camera on the pole. The clip showed the Camaro leave the house again. It was a new event, not the same clip he'd already seen, because this time the driver's window was rolled up. But he hadn't seen the car coming back. When he checked the list of videos, though, it was there—he'd just missed the alert.

That coffee place where he'd met Chad was a couple of minutes from here. Tanner could be headed anywhere, but there was a chance that he hung out there too.

Pulling into the street, he drove over and cruised the strip where the coffee place was. Sure enough, the Camaro was parked at the end of the block. Slater turned the corner and found a meter, then pulled on a pair of black latex gloves from the box in the backseat. From the trunk he retrieved the vehicle tracker, and clicked on the little recessed power switch, and palmed it as he walked back to the corner. This was a better use for it than putting it on Bucky's car—that idiot hardly ever left his house.

This was the right vehicle—the plate said LFH. It belonged to the loser football himbo. The street was busy, with a steady stream of cars rolling by, but there was no stoplight to let drivers ogle him while they idled, and no pedestrian traffic at the moment. He was far enough from the coffee place that Tanner wouldn't be watching. Still, it felt risky.

Slater stepped into the street and crouched next to the Camaro's rear tire, then reached up into the wheel well, moving the device over the surfaces. It couldn't find any steel to attach to. Freaking modern cars were mostly plastic.

It was taking too long. He could feel the sweat trickle out of his hair onto the back of his neck. The longer he squatted here, the more likely it was that someone would challenge him. He was about to give up when he felt the magnets tug and adhere.

Rising, he looked around the street, at the cars rolling by, a couple of pedestrians on the sidewalk. Nobody seemed to be paying him any attention. As he walked back toward his vehicle, he peeled off the gloves, and tossed them in the backseat as he climbed in.

Traffic on the parkway was stop-and-go, and as he drove, the daylight faded to dusk. Eventually he pulled into his garage, and went upstairs, and found Pike in the back bedroom, where he'd set up a desk for the days when he worked remotely. When Slater stepped in, he folded his laptop closed and swiveled around to face him.

"So I had an interesting experience today," Pike said. "I found twenty grand in a plastic bag stashed up under the bathroom sink."

Slater put his hands on his hips. "I put it there."

"I figured."

"Did you put it back?"

"Why do you have twenty grand stashed in the house? What's wrong with the bank?"

"I need to stay nimble," Slater said. "If someone's coming for me, I'm not going to have time to drive downtown before three o'clock, and stand in line, and fill out all the little slips of paper."

"That's not how banks work anymore. What if I hired a plumber and they found that bag and jacked it?"

"Now that you know about it, you can pull it out of there before you hire a plumber."

"Are there any other cash stashes?"

"Not that I'm aware of."

Pike chuckled as he rose and embraced him. "I

wish they all could be California boys."

He kissed him, and mouthed his neck, and relished the warmth of his body. Eventually Slater pulled back.

"I need to eat."

On his phone Pike ordered Thai, and they ate upstairs at the dining table. Afterward they stretched out together on the sofa, and Pike put on the radio, as there was good music on Friday night.

He dozed for a while, comfortable in Pike's arms, and then checked his tracking app. Chad's phone was at his place in Pasadena. Looking through his text messages, Chad had texted someone listed in his contacts as MW: "Be at the club tonight." MW sent a one-word reply: "Busy." Chad's response was, "You're a purpose guy. Don't forget your purpose."

Earlier he'd exchanged texts with a contact named Door. Chad wrote, "You on tonight?" and Door replied, "From 8." Chad's response was "T tonight," and nothing more was said.

The vehicle tracker on Tanner's car was working, he saw when he checked the app, and from the coffee place he'd gone home, then driven to Hollywood. The car was in a parking structure, and the structure was a block from Electric.

Chad had been at the place last night, likely with Liz helping him, and Tanner was there now. MW sounded like someone in the same role as Liz, coerced by Chad into working the grift with them. Thinking about it, maybe Door was the doorman at the nightclub. Their racket would run a lot smoother if they had the club's security on board.

He took a minute to set up a fake outgoing

number on his phone with the spoofing service that he and Max used. They needed it often enough that they had a subscription. It was a powerful tool, and considering all the illicit tools he used, all the hinky stuff he did, it was hard to believe that spoofing a phone number was perfectly legal.

When he dialed Door's number, someone picked up, with a gruff "Hello."

"Are you working tonight?" Slater said.

"Who's asking?"

He ended the call and thought about it. The deep voice made him sound like a beefy guy. It had to be the club's doorman. Chad was paying the guy off to look the other way when they were running their squeeze play.

Pike stirred and mumbled, "Who's working to-night?"

"I am. Do you want to go clubbing?"

He opened his eyes. "For work?"

Slater explained about Chad and Tanner and how they ran their grift. "I kind of want to see them in action."

"Won't they remember you?"

"I've only met one of them, and he's not there tonight. The other one is."

"How do you know where they are?"

"I can't really get into it. It's what you might call a trade secret."

Pike watched him for a moment. "Not my circus, not my monkeys."

"Exactly."

"I'm down for going out. What's the name of the club?"

"Electric."

Pulling out his phone, Pike tapped at it and studied the screen. "It looks kind of straight. No go-go boys. We have to dress up for it."

"Fuck that."

He chuckled. "They won't even let you in wearing jeans. Just wear what you had on for Doris last night."

They went downstairs, and Slater pulled on the black trousers and the derbies, plus a green shirt with a bit of sheen to it.

"Can I wear this?" Slater said, holding up his black faux-leather jacket.

"I think it's dressy enough."

He pulled it on and watched as Pike stepped into a pair of the pants he wore to work, and a shirt with a pattern of tiny red and blue flowers. He'd never wear that for work—it was specifically for nights out.

"You're so fucking hot," Slater said.

He grinned. "You like the shirt?"

"I love the shirt. I love the way it makes your body look. I love your body. I love you."

Pike embraced him and mouthed his neck. "You're just saying that to get me to put out."

He scoffed. "Like you need any prodding." He pulled on the sides of Pike's belt, grinding into his crotch. Under his breath, he said, "Feel that? That's what's waiting for you."

"Great. Now I'll be walking around with a stiffy."

"Suck it up," Slater said, and stepped back. "Wood looks good on you."

They took the Continental, cruising the freeway to Hollywood, and parked in a structure around the corner from the club and across the street from where

Tanner had parked. It was impossible to miss the nightclub—the entrance was in an alley under a big blue neon sign that said ELECTRIC.

At the door they joined the short lineup along the building's wall. A burly guy dressed in black was checking IDs but letting everyone in. The men in the line were in suit jackets or slick shirts, the women in short dresses despite the cold.

"You were right," Slater said. "People are dressed all snappy."

Digging out his phone, he dialed the number for the contact named Door on Chad's phone. As he watched, the guy checking IDs pulled his phone out of his jacket, and glanced at it, and tucked it away again.

"You just called the bouncer," Pike said.

"You don't miss a trick. I wasn't sure if it was his number. Now I know."

As they got closer to the door, Pike dug out his driver's license, and Slater pulled out his fake ID. His brow furrowing, Pike took it from his hand and studied it.

"Salvatore Moreno," he read aloud. "República de Honduras: Registro Nacional. That's your face, but you're not really a citizen of Honduras."

"My name isn't Salvatore Moreno either."

Pike lowered his voice. "Do you know how illegal this is?"

"A tool of the trade." He took it back. "I can't go flashing my own name around."

"It's a felony."

"Not your circus, remember?"

"It will be when I get the call that you need to get

bailed out of jail."

"I'm not that guy." Slater squeezed him around the waist. "You know me."

The bouncer had a bored look on his face when they stepped up. In the voice that Slater recognized from the phone call, he said, "IDs." Once he'd glanced at their cards, he waved them inside.

The dance floor was on the same level as the entrance, with tables around the sides, and a few steps higher was the bar. The music was loud. It was house music, but it was dead-ass, and nobody was dancing to it. There were a lot of people here, standing and scattered around at tables, but he didn't see Tanner.

Pike led the way up the ramp toward the bar and leaned in to order drinks. When the bartender set two highball glasses on the mat, he handed one to him. Gin and tonic, Slater decided, taking a sip.

Pike stood looking out at the room, and leaned close to be heard. "It almost has a gay vibe."

"I'm told it's mixed," Slater said, raising his voice. "We need a spot with a good view of the room."

"How about there?" Pike gestured to a table with a lone occupant and a couple of empty chairs. It was positioned at the edge of the higher floor, ideal for surveillance. Not waiting for an answer, Pike stepped over and leaned in to talk to the guy. He had close-cropped dark hair with a lot of gray in it, and sun-weathered skin, wearing a Hawaiian shirt with gold chains. He gestured languidly to the other chairs. Pike set his drink on the table and sat next to the guy, leaving the chair with the best view of the room for Slater.

The guy eyed Pike. "Are you two together?"

"A-yup," Pike said, and nodded.

His eyes went dead, and he looked away. The guy had no imagination, Slater thought. Otherwise he would have tried to set up a three-way. Like Svetlana said, he was leaving money on the table.

There were lots of gay guys, he saw, surveying the room, but it wasn't a diverse crowd, like the bars downtown or in East Hollywood. More like WeHo, with all the white guys, and it definitely skewed older.

Hawaiian shirt raised his voice and waved a hand at the room. "There's so damn many women."

"So what?" Slater said. "They're not going to out-compete you for guys. The guys are here for you."

"It's not a women's place."

"To me it looks like it's for everybody."

"We'd be lost without them," Pike said. "It's always the women that step up. Remember that serial killer that was picking off gay guys? The lesbians jumped into action to defend us. The men were still sitting around with their dicks hanging out waiting to get murdered."

"These look like straight women," the guy said.

"Imagine having to deal with straight guys all the time," Slater said, and raised his eyebrows. "Like, inside your house. Crumpled beer cans everywhere, and sports memorabilia, and tighty-whities with scorch marks strewn all over the carpet. You'd need a night out too."

Pike laughed at that, but Hawaiian shirt just shook his head and looked away. Slater turned to scan the room again. And there was Tanner, over by the entrance. Wearing a sharp dark-green suit, his shirt was open to the middle of his bare torso. Focusing on him, he tuned out whatever Pike and Hawaiian shirt were yapping about.

Tanner stood with his feet apart, phone in hand, and scanned the room. The guy was actually hot, with the football build, and he knew how to dress to accentuate it. Within a minute he walked over to a guy with gray hair and a trendy-cut suit, standing alone near the dance floor. Whatever Tanner said worked, as the guy guffawed, tossing his head back. They chatted for a minute, and then he walked away, leaving Tanner on his own.

Over by the entrance a familiar figure caught his attention: Bucky. Dressed in a black suit, he was wearing a pink shirt under it, and eyeglasses with pink lenses. He briefly glanced around the place but didn't spot Slater in the higher part of the room.

Bucky walked over to Tanner and stood next to him, elbow to elbow, both of them facing the dance floor. Neither one of them looked surprised to see the other. They were talking, he saw, Bucky leaning in to be heard.

"That little rat-fuck," Slater muttered.

This was who Chad had texted today. MW was short for Bucky's last name, Mainwaring. Why hadn't he thought of that? More important right now, it was only a matter of time before Bucky spotted him. He forced himself to look away, and turned to Pike, and interrupted his conversation with Hawaiian shirt.

"I have to bug out," Slater said. "If that guy spots me, it'll blow my cover."

"Which guy?"

"Black suit, pink shirt, pink glasses. That's Bucky. The guy from the airplane."

"Who's the blond?"

"Part of the crew that's blackmailing Bucky."

"I like his suit," Pike said. "Jade green. Do you want me to try to eavesdrop on them? They don't know me."

"Fuck, yeah."

He drained his gin and tonic, then got up and walked out, keeping his head down. With any luck Bucky hadn't noticed him.

Once he was out on the sidewalk he was glad he'd worn a jacket. Despite the gin warming his belly, it felt cold out. He stepped into the tiendita around the corner and winced at the bright fluorescent lighting. A trio of drunk twenty-something women with long hair and short skirts were at the register, laughing and chatting with the clerk, their voices loud. He surveyed the snack-treat aisle, then pulled a bottle of tomato juice out of the cooler. That should get the smell of gin off his breath.

Once the women finished their transaction, he put the bottle on the counter, and dug out a fin, then walked back to the parking structure and the Continental. Sitting in the dark, he sipped the tomato juice. A different group of women in party dresses walked in front of the car toward the stairs that led to the street. Still sober, they were a lot more subdued than the ones at the tiendita. They looked young for Electric, but they were likely headed elsewhere, as there were a lot of other nightclubs around.

On his phone he checked his trackers. Walter was at his place in South Pas, which seemed boring for a Friday night. Chad's phone was somewhere east. When Slater zoomed in on the map, he saw that it was at Chalo's Rims. What was he doing there again? He was inside the building. The location was so precise that he could tell the device was in the office, not one of the garage bays. No way was he there for a retail transaction at this hour.

A minute later Pike appeared, and climbed in the passenger side.

"Did Bucky spot me when I left?" Slater said.

"He was oblivious. I didn't have much luck. I got as close as I could, but the music was just too loud."

"I figured." He started the engine, and headed toward the exit.

"I got the sense they know each other pretty well," Pike said. "Like they're collaborating. Blondie is definitely the boss."

"That's actually a useful insight."

"You said the blond is part of the crew that's blackmailing Bucky. But they're hanging out together."

"I was not expecting that," Slater said.

"So what are they up to?"

"I plan to find out." He glanced over at him. "I got a lead on the other blackmailer just now. I'm going to track it down after I drop you."

"You want me to come with you?" Pike said.

"The last thing I want is to get you involved in something shady that you'd have to explain to your bosses."

"When you say that, it makes me wonder what you're getting into."

"You can't worry about that," Slater said. "It's my job. Just like I can't worry about you hanging out with biker gangs."

"They're motorcycle clubs," Pike said. "And I can't

really switch off how I feel."

"You should read that twelve-step book you made me read. It talks about letting people do their thing without getting hung up on it."

"It's so great that some of that sank in." He laughed. "But I have to say I'm not loving having it quoted back at me."

SEVENTEEN

WHEN THEY GOT TO the house, Pike popped the door handle, and leaned in to kiss him. Slater waited for him to climb out, then headed for Chalo's Rims. The obnoxious blue Subaru was parked at the curb in front, and once he'd parked around the corner and walked back, he checked the plate—the letters in the middle were ERD. It definitely belonged to the extortion racket dick-smack.

The gate to the street was open, and the garage bay doors were down, but through the row of grimy glass panels in them he could see there were lights on inside.

The door was unlocked, he found, trying the handle, and gingerly opened it and stepped in. Closing it behind him, he could hear voices in the office, and he walked toward the office doorway. The mess of paper that had been strewn around earlier today had been cleaned up.

Through the big window onto the shop he could see that the lights were on in the office. From this angle he could only see one side of the space, the file cabinets and the far corner of the desk, with no bodies in view. He stopped to listen, and could hear what they were saying now.

"It's too much," a man's voice said. "It's not working."

That was Gonzalo. A woman spoke next, her tone impatient.

"Just give it a minute."

He knew that voice. Not Vivi. Slater stood listening, trying to place it, but they'd stopped talking.

"If it isn't the state inspector," Gonzalo said, raising his voice.

Was he talking to that idiot redhead with the attitude problem?

"I know you're out there, *payaso*," Gonzalo said. "You tripped the security camera. I'm looking at your stupid face right now. You should have dressed like that when you came here before. I would have believed you worked for the government."

His heart started to pound. The guy was talking to him. He should have worn Svetlana's glasses. Why hadn't he thought of that? Standing up straighter, he stepped into the office doorway.

The place had been tidied up, with no evidence left of the ransacking. Gonzalo sat straddling the corner of the desk, his phone in hand. A handgun was shoved into the front of his belt, its ugly black butt visible against his shirt. Why did guys do that?

It seemed like a great way to accidentally blow your dick off.

Chad sat in one of the stacking chairs that had been moved to the open part of the floor, slumping with his chin on his chest. His arms were behind the chair, and Slater could see the glint of metal at his wrists. The guy was handcuffed. On the other side of Chad stood Mara, her glasses pushed up into her dark hair.

"Hey, guys," Slater said, affecting a casual tone. "How's everybody doing?"

Mara's eyebrows shot up. "Ibáñez? What the fuck are you doing here?"

"You know this fool?" Gonzalo said.

"He told me he was investigating the extortion racket."

"I am investigating the extortion racket," Slater said.

Gonzalo gestured to Chad. "Should we juice him up too?"

"First I want to know what's going on."

"What's up with the frat boy?" Slater said. "It doesn't look like you've roughed him up, but he's definitely out of it."

"I never touched him," she said. "I'm not an animal. He's on a little trip right now."

"Why?"

"It only seemed fair. He gave me molly, so I gave him ketamine."

"You might have overdone it," Slater said. "He looks like he's deep in a k-hole."

"He'll talk." Mara stepped in front of the chair, and leaned in to pull up his chin, and raised her voice.

"Where are the pictures, Chad?"

His eyes glassy, Chad smiled at her. "Hey, girl."

Mara stood erect. "It might take him a minute."

"You want him to hand over the blackmail photos?" Slater said. "You know he's going to have copies stashed somewhere else, right?"

"I'm sure he'll tell me about those too. We just have to ask the right questions."

Slater looked the guy over. A thin line of drool dripped from the corner of his mouth, and his eyes were closed again. He was definitely in a k-hole.

"You should have used GHB. It makes people chatty."

"What I want to know," Gonzalo said, "is why you keep coming around my shop."

"I knew there was a connection to this idiot's racket. I thought you might be working with him. I'm glad to see you're on the right side of it."

"You don't know me, *cabrón*. You don't know anything about me or what my side is."

"Well, I know you didn't draw down on me just now," Slater said. "That means either you don't think I'm a threat, or you've got ice water in your veins."

Gonzalo laughed. "The only reason you're still breathing is that you played fair in that dustup a few days ago. The fuck are you, anyway?"

"I'm working for another one of this knucklehead's victims. I'm totally down with deleting the photos too," he said, and waved at Chad, "but I don't think this technique is going to work."

"It takes time," Mara said.

"How long has he been in k-land?"

"Less than an hour."

"I'm not sure you're going to get anything."

He started to step over to the chair, and Gonzalo straightened up, putting his hand on the butt of his heater. Slater showed him his palms. "I'm just going to say hello."

Squatting in front of Chad, he put a hand on his cheek, his thumb under his chin, and lifted his head. The half mustache thing really made him look sleazy.

Chad's eyes gradually focused on him, and his brow furrowed. "Do I know you?"

"Where were you just now?"

"I think I died. Dad was there."

Slater rose. "I'm no junkie, but he's hallucinating. He's past the point of being able to make sense. You're not going to get anything useful."

"Fuck," Mara roared.

"So what now?" Gonzalo said. "Do we croak the guy?"

"That wasn't the plan," Mara said.

"It would be a warning to his crew. They'll back off if one of them goes missing." Gonzalo gestured to Slater. "We'll have to do this one too."

"Slow down, *jefe*," Slater said. "You don't need to croak anybody."

"The *mocoso* will squeal," he said, "and so will you."

"This idiot won't remember much of tonight. Even if he does, he's not going to go to the cops. That would expose his racket. Extortion means serious prison time." Slater raised his eyebrows. "Kind of like croaking people."

Gonzalo jutted his chin. "What about you? Why wouldn't you talk?"

"Our interests overlap, man. I'm being paid to

shut this dirtbag down, so my loyalty is to my client. I have no incentive to rat out his other victims." Slater waved toward Chad. "The interrogation thing is actually not a bad idea. Next time maybe we can try it with GHB. I think we'll get better results."

"There's no we," Mara said. "You and I are not collaborating." Eyeing Gonzalo, she added, "We're also not going to croak anybody."

"I don't trust the *pocho*."

Slater jabbed a finger at him. "I'm not a *pocho*."

"Just chill out, both of you," Mara said. "I need to think."

"How about this," Slater said. "The ketamine didn't work out, so we just take him home. I'm running my own operation with the same goal. To shut them down. I'm going to put the squeeze on the other brother."

"How do you know about his crew?" Gonzalo said, frowning at him.

"He seems to know a lot," Mara said. "Let him talk."

His plan was only a vague half-baked idea, but he laid it out for them. "I'm going to let Tanner pick me up at the nightclub and photograph me. He'll send me the photo and ask for cash. I'll take it all to the cops. Whether they go to jail or not, it'll be the end of their operation."

"But then the pictures of me will come out too," Mara said.

"I doubt it. Even if the cops find them, they won't just pass them out. The prosecutors might ask you to testify against them, but you don't have to do that. Benching them both will be more effective than croaking him tonight." Slater shrugged. "Your other option is to keep paying him."

"Or we could ice you both," Gonzalo said.

"Wait a minute." Mara folded her arms. "There's nobody they can blackmail you with?"

"I'm going to tell Tanner that there is, and let him come at me." He waved an arm. "I've got raunchier photos of myself on hookup apps than anything these tyros could come up with."

"When are you planning to do this?"

"As soon as I get the opportunity."

Mara nodded. "OK. How do we get him home?"

"Are you sure that's what we're doing?" Gonzalo said.

"We'll know soon enough whether Ibáñez's plan is going to work. If it doesn't, we'll pick up Chad again."

"It'll be harder," Gonzalo said. "He's not going to trust you next time."

Mara met his eye. "This is what we're doing."

"I know where Chad lives," Slater said. "I can drive him and his car to his house. One of you can follow me and bring me back here for my wheels."

"Or you could take a rideshare," she said, and raised her eyebrows.

"If you pick me up, there'll be less evidence. Just in case Chad overdoses in his driveway and the cops start looking for the chauffeur."

Mara eyed Chad and frowned. "You think that might happen?"

"I doubt it. He would have stopped breathing already."

"So let's go."

She squatted behind the chair, and unlocked the cuffs, and tossed them on the desktop. Chad's arms swung down to his sides and he slumped forward.

"His ride is right out front," Slater said, eyeing Gonzalo. "We can carry him."

Gonzalo stood up. "How do you know his car?"

"I've been running surveillance on him. That's how I got here."

"He's deep into this," Mara said, "like we are. Just do what he says."

"Can you turn off your cameras for a minute?" Slater said.

"Good idea." He frowned as he tapped at his phone's screen. "You're smarter than you look, *pocho*."

They went to either side of Chad and lifted him by his armpits. He was able to stand, and took a wobbly step. Staying with him, arms around his back, they walked him out to the curb.

When they got to the sidewalk, Slater groped around in Chad's pants pockets, and found a key fob. He pressed it to unlock the Subaru, and they loaded him in the passenger side. Gonzalo reached in to fasten the seat belt around him.

"Where is his place?" Mara said. "In case I can't keep up with the penis car."

"Pasadena." Slater rattled off the address.

"How did you know that off the top of your head?" Gonzalo demanded. "It's suspicious, bro. Like you're working with this guy. I mean, you talked us out of croaking him, and now you're driving him home."

"You need to chill out. Like the woman told you, I've done a lot of work on this." Slater jabbed a finger at him. "Don't grease anybody."

He stepped around to the driver's side, and climbed in, and pressed the starter button. The engine was loud, like there was a hole in the muffler, but more likely it was intentionally set up that way because Chad liked to make noise.

Gonzalo strode back toward his shop. In the rearview he watched Mara walk back to a boxy little SUV parked at the curb, and when she flicked on her headlights, he pulled into the street, and drove to the next corner, and stopped next to the Continental.

Climbing out, he left the door open, and from his own ride grabbed Svetlana's camera-jamming glasses. There was a good chance Chad's front gate was monitored by video, and he knew lots of streets and freeways were. Back behind the wheel of the Subaru, he clicked on the glasses' power switch and put them on his face, then pulled a U-turn and headed for Pasadena.

It was well after midnight but there was still lots of traffic. Even though the seat belt kept him upright, Chad's head hung forward. It was coming up on the witching hour, when the bars closed, so hopefully anyone who noticed the guy would just assume he was drunk. At any time of day a car with a scoop and a spoiler and noisy exhaust felt like a police magnet, so when he got on the freeway he drove the same speed as the other vehicles in lane 3, where he'd attract less attention than in the left lanes.

Chad's street was dark and quiet, and he pulled into the driveway of his house and stopped in front of the gate. Wiping his prints off the steering wheel, and then the key fob, he tucked it into Chad's front pocket. The guy groaned and smacked his lips but didn't lift his head. He was still completely out of it.

Mara had definitely overdone it with the dope. At least when he pressed a couple of fingers to his neck, the guy's pulse was solid and steady.

Once he'd cracked both windows half an inch, he climbed out, and gently closed the driver's door, and walked up the block. He hadn't seen Mara behind him most of the way, and thought she might have ditched him, but here was the little gray box, waiting at the curb, its parking lights on.

He climbed in the passenger's side, and Mara pulled into the street and headed toward the parkway.

"I sell frames for a living, and I've never seen a pair like those," she said. "They look heavy."

"They're a custom job. They have tech built into them that interferes with security cameras. To obscure my face."

"Was trash boy still breathing?"

"He's hallucinating," Slater said. "But it's been so long since he took the drug, there's no way he'll OD now."

"You saved his ass tonight."

"You would have let Gonzalo murdertize him?"

"Probably not." She sighed. "It's hard for me to be rational about it."

"It doesn't really make sense that the first solution you try is the one with the most prison time. Let's see how my way works out."

Mara shoulder-checked as she accelerated onto the freeway. "I hope you're serious about nailing that fucker."

"I can't promise anything. I might not be white enough to attract his attention. I can fake the wealth, but not the Aryan part."

"Why did you volunteer to drive him home? It's a big risk. You could have been pulled over."

"I figured if Gonzalo drove, he might change his mind and just grease the guy on the way there, and dump his carcass on the side of the freeway." He looked over at her. "It was also a way to demonstrate that I'm not a threat to your business. To show Gonzalo I wasn't going to rat you out. I can't do that if I'm participating."

"That's actually smart."

"My priority tonight was to save my own ass."

She scoffed as she changed lanes.

"Did Gonzalo explain why the place got tossed?" Slater said. "The unconscious guy at his shop? That was just today. Somebody cleaned up since then."

"I didn't ask him about it, and he didn't mention it. It's like I told you—he does business with some scary people."

"Are you in business with him?"

"Yes and no. We were involved for a while."

"Like romantically," Slater said, "or like a fuck buddy?"

"Both. That still happens now and then."

"I can see why. He's pretty damn hot."

Mara chuckled. "You have no idea."

"It also explains why Gonzalo let you call the shots."

"He trusts me. Trusts my judgment."

"That kind of relationship is like a gold nugget," Slater said. "Rare and valuable."

When they pulled up on the repair shop, the gate was rolled closed. Slater popped the door handle.

"Let me know how it goes," Mara said.

"Get some sleep."

As he walked toward the corner, she zoomed past him in the little gray box. He climbed into the Continental, and pulled off the glasses, and headed for his house.

When he got upstairs, the bedroom door was closed, the gap beneath it dark. Pike was asleep. He went up to the kitchen to slam his ration, savoring the burn in his throat. It had been a long freaking day. He poured another slosh from the bottle and slammed it before he headed down.

Enough light filtered in through the bedroom windows to make out the furniture and the closet, and he ditched his clothes without switching on the room light.

"You're back," Pike mumbled, shifting in the bed. "No bullet holes?"

Slater chuckled as he climbed under the covers, and wrapped his arms around Pike's torso, burrowing his nose into his hair. Pike shifted back, pressing the contour of his butt and his thighs into Slater's. The warmth of his body was heady, and he relished it, with the burgeoning warmth of the bourbon in his belly, and he sank into it.

"Why do you do this to me?"

"What did I do?" Pike said, his tongue thick.

"You make me fucking crazy. I can't think straight. I love you so hard."

EIGHTEEN

<hr>

SLATER GOT UP EARLY and found Pike upstairs, cooking oatmeal, coffee already in the pot. He was dressed for the weekend, wearing his fugly cargo shorts and a T-shirt. Slater embraced him from behind and kissed his neck.

"You want some of this?" Pike said. "Grab the blueberries in the Frigidaire."

He threw some berries on the oatmeal and they carried the bowls out to the deck. As they walked through the main room, Slater eyed the flowers on the dining table.

"Those goddamn roses still look fresh."

"Right?" Pike said. "They must have put something in the vase."

Sitting at the patio table, he squinted at the bright daylight, and slurped at his coffee, and looked at his phone.

He found the number for MW that Chad had texted yesterday, then looked up Bucky in his own contacts. It was the same number. In the tracking app he checked for Bucky's phone. The guy was at his house.

Pike was leaning over the table to eat his oatmeal, and he gestured with his spoon. "Brewster's coming over today. She's going to look at the electric panel."

He knew her, one of Pike's colleagues that wasn't trying to get into his pants.

"Why?"

"She knows about wiring and all that. If my next car is going to be an EV, I'm going to need to put a charger in the garage."

Slater furrowed his brow, and pushed his bowl away, watching him.

"I can see the wheels turning," Pike said. "I'm happy to park my hooptie on the street, but not a new car. You know there's room in there for two vehicles, right?"

"Theoretically, sure. But the Continental needs a certain amount of breathing room."

Pike chuckled. "I can park carefully. I took a whole emergency vehicle course."

"That just means you can roll priority and get into car chases with crooks, not that you're any damn good at parking."

"It'll be a while before I get another car. There's no cause for stress just yet."

Sliding off his chair, Slater knelt in front of him, and wrapped his arms around him, and pressed his face into his belly.

"You can park anywhere you want," Slater said.

"Take the whole garage. You can tow the Continental up to the Angeles Crest Highway, and push it off a cliff, and watch it burst into a fireball. You can beat the shit out of me and lock me in the trunk, or leave my battered bleeding body on the side of the road to be scraped away by a snowplow. It wouldn't matter. I'd still love you."

Pike ran a hand into his hair, and Slater looked up at him. He had an odd look on his face, a half smirk, his eyes bright. He caressed Slater's cheek with a thumb.

"I don't suppose I'll need to do anything quite like that."

Leaning in to squeeze him again, Slater lingered in it a moment, then got up. "I have to go."

"You're working today?"

"I need to give Bucky a tune-up."

Pike winced. "I don't want to tell you what to do, but go easy. He is your client."

Hustling down to the garage, he backed the Continental into the street, then drove the few minutes to Silver Lake. There was no vehicle in front of Bucky's house. The fact that he hid it in his garage even though he had a big driveway meant it was either too flashy to leave in plain view or he was driving a junker.

When he rang the bell, Bucky pulled open the door and flashed a smile. He was dressed in dark-red jeans and a snug athletic top with a black-and-white checkered pattern.

"I wasn't expecting you," Bucky said, and waved him in, walking through to the kitchen. "Want some OJ?"

"That's quite the shirt."

"Thank you," he said, and picked up a glass from the counter.

He hadn't meant it as a compliment. Staring at that pattern for too long would give anyone a seizure. Slater put his hands on his hips.

"How was your night, Bucky?"

"Fine." He held his gaze. "Why are you asking?"

"Life must look sweet through those rose-colored glasses. Tanner is quite the looker too. Are you fucking him?"

His eyes grew wide. "I can explain."

Stepping closer, Slater slapped him hard, a rapid kovac. Bucky screamed and dropped his glass. It hit the floor with a hollow plastic *clunk* and bounced into the corner, splashing juice all over the tiles.

"Why do you make me do this to you?" Slater said through his teeth, and slapped him again. "Why do you do it?"

Bucky shoved him back. "Stop it."

"You lied to me."

He lunged at him again, and Bucky raised his forearms to fend him off. Slater grabbed his shoulders and started to shake him.

"Stop it, stop it." His voice broke, like he was sobbing.

Finally Slater pushed him away and stepped back.

"Start singing, brother."

Bucky was panting. "Just give me a minute."

"You don't need a minute to think about the truth. It's the bullshit that takes the thinking. Are you really going to make me crack you? You know I'll do it." Raising his voice, he said, "Talk."

"I'm not really part of it," he said quickly.

"Why were you hanging out with Tanner? A couple days ago you'd never heard of him. You told me Chad works alone."

"It's part of their racket. If I help them with the work, it means they charge me less. I didn't volunteer for it."

Slater studied his face. "I actually think I believe you. Lo, he finally speaks the truth. The golden thread that stitches the world together."

"Of course it's the truth."

"You looked pretty comfortable last night. Not like you were under the gun."

"I'm in a jam here. I don't have unlimited resources."

"Tell me exactly what you do for them," Slater said, "or I'll bust you open."

"I don't set up the targets. They do that. I just help them identify closety guys. Chad can tell if they have money but he's got no gaydar. I'm like a consultant, not a player."

"I just loaded them into the boxcars," Slater said. "I just drove the train."

"What are you talking about?"

"You work with both Chad and Tanner?"

He looked away. "Sometimes."

"What about Liz?"

"I don't know that name."

"Why would I believe you now?" Slater demanded.

Bucky gestured helplessly.

"You work at Electric. Are there other clubs too?"

"Only that one."

"What do you know about Chad and Tanner? All of it this time."

"Tanner's aura is muddy green. Chad's is even darker. I should have known they were bad news."

"Spare me the New Age bullshit," Slater snapped.

Bucky huffed. "Chad is the smart one. Tanner does the grunt work. You asked about guns before. They don't have those. They keep people like me in line with the threat of exposure, not violence."

"When are you supposed to work with them again?"

"Next week, tentatively. But Tanner said he was working tonight at Electric."

"Not Chad?"

"He's collecting payments at the Blue Dragon. They think Tanner is hotter, so he's doing more of the frame-ups."

Slater stared at him for a moment, then gestured to the floor. "You shouldn't let that OJ dry up. It'll get all sticky." He turned to walk out.

"That was your fault," Bucky said, and louder, "What am I supposed to do?"

Slater paused and turned back. "I don't know, man." He threw up his hands. "You could stand up to those lowlifes."

"I'm paying you to help me, remember? I hired you to get me out from under them."

"When you lie to me, you're hobbling my work, and wasting your best resource." He took a breath and lowered his voice. "I've got a plan to shut them down. I'll let you know how it goes." He jabbed a finger at him. "Do not tell them about me."

When he climbed into his car, he looked at his phone and called Jack, glad that he picked up.

"I need help with clothes," Slater said. "Can I

take you shopping today?"

"I would absolutely love that, but your timing sucks. I'm on my way to New York. I'm at the gate already."

"Who the fuck goes to New York in January?" he demanded. "It's buried in snow. Is it even open?"

Jack laughed. "It's my crazy jet-set life."

The guy lived in a studio over an Italian restaurant, but he didn't need to remind him of that.

"I'm disappointed in you, Jack," he said, and ended the call. "Idiot," he muttered.

Thinking about it, he had other options. A phone call with Max was easier than texting with him, as it took him forever to punch out terse messages with those stubby fingers. Plus Max usually answered his calls.

"When is that street-naming ceremony in Lennox?" he said when Max picked up.

"Today," Max said. "Later this morning."

"Do you know where?"

"The doughnut shop where it all began," he said, and named the cross streets.

Once he'd ended the call, he sat for a minute and thought it through. His plan was coming together, but he needed some help. A while back he'd put Svetlana's stealthy tracking software on Della's phone. She was his handler at Cudahy Mutual, and pulled him in to investigate insurance claims when the desk jockeys suspected fraud but didn't want to get their own hands dirty.

At the time he'd done it with her permission, as he'd been helping her out, but he'd never deleted the connection to her phone. When he checked the tracking app and tapped her name, he saw that it was still functioning. The green dot was on Rossmore. That was her apartment. She hadn't gone out for the day yet. He dialed her number.

"The goddess is smiling on me today," Della said when she picked up. "Hearing from my favorite investigator on the weekend."

"Do you have a minute for me? We need to talk."

"That sounds ominous."

"It's not. Nobody's going to try to borrow money from you."

She laughed. "I'd be thrilled to see your pretty face."

"You said once you lived on Rossmore."

Della recited her address. "I'll put the coffee on."

Once he'd punched it into his navigation, he started the engine, and headed west, soon cruising up the boulevard. He never came out here. There were some great old buildings, and Della's had deco styling, with the ziggurat cutouts, and period tattersall windows with the black frames, and elegant planter urns flanking the entrance.

As he walked up he paused to look them over. They were planted with pink *Aeonium* succulents. Those were expensive, and fickle, but someone was making them thrive here. He clicked his tongue. The things you could do when you had money.

There was no directory outside, so he tried the door. It wasn't locked. Parked behind a desk was a woman in a dark suit jacket. She looked up and greeted him.

"This place is tony," Slater said. "Staff instead of an intercom."

She laughed. "It fits the vibe of the building, don't you think?"

"I'm here to see Della Van Ness in 902. The name is Ibáñez."

She nodded, and picked up her desk phone, and murmured into the receiver. Replacing it, she looked up at him. "Take the elevator on the left."

As he walked toward it, the door slid open well before he was anywhere near it. That meant the desk clerk had control of it. A rich-folks security measure, he realized. No riffraff were going to get in and have the run of the place, but the mechanism to ensure that was invisible—the place still felt open and accessible.

When he knocked on Della's door, she pulled it open and smiled. Dressed casually today, in capri pants and a gray sweater, her hair was brushed back around her ears. Tall for her age, she had to be in her sixties.

"You've never been here before," Della said.

"This place is money, Della," he said, looking around. "You're going to have to start paying me more. They're clearly paying you more."

"It's a condo. My monthly isn't that high."

The windows in the main room had a view west toward Century City and the hills. Nearby sat a set of lounge furniture, all in mid-century style. He recognized the coffee table—ebony, maybe, or rosewood in two curving parts with a glass slab on top, by some big-name designer. There was no clutter anywhere.

"Viva la modernism," he said.

"My decorator said it was coming back."

"It never left." He waved at the room. "This place is beautiful."

She preened a little, and nodded for him to follow her.

In the kitchen the counters and cabinetry were new but fit the modernist vibe. Della waved him to a breakfast table with tall chairs around it.

As he sat, Slater said, "What's the square footage on this place?"

She poured coffee from a carafe into two mugs. "It's not that big. Two beds, two baths."

He folded his arms. "Must be nice."

Stepping over to the table, she set a mug down for him. "You can't out-poverty me, Slater. I looked up your place when you bought it." She climbed on the opposite chair. "I know how much space you have, and what you're paying for it. It's a lot more house than this place."

"That seems snoopy."

"Wouldn't you have done the same?"

"Of course, but snooping is kind of my job." He sipped the java. "I know it's a lot of house. I had to buy that place. To make room for Pike and our narrative complex."

"How is that long drink of water?"

"He's all gravy. And then under the gravy there's more gravy."

"It sounds like it's still intense."

"For a long time it felt like there were towering flames all around me. Like those videos of people driving through a wildfire." He waved a hand. "He dances. We went to a swing class. He's actually got me reading the *Odyssey*."

"I'd say he's enriching you," Della said. "New ideas, new experiences."

"It's my life now. It's hard to be objective about it."

"If things ever get routine, you should consider introducing a feminine element. I could teach you old dogs some new tricks." She flashed her palms. "No strings."

"If I did that, it would be a hot minute until you hated me. Despised me, and saw me for the trash that I am. Then you wouldn't give me any more work, and I'd have to move into a tent along the railroad tracks."

Della chuckled. "How could I ever hate the way those jeans fit?" She rose and went to the counter. "Want some sugar?"

"I don't." He watched as she grabbed a box and shook some into her mug. "I'm working on shutting down an extortion racket. How would you like to pose as my wife?"

She laughed as she sat down again. "Explain."

"I need a verifiable name and workplace. Somebody they can threaten to expose me to."

"That's exciting. I guess it's OK."

He hadn't actually come to ask permission. It was more of a head's up. But he could roll with it.

"Nobody's going to contact you," he said. "That would be cutting off their potential revenue stream. But if they look you up, you're a real person."

"I am indeed. You're sure you don't need me as arm candy? I'm good at parties."

"I know you are. You're the best. But not this time."

They chatted a while longer, and he finished his coffee, then slid off the chair.

"I should go."

Della followed him to the door. "It was great to see you."

"Give me some work and you'll see more of me."

Once he was back in his car, he checked his phone. He needed to head to Lennox soon, but first he'd need a phone number that couldn't be traced to him. Getting a fake outgoing number from his spoofing service was easy, but an incoming number took more effort. Eventually he had it figured out, and set it up, then stuck his phone in the dash mount and pulled into the street.

The navigation app sent him on Crenshaw most of the way, and a half hour later he was cruising the boulevard in Lennox. It was a low-income neighborhood, and low-rise, with multiple car lots, a Latin mercado, a pawn shop between a storefront church and a taco stand. He rolled through the intersection Max had named and saw a small crowd of people gathered on one of the corners. That was the street-naming event. The curb lane had been coned off.

Once he'd parked, farther up the block, he walked back to the intersection. A blue curtain with a rectangular shape underneath it was hanging high overhead. It was on a light pole, just a few yards from the traffic signal at the corner.

As he stepped up to the edge of the small crowd, he saw there was a news crew. A video camera that bore the channel 6 logo sat on a guy's shoulder, and standing with him was a TV reporter with way too much makeup, her hair freshly blown out, holding a big mike down at her side.

The camera and the crowd's attention were trained on a woman in a gray suit at a little lectern, her voice amplified through a sound system. He recognized her as a county supervisor. Standing behind her were several drag queens in full glam, with dramatic curves, their hair piled high, and even more makeup than channel 6. It took him a minute but he finally figured out which one was Gladys Rayon.

Her blond hair was styled to look windblown, and her lashes were so long that they obscured her eyes. The long gold lamé gown accentuated her curves, with hips that were way out of proportion to her lanky frame. Pushed-up balloon breasts created cleavage that looked real.

After the supe finished yapping there was polite applause, then a guy in a dark suit stepped up to the mike. He looked like another politician, and sure enough he introduced himself as the mayor. After the suit finished his spiel, Gladys made a camp-inflected speech, explaining a little about the sit-in and the confrontation with the cops.

Eventually she pulled a cord that dropped the blue curtain to reveal the sign: GLADYS RAYON SQUARE. There was applause and hooting, and one of the other queens whistled loudly through her fingers. He should have timed this better, Slater realized. Gladys was going to have to press the flesh, schmooze the politicians, talk to the journalist.

It took a while, but he finally got a break to approach her.

"You don't look like Bill at all," Slater said.

"I remember you." Gladys smiled. "I guess Max didn't throw me under the bus, seeing as the city went ahead with all this." She gestured at the new sign. "You like?"

"Not everybody gets their name on a street sign," Slater said, glancing up at it. "Listen, I know you're retired, but I wanted to hire you as a consultant."

"By trade I'm a plumber." She arched her carefully painted eyebrows. "You want me to assess your pipes, honey?"

"I want you to dress me in man drag to look like a rich-ass desk jockey."

"A makeover," she said in a singsong voice. "I never retired from being fashionable. This day just keeps getting better."

"You can do boy looks?"

"Of course. A makeover starts with a purge. We'll have to throw all this away." She swirled a palm at him. "Everything in your closet must go."

"I don't want a makeover. I just need to create a look."

She frowned. "What exactly do you need to do?"

"I want to attract the attention of a guy who's very into closety rich guys. It needs to happen today. I have an opportunity to see him tonight."

"Can I ask why?"

"That's need-to-know type dope, Gladys, and you don't need to know."

"Well, first you're going to need your hair cut. I'll see if my stylist friend can do an emergency visit. It's going to cost you."

"Is that really necessary?" Slater said. "I can just put some gel in it."

Gladys pursed her luridly red lips into a pout, and reached for the side of his head, and ruffled his hair. "Trust me, honey—to look stupid rich, you're going to need to put in the work." She looked past his shoulder. "I need to talk to channel 6."

Digging a business card from his hip pocket, Slater handed it to her and said, "Call me."

He watched as Gladys stepped over to the camera, and sparkled in the glare of its floodlight, and chatted with the reporter like they were old friends. As he walked back to his car, he had to grin. She hadn't asked him what he was going to pay her. He might get off cheap.

NINETEEN

⌐⌐⌐⌐⌐⌐⌐⌐⌐⌐⌐

A FEW MORE THINGS NEEDED to come together, and as Slater climbed behind the wheel of the Continental, he dug out his phone and texted his operative Etta:

You around today?

Her reply came a moment later:

Doing some work for Max. In the office later on. What up, pup?

Slater thumb-typed a response:

I'll see you at the office.

He started the engine, and pulled into the street, and drove to his house. The garage door was up, and as he nosed in he saw Pike and Brewster standing at the back, next to the laundry machines, with the electric panel open.

She was about Pike's age, and wore her longish hair tied back, today clad in a puffy dark winter jacket, even though it wasn't that cold out. Slater killed the engine, and climbed out, and walked toward them.

Brewster called out a greeting as he approached. "You're good to go for an EV charger. There's room on the panel."

"So Reddy Kilowatt can charge up at his leisure," Slater said.

"Brewster brought us some avocados," Pike said, and handed him a plastic bag.

Slater pulled one out and looked it over. "These are from a backyard tree."

"You're right. From my neighbor."

"You need to ingratiate yourself with this person," he said. "Become indispensable in their life, and get more of these."

"Are they so different from supermarket ones?" Pike said.

"That's like comparing you and your electric car to a chimp on a unicycle. The only good avocados come from backyard trees."

"Same goes for oranges and lemons," Brewster said.

"Preach, sister." Slater gestured with the bag. "I'll take these upstairs. They'll be in a secure location on a need-to-know basis."

Brewster chuckled. "So why do you have a gun safe in here? Pike says you're not a firearms guy."

"Who says I have a gun safe?"

She gestured to it. "It's sitting right there. Don't

blame Pike—he didn't point it out. I've seen that particular model before."

"I have a lot of tools. Some of them are damn expensive." He gestured to the wall rack. "I figure if the junkies break in to steal stuff, they can take the string trimmer and the chainsaw. I left those out as the easy pickings."

Her brow furrowed. "OK."

"You don't need to be inspecting my stuff, woman. Do you have any idea what a decent post-hole auger costs? It would make your eyes water."

She flashed her palms. "Just curious."

"Nobody's touching your stuff," Pike said.

"See, this is what happens when you bring law-enforcement types around."

"I hate to say it, but that's on you," Brewster said. "You married one."

Slater narrowed his eyes. "Not yet. But point taken."

"It sounds like I've got a chance," Pike said, and laughed.

"You're the only man for me," Slater said, and waved an arm. "You know that. You're the sun in the day and all the stars at night. The land and the sea and the sky. I don't see any need to get something as mundane as the government involved in all that grandeur."

"Such a romantic," Brewster said, and put her palm over her heart.

"We were going to get lunch on Sunset," Pike said. "You're welcome to join us."

"I've got stuff to do." He gestured to his gear cabinet. "There's no point trying to get into it. The door has a multipoint lock. It's sealed up tight."

Brewster chuckled. "I won't waste my time, then."

He pointed two fingers at his eyes, then jabbed one at her, a tacit *I'm watching you.*

Walking back to the front of the garage, he headed up the stairs to the kitchen, and set the avocados on the counter, then stepped out onto the deck and sat on one of the loungers, straddling it to face the morning sun.

Chad's phone was at his place, he saw when he checked his trackers. The guy had had a rough night—he'd definitely be sleeping it off. Tanner's vehicle was at the coffeehouse near their house. It was hard to believe they lived in a house like that and couldn't make their own damn coffee. A few minutes ago Chad had texted Tanner:

> Checked the video. It wasn't four-eyes. Some guy. Couldn't see his face. He was wearing a spotlight on his head.

That was about Slater—there was a security camera at the front gate to Chad's house, and the stealthy glasses had done their job and obscured his face. Thank you, Svetlana. They were trying to figure out who'd driven the Subaru back to his place. Four-eyes had to be Mara. That meant Chad knew he'd been with her last night. That made sense—his memory would be intact up until they'd given him the ketamine.

Finding Liz in his contacts, he dialed and got her voice mail.

"We need to talk," Slater told the machine. "Today."

She'd call back, he knew. Slater had something she wanted—she'd asked him to warn her if Chad's racket was in danger of being exposed so that she could distance herself from it.

Rising, he went inside and down the stairs to the bathroom. He sat on the floor in front of the sink and reached up behind the drain pipe. The freezer bag of cash was still here, tucked into a gap, and he pulled it out. What was Pike doing digging around in here anyway? Everything was dry, and nothing was dripping. The bag had been pretty well hidden.

He wasn't sure what working with Gladys was going to cost him, and he counted out three grand, then resealed the bag and wedged it into its place again. His phone buzzed in his pants, and as he stood up he pulled it out to check—Liz.

"What do we need to talk about?" she said when he picked up.

"It has to be in person."

"Why?"

"I'll tell you when I see you."

"I don't work Saturdays," Liz said. "I'm at a thing in Grand Park."

"Meet me by the coffee place. I'm a few minutes from there."

Slater stuffed his phone in his jeans and trotted down to his car. The garage door was closed now, and Pike and Brewster were gone. He backed into the street and waited for the door to descend, then headed to Grand Avenue. If there was an event happening, there'd be no open meters on the street, but there was always room under the Music Center. He nosed onto the ramp, and minutes later emerged on foot from the stairwell into the park.

There were a lot of people around, and lively music was thumping from a stage set up at the far end, down by city hall. It sounded like old-school roots music, with a fiddle and a guitar. He could see a crowd gathered there.

He spotted Liz slouching on one of the park's hot-pink chairs, facing the splash fountain and the bare-foot kids playing around the shallow water. Wearing jeans and a tweed jacket, her hair was pinned back in a messy bundle, with big dark sunglasses obscuring her eyes. Her feet were up on a second chair, and when she spotted Slater approaching, she sat up and gestured to it.

"If you're looking for a date," Liz said, "the woman in the black hoodie was checking out your butt."

"No thanks." He shifted the chair next to her and sat down, looking to where Liz had nodded. The woman in black was one of the adults hovering over the kids at the fountain, holding hands with a toddler who was stamping her feet to splash the water.

"You're not into women with kids?"

Slater frowned. "I'm on dick, sister."

"Got it."

"This place is hopping on Saturday. You came for the band?"

"That guy is a hack. I like the opening act. They're pure Appalachia." Liz waved a hand. "So what's going on that can't be said on the phone?"

"When the trash brothers pick up men at the nightclub, is it always drugs in the toilet stall, or do they have other scenarios?"

She looked away, toward the splash fountain.

"Gay guys are usually down for a quickie in the stalls, especially if they take the ecstasy. But straight guys usually want to go somewhere more comfortable."

"I'm thinking Chad and Tanner prefer the stalls because it's easy and safe. They pay the security guys to look the other way."

Liz looked at him. "How did you know that?"

"If the mark insists on going somewhere else, where do you take him?"

"Oh, man." She huffed audibly.

"If you want to shut them down, sister, I need to know. So squawk."

"They rent a room in one of those micro hotels. It's not far from the club they use."

"Electric."

"That's the one. They haven't found any new suckers for a while. I think they're getting antsy about it. They're working the place more often. Several nights this week already."

"The room is wired with cameras?" Slater said.

"Just one, I think. The photos I've seen are always from right over the bed."

"You must be in lots of them."

She sat gazing at the kids and the fountain. "I get out of it sometimes by telling those idiots I'm on my period. That tends to freak men out."

"I've heard that one before," Slater said. "Don't you dare treat me like I'm impaired because of my period, but cut me some slack because I'm on my period."

Liz chuckled. "It's a powerful tool, isn't it? It's only a disability if I say it is. And when the job is about sex, it does change things. The problem is, even straight guys can count. I can't use that excuse more than once every few weeks."

"Tanner and Chad both take guys to this micro hotel?" Slater said.

"Mostly Tanner. I think he's got more gay in him." She pulled off her sunglasses and frowned at him. "I never told you about Tanner."

"You just remembered that?" He scoffed. "It's a lot easier to keep track of stuff if you just tell the damn truth."

"How did you find out about him?"

He stood up. "You're not the only patsy in this case."

"Why are you asking all this?"

"I need all the dope on those knuckleheads that I can get," he said, and walked away.

On his way to the stairs down to the garage his phone buzzed in his jeans, and he pulled it out to check. It was a 323 number, and he picked up.

"My stylist can see you today," Gladys's familiar voice said. "How close are you to Mateo Street?"

"I can be there in a few minutes."

"Excellent. I'll text you the address."

Rolling up onto the street, Slater headed to the Arts District and pulled in when he spotted a meter. The building at the address Bill had sent didn't look like a salon, or even like a retail venue, with no windows out front, no signage, just big aluminum street numbers mounted next to the door.

Before he could pull on the handle, he heard someone call "Ibáñez." He saw Bill trotting up the sidewalk, out of drag now.

"How did it go with channel 6, Bill?" he said as he approached.

He grinned. "The name is Gladys."

"Put the dress on again and I'll call you Gladys."

Bill briefly put a hand on his shoulder and met his eye. "You never have to be ashamed to admit that you need help. I'm really glad you asked."

"Shame has nothing to do with it," Slater said. "I figured drag queens know fashion. I have some sense of it, but not enough."

"I'd call that a shame." He waved a hand. "Fernande usually charges four, but it'll be more because of the urgency. Can you handle that?"

"It seems like a lot of dough for a haircut."

"You want to look stupid rich. Fernande will make you look stupid rich."

"He cuts yours?" Slater said.

"Fernande is a she. Of course not. I don't have any." He ran a hand over his sparse gray hair, cropped short and slicked back. "At least not the kind that's attached without wig tape. Come on." He pulled the door open and stepped inside.

Like the facade, nothing about the interior gave any indication of what business they were conducting. It looked more like a cigar lounge—there was a desk with a woman sitting behind it, a bookcase full of hardbacks, and a fireplace to one side with what looked like real wood burning in it. In front of the desk and facing the fireplace was a pair of burgundy leather club chairs.

The woman smiled and stood up as they stepped in. "Mr. Slater?"

"It's just Slater," he said.

In his experience, upscale retail was either warm and friendly, to make you spend more, or aloof and rude, to make you want to prove you were worthy of the merch by spending more. From her demeanor this place seemed to take the friendly approach.

"Fernande will be available shortly," she said. "Come with me."

She led them down the hall and into a space with just one adjustable chair. This room finally looked the part, with mirrors, and a sink, and a rack with towels and a blow-dryer and other tools of the trade. Slater sat in the salon chair, and Bill perched on one of the stools.

"Can I get you an espresso or a cappuccino while you're waiting?" the woman said. "I also have a nice pinot noir."

"Hit me with the joe," Slater said.

She looked to Bill. "For you?"

"An espresso would be lovely."

The receptionist closed the door gently behind her, but there wasn't any wait, as a woman stepped in moments after she left. In her fifties, maybe, with an athletic frame, Fernande was wearing a dark-blue jacket and black trousers, her blond hair casually tucked behind her ears. She greeted Bill with a familiar embrace, then introduced herself to Slater. Her speech had just the faintest hint of an accent.

Swiveling Slater's chair to face the mirror, she ran her hands into his hair. "So what's the style we're looking for?"

"He needs to look Westside wealthy," Bill said.

Fernande nodded sagely, meeting Slater's eye in the mirror. "That, I can do. I'll have Bethany wash your hair, and I'll be back in a few minutes."

The woman from the front desk came in briefly

with a couple of little demitasse cups, complete with a cube of dark sugar and a twist of lemon rind on the saucer. Handing one to Bill, she set the other on the counter in front of Slater.

"Sweet caffeine," Bill said. "This will get us amped up for shopping after."

"Keep in mind that I'm not made of money," Slater said.

He'd only just spritzed the lemon rind and taken a couple of satisfying sips when Bethany came in. She looked to be in her twenties, and had glowing skin and curly brown hair. Once she'd introduced herself, she swiveled Slater around and lowered the chair back to wash his hair in the little sink. Afterward she gently dried it with a towel.

Once she'd left, he sipped his espresso again, and a moment later Fernande stepped in.

"I'm sorry to keep you waiting."

"I wasn't waiting," he said. "Bethany just left."

"You're easy to please." She grinned at him in the mirror. "We're going to get along fine."

She ran a comb through his hair and set to work. Sometime later, when her labors were complete, she met his gaze again.

"How does that feel?"

"I'd say it's perfect," Bill said. "All you need now is a polo pony and a sports car."

Slater turned his head to get a better look. It was short on the sides and longer toward the front. "I guess I trust your judgment."

"Can we spray it into place?" Bill said.

"Of course." Fernande reached for an aerosol can on the supply rack.

"Hairspray?" Slater said. "Seriously?"

"It means you won't have to style it again," Bill said.

"Fine," he said flatly, and screwed his eyes shut while Fernande sprayed and brushed.

"I hope we'll see you again," Fernande said finally, smiling at him in the mirror as she left.

Slater got up and drained the last of the cold espresso from the little cup, then followed Bill out to the front desk.

"What's the damage?" he asked the receptionist.

The woman smiled politely and said, "Five fifty."

Digging out his wad, Slater riffled off the bills. "Is this Fernande's own shop, or does she work for someone else?"

"It's her place."

"That means I'm not going to tip her." He set the cash on the counter. "That was good java, by the way."

TWENTY

▨▨▨▨▨▨▨▨▨▨▨

ONCE THEY WERE OUT on the street, Bill looked him over. "It's really good."

"Hairspray," Slater said. "Now I can't touch my head. I can already feel it starting to itch."

"That's psychosomatic, you big baby. You can wash it out in the shower before bed."

"All right, Gladys. What about the clothes?"

"To the Fashion District. We can walk from your office. Where should I park?"

"In the surface lot across the street."

Slater drove over and parked along the fence. As he was climbing out, a silver Lexus pulled into the next stall. Bill got out and gestured to the Continental.

"How can you drive such a glamorous car and be clueless about clothes?"

"I'm not clueless about clothes," Slater said. "I'm

clueless about what one-percenters do."

They crossed the street with Bill leading the way. There were a cluster of men's suit stores on the next block, and he looked into the first store they came to, not breaking his stride.

"Not here. Next one." They passed two more before he said, "This place will work."

"You can tell enough about the inventory from the display window?" Slater said.

"I can tell who's working." He pulled open the door. "We have to find a clerk that I can bend to my will."

A guy stepped up and greeted them. In his twenties, his Black hair was cut short with a fade at the temples, and he wore a blue suit without a necktie.

"We need something in black satin for my client here," Bill said, gesturing to Slater. "In a sharp cut."

"We have just the thing," he said, his tone genial, and to Slater, "What size do you wear?"

Before Slater could reply, Bill said intently, "Sizes change every single day. You need to measure him."

His eyebrows shot up. "I can do that. Follow me."

Suppressing a grin, Slater followed them toward the middle of the store. The clerk found a tape and gestured for him to raise his arms, then measured his waist, and his chest. Stepping over to the rack of jackets lining the wall, he flicked through several, checking the tags.

"I have your size in the stockroom. Give me a minute," he said, and went into the back of the store, emerging again a minute later with a dark suit on a hanger.

Bill intercepted him, stepping in front of Slater as he approached, and ran his hand under the arm of the jacket. "I hate this fabric. Do you have anything that's less cheap-looking?"

"Right—let me see what I can come up with," he said, and turned on his heel.

While they waited, Slater looked through the rack of jackets the clerk had first dug through. "There are so many different versions of black."

"That's why I'm here," Bill said. "To cut through the crap."

When the clerk came back with a different black suit, Bill assessed it.

"Better," he said, and to Slater, "Try it on."

Slater took the suit jacket from the clerk and shrugged into it.

"Button it," Bill instructed. "Top button only."

"Would you like to look in the mirror?" the clerk asked.

Before Slater could reply, Bill waved impatiently, stepping up to him to pull the hem of the jacket down. He took a step back and looked him over.

"We'll need it half a size smaller."

"Are you sure?" the clerk said. "This one fits him pretty well."

Bill turned to him and arched his eyebrows. "Do you have this jacket in the correct size?"

"Of course," he said, and went into the back.

Slater took off the jacket, and when the clerk returned, he put on the new one, then buttoned it. Bill adjusted the hem, and the sleeves, and stood back, looking him over the way an artist would scrutinize a half-finished painting.

"I suspect that's as good as it's going to get," Bill said.

"Am I allowed to look at it?" Slater demanded.

The clerk grinned and waved him to a wall mirror, and Slater spent a minute checking out the fit.

"It looks a little puckered," he said.

"That's the style right now," Bill said.

"He's right," the clerk offered. "It looks great on you."

Bill nodded. "Try on the pants."

Slater unbuckled his belt and pushed down his jeans, then stepped into the suit pants. Bill adjusted the fit, not shy about touching his butt or shifting his junk around. When he was satisfied, he looked to the clerk, who was hanging back to watch him work.

"This is satisfactory," Bill said. "We'll need to mark these hems."

After he'd pinned the pant legs, and Slater changed back into his jeans, the clerk led the way to the register at the front of the store, where Slater paid for the suit with cash from his wad.

"There's a tailor shop in the next block," the clerk said, ringing up the sale and then tucking the suit into a garment bag. "They can do the work the same day."

"I'm aware," Bill said.

"Are you in the fashion industry?" the clerk asked, handing the hook at the top of the garment bag to Slater and keeping his eyes on Bill.

"I'm not," Bill said, "but I know the business, and I don't mess around."

The clerk nodded. "We should hang out sometime. Have a drink and stream some tunes."

Bill's eyes narrowed, and he studied him for a

moment, then reached into his pants pocket, producing a business card, and handed it across the counter. "You may call me."

As they stepped out to the street, the clerk stood engrossed in studying Bill's card.

Once they were headed up the sidewalk, Bill said, "Wasn't he cute?"

"I can't believe he wanted your number. You were pretty hard on him."

"And yet he asked me out anyway. He could be my grandson. Don't get me wrong—that's not going to slow me down."

"He didn't ask you out," Slater said. "He asked you in. 'Stream some tunes' happens at home."

"Even better." Bill chuckled. "Stream some tunes. I remember when it was CDs. Those came after vinyl. Before that we'd crank up the gramophone, and put on a 78, and sit bolt upright in a hard-backed wooden chair to listen to it."

"I heard some Bessie Smith music this week. I bet she was on your 78s."

"Good god, man, how old do you think I am?" Bill said, glancing at him sidelong.

"Dude—you're the one who said it." He paused on the sidewalk. "This is the tailor shop."

"I have my own tailor. We need this done fast."

He gestured for Slater to catch up, and they crossed the street at the corner and walked into the next block. Bill ducked into a narrow doorway without a sign over it, and Slater followed him inside. The space looked more like a walk-in closet than a place of business, and the heat was up high, making it feel close and stuffy. Taking the suit bag from him, Bill laid it on the counter. A man with rounded shoulders and slick gray hair approached.

Bill explained what he wanted, and the tailor gestured to the plastic chairs by the door.

"Sit. It'll just be a few minutes."

Taking the chair beside him, Bill waved a hand. "To really look money, it's about the shoes."

"I have a pair of black derbies."

He shook his head. "No way."

Slater glared at him sidelong and took a breath. He'd asked for this, he reminded himself. He couldn't very well just punch the guy in the face, as much as he wanted to right now.

"Well, I'm not going to buy anything made of leather."

"There's a vegan shoe store back in the Arts District," Bill said. "They'll have what we need."

While Bill inspected the work on the pant cuffs, Slater paid the tailor. Satisfied, Bill zipped the bag closed and handed it to him, and they walked back to his office. Even on Saturday the neighborhood was busy, with the small sewing factories and fabric suppliers and wholesalers open and hustling.

He hung the garment bag in the backseat of the Continental, and Bill climbed in the passenger side.

"You could host a mah-jongg game in here."

"This is what a car should feel like," Slater said. "Cars aren't good anymore."

"That depends on your definition of good. I bet it breaks down more than mine."

"It's worth it, because it doesn't feel like my soul is being crushed when I drive it."

He cruised the few blocks to the Arts District,

and Bill pointed out the shoe store. Once he'd circled the block he found a street space, and parked, and they climbed out.

Inside the shop, a young woman with long hair greeted them, and Bill held up a finger, not looking at her but surveying the footwear on display.

"These," he said finally, seizing a shoe.

It was black, and an odd shape, with an alligator-skin finish.

"Excellent choice," the clerk said. "What size do you wear?"

"Oh, god—I wouldn't wear that," Bill said, and jutted his chin at Slater. "What's your shoe size?"

Slater told her, and when she brought the box from the back, he sat on the little stool next to the register and tried them on, walking over to the mirror once he'd knotted the laces.

"These are so damn ugly," Slater said, frowning as he studied them. The toes curled upward and into a weird slanted point, making his feet look bigger than they really were.

"Hike up your skirt, Alice," Bill said.

"Is that some drag code I haven't heard before?"

"It means suck it up and do the work."

Slater gritted his teeth and groaned, studying the shoes.

Stepping behind him, Bill met his gaze in the mirror. "Do you trust me?" he said gravely.

"On this, yeah. You're the authority."

"Then quit futzing around and pay the woman."

Slater sat down again to pull the shoes off, and the clerk put them back in their box, unable to conceal her amusement. As she rang up the sale, Slater pulled out his wad.

"You're packing a lot of cash," Bill said, watching him peel off the C-notes. "Did you rob a bank?"

"My business runs in cash."

They walked back to the car, Slater with the shoebox in a bulky shopping bag dangling from one hand.

"You're good at this," Slater said. "I thought it might take all afternoon."

"What about a watch?" Bill said.

"I don't have one."

"Rich idiots always wear forty-thousand-dollar watches when they go to nightclubs."

"I'm not spending that on a watch," Slater said as they climbed in the Continental.

"I can get you one for two hundred bucks. But we have to go out of town."

"How far out of town?"

"Monterey Park."

"That's not far."

He started the engine, and navigated to the freeway, and sped up the ramp. The traffic was stop-and-go, and Slater rode the brakes as he gradually merged across several lanes to get onto the 10, headed east.

"It's like this all day now," Bill said.

"I just don't get why people need to be out here on Saturday. 'Let's go hog up the freeway.' It makes no sense."

Bill looked over at him. "People can be so inconsiderate."

"Preach, brother."

Once they were in the San Gabriel Valley, Bill directed him where to exit, and then into the parking lot of a sprawling strip mall. The low-slung architecture was classic suburban 1960s, and the signage on the storefronts was almost exclusively in Chinese.

As they walked toward the shop, Bill spoke. "Negotiating is one of the skills of my people, so just keep your mouth shut."

"You mean drag queens? I thought shoplifting was their preferred retail technique."

"That's slander," Bill said. "And we call it mopping."

Even though it was broad daylight outside, Slater winced as they stepped into the even brighter interior. Lit from above with spotlights, the display case lining the narrow shop was loaded with watches, gleaming gold and silver. The guy behind the counter was Bill's age, and Bill engaged him as soon as they stepped in, pointing into the case at a bulky model with a gold band.

"That one looks damaged," he said. "What's your salvage price?"

The clerk chuckled, and pulled it out, and got into it with him. Bill actually was good at haggling, Slater realized, watching him alternately cajole the clerk and then act offended. Bill took the watch and peered at it, then grimaced and set it down on the counter, wiping his fingers on his shirt, as if it were somehow tainted. It took him a while, but eventually the price came down from four hundred to two-fifty.

"Does it fit?" Bill said finally, turning to Slater and handing him the watch.

He pulled it on and closed the clasp. "It's a little loose."

"It's supposed to be," Bill said, manipulating his wrist to check the fit.

"It's so heavy," Slater said. "It feels like an exercise weight."

"But the look is right, and it fits you."

"Won't it make my arm muscles all asymmetrical?"

Bill glared at him. "Pay the man."

Slater chuckled and riffled off the bills, handing them to the clerk. As the guy tucked them into his pants pocket, Slater raised his eyebrows. "No receipt? Maybe a warranty card?"

The guy just laughed.

Bill was already outside, and Slater followed him, holding out his wrist to inspect his new purchase. It was way too flashy for him, but it was definitely the right look for a nightclub.

"Don't wear that thing on the street," Bill said, eyeing him as he climbed in the passenger side. "People might think it's real."

TWENTY-ONE

<hr>

ACK DOWNTOWN, SLATER PULLED into the lot across from his building and parked next to the Lexus.

"What do I owe you for your work today?"

"Oh, honey, we're not done," Bill said. "I need to show you how to strike a pose."

"I'm going to a dimly lit nightclub. How hard can it be to stand around and drink a margarita?"

"Straight guys call them 'ritas. You need to act money, not just look money."

He took a breath. "Probably a good point. We can do it in my office."

As he climbed out, Bill said, "Bring the clothes and the shoes."

No one was in the office when they got upstairs, and Bill stepped behind the front desk and whirled a finger in the air. "Let's get you changed."

He hung the garment bag on the coatrack inside the front door and unzipped it. While he was dressing, Bill pulled the bizarre slanted alligator shoes out of their box and set them at his feet. Once he had the suit on, and stepped into the shoes, Bill adjusted the jacket, and showed Slater how to get the right look in the shoulders and the waist.

After that Bill demonstrated a standing pose, and had Slater mime it, then practice it again.

"And never lean on anything. It makes you look stupid."

"Got it," Slater said.

"Next, picking up women."

He frowned. "I'm not going to be doing that."

"Still, you might need it in your repertoire. You have to look at them from under your eyebrows, like this." Bill dropped his chin and held his gaze, his eyes steady and piercing.

"You look like a sociopath," Slater said. "I just need to look like a married guy who's trying to look single."

"That's what I'm doing here. Try this."

He turned his head and gave Slater the side-eye, then dropped his chin. Slater mimed the action back to him.

"Ooh, I've got wood," Bill said, and slapped Slater's arm.

"I think I can handle the standing around."

"Show me your ring."

He held up his left hand, and Bill grasped it and peered at it.

"Simple. That'll work. What about makeup?"

"Too much work," Slater said. "Plus I'm trying to look boring."

"So just a little around the eyes, then," Bill said, peering at his face.

"I respectfully decline."

"You're missing out on my best skills."

He unbuttoned the suit jacket and pulled it off. "What do I owe you?"

"Considering my intricate skill level, can we say four hundred?"

"I can do that."

Once he'd ditched the suit pants, and stepped into his jeans, he dug out his wad and peeled off the C-notes. As he took them, Bill held one up to the light.

"Where did you get these?"

"They're real, toots," he said sharply.

Bill chuckled and tucked the cash away. "Does that gold band mean you're exclusive?"

"Mostly. I need to keep my dick out of my work."

"What about a simple blow job? I've been thinking about it all day. It's your fault, wearing those jeans. And then you keep taking your clothes off and flashing all that flesh."

"What is it about drag queens and blow jobs?"

He raised his eyebrows. "It's free sex, Slater."

"Sure, but then what are you going to want in return?"

"Unfortunately I can't reciprocate. With age the will is still there but the flesh needs chemical assistance. Even that fades."

"I guess you can smoke me," Slater said, "if you give me back one of those C-notes."

He scoffed. "Such an egomaniac." Stepping closer, he held his gaze, and unbuckled his belt.

"Let's go into my office."

They stepped inside, and Bill pushed him back against the front of his desk, and dropped to his knees, and popped his fly. Soon he had his junk out, flaccid at first, but Bill knew what he was doing. In a minute he had solid wood, and Bill worked him hard.

Closing his eyes, Slater braced his hands on the desk and tilted his head back, getting into it. When he came, he put a hand on Bill's head to get him to stop.

Rising, red-faced, Bill gave his cock a squeeze. "It seems like you enjoyed that."

"When a man is tired of blow jobs, he's tired of life."

Bill chuckled and leaned into him, and Slater pulled him close, his arms around his waist.

"I wish there was something I could do for you," Slater said. "Do you want to try?"

"Would you kiss me?"

Moving his hands to his neck, Slater met his mouth. The guy was good at this too. Eventually Bill pulled back to catch his breath.

Slater smacked his lips. "Butterscotch."

He laughed. "Stop that."

Pulling him in, he mouthed his jaw and his neck, moving his hands over his back, and explored his mouth some more. Then came the sound of the front door opening, and Etta's voice called a greeting.

Bill took a step back, his face red, and spoke under his breath. "Busted."

Slater quickly buttoned his fly and buckled his belt.

When Etta stepped into the doorway, her eyes narrowed. "What's up, fellas?"

Not much got past her—she knew they'd been up to something. Curvy, with her black hair butched short, she was wearing a plaid shirt and jeans.

"Etta's one of our operatives," Slater said, and Bill introduced himself.

Etta snapped her fingers. "Gladys Rayon Square. I didn't work on the case myself, but hey, congrats on that."

Bill made a fluid little bow from the neck. "Much like myself, the square has a palpable touch of class. There's a car wash on one corner and a strip club across the street."

She chuckled. "I hope I can see you perform one day."

"I should go. I've got a party tonight. For the new street sign." He gave Slater's arm a squeeze. "Fly free, little bird. You're going to look fabulous." As he walked out, he called back to them, "Later, darlings."

Once they heard the front door close, Etta frowned at him. "What happened to your hair?"

"I need to look affluent and square for the case I'm working," Slater said, and sat behind his desk.

"It's definitely both of those. You'll have to up your fashion game."

"I'm already on it."

"The garment bag in the front office," she said. "Bill took you shopping."

"You could be a detective." He sat back. "Have you got a minute, or are you working?"

"I've got time." She sat in the guest chair. "I did

some shagging for Max. I came in to type up my notes."

Slater nodded. A civilian would have called it surveillance, or just plain following someone. Etta had learned the lingo like the old-timers. She didn't do the work full-time, but she was good at it, and had the requisite sangfroid. He'd seen her walk up to a target and spin a stream of outlandish jive without even breaking a sweat.

"When we were on that super boring stakeout," he said, "you talked about a lesbian friend who works in banking."

"Ray-*hee*-na," she said, and spelled it—Regina. "She's a teller."

"Would she do something slightly unethical?"

"It depends on the risk to her. It's basically a minimum-wage job. I can't imagine she feels obligated to protect the billion-dollar corporation that treats her like they treat the furniture." Etta chuckled. "They actually laid her off last year, and three days later they hired her again. The catch was that in the new contract, half her benefits had disappeared."

"That's how gangsters operate."

"Ethically the syndicates are no different than corporate America."

"Can you ask her if she can get me one of those dye packs they put with the cash when somebody robs the bank?" Slater said.

"I can ask. What are you planning to do with it?"

Lacing his fingers behind his head, he outlined his plan.

"It might work," Etta said finally. "It's not the craziest thing I've seen you do."

"Let me know." Slater got to his feet.

"Before you go, I want to show you something," she said, and dug out her phone.

As she tapped at it, Slater stepped around the desk and leaned in. She pulled up a photo on the screen: a bored-looking woman with big hair, lounging in the back of a car, a prominent Rolls-Royce logo on the red leather headrest beside her. Sitting next to her on the seat was a gray pit bull. They were both facing straight ahead. It looked like a paparazzi photo taken through the open car window.

"Recognize him?" Etta said.

"I know her. That's Artémise. The most overphotographed pop star ever."

"I mean the dog. That's Rocky. The pup you found out on the rocks."

He leaned closer. "It does look like him. What's he doing with her?"

"So Artémise wanted a dog." Etta turned to meet his gaze. "She showed up at my friend's rescue and met some pups. She picked Rocky because he was so chill." She gestured with her phone. "His life from now on is going to be mansions and limos and private jets."

"Dogs need grass, and dirt, and stuff to sniff. I hope he doesn't get bored with her."

"He'll be fine. Isn't it a great story, though? Rags to riches. From stranded like a castaway in the Pacific to riding in a limo with the richest woman in the country."

"Good for him, landing on his feet," Slater said. "I knew he was smart."

When he got down to the parking lot it was

already dark out, and he flicked on the Continental's headlights for the drive to his house. Traffic was heavy, and the navigation sent him on surface streets. He hauled the new shoes and the garment bag upstairs to the bedroom, then climbed the stairs to find Pike on the sofa, wearing jeans and a navy-blue sweater, stretched out with a hardback. The guy loved that sweater, and kept it even though he couldn't wear it out of the house, with the frayed cuffs and all the pills on the fabric.

"You've been to that used bookstore again," Slater said.

Pike sat up. "Whoa—what's with the haircut? And a new watch? That looks expensive."

"The watch is fake." Slater sat next to him and kissed his neck. "I want to look like the kind of guy the blackmailer would hit on. Like Walter. Square and affluent and closety."

"That blond dummy from last night," he said, and frowned.

Slater shifted sideways and took a breath. "He's the one running the squeeze play."

"Are you going the whole way? You're going to let that knucklehead take photos of you fucking him?"

"That's the plan."

"Damn it," Pike said intently.

"It's part of the sex rules we agreed on," Slater said. "I can sleep with other people if it's for work."

"That doesn't mean it doesn't bug me."

"It's just sex. It doesn't mean anything."

"Well, if you're going to just-sex that gonif," Pike said, "while you're doing that, I'm going to just-sex somebody else too."

Slater stared at him. "Fuck that."

"You can't have it both ways."

Breathing hard now, he couldn't say anything to that. He watched him for a moment. "Are you going to call Davis? He wants into your pants so bad."

"You're wrong about that."

"Anton, then. I've seen the way he looks at you."

"You're delusional," Pike said. "Maybe I'll call Andy, and set up something with him and Kyle."

"That would definitely piss me off." He looked away. "Maybe not quite as much as knowing you hooked up with Davis."

"At least there'll be souvenir pictures of your little escapade."

"I have to go."

As Slater got up, Pike stood and stepped in front of him, and grabbed his waist, and pulled him close. He mashed their mouths together and wrapped him in a tight bear hug.

"Whatever you do," he said in Slater's ear, "you have to think about me while you're doing it."

"You're the only man in the world. You know that."

He kissed him again, then walked through the kitchen, and checked his tracking app. The green dot for Chad's phone showed it was still in Pasadena. The guy was likely still recovering from his ketamine trip. The tracker on Tanner's Camaro was in Hollywood, a couple of blocks from Electric. He was already at work. Either they were getting desperate, like Liz said, or the squares they targeted went clubbing early.

In the bedroom he pulled on the black suit, and the stupid pointy shoes, then checked the look in the floor mirror, adjusting the jacket and his shirt collar. Bill was right: with hairspray on it, his hair still looked the way Fernande had styled it.

He trotted down to the garage, and drove to Hollywood, and parked in the same structure he'd used last night. As he walked toward the stairwell he stopped short and looked down. For a split second he thought he'd glimpsed a rat or a cockroach at his feet, but it was just the fugly pointy shoes. They were going to take some getting used to.

Out on the street his legs felt cold in the night air. The sheer suit fabric was like wearing nothing at all. He walked toward the doorway under the blue neon ELECTRIC sign and saw there was no lineup this early. As he walked up he handed the bouncer his fake ID. The guy's bored expression didn't shift, and he spent less time looking at the card than he had assessing him as he walked up. Handing it back, he waved him in.

TWENTY-TWO

SLATER PAUSED INSIDE THE nightclub's entrance to survey the room. There were a surprising number of people here, dressed up like last night, and there were definitely more men than women. The music was totally dead-ass again. They must really not want people to dance.

Standing at a table beyond the dance floor he spotted a familiar face—Liz. She looked a lot different than in the park today, with her hair up, and makeup, and a tight black dress with sequins. She was alone, with a cocktail in front of her, and he waited for her to spot him. When she did, he held her gaze.

It took her a moment, but he saw the flash of recognition as her eyebrows shot up. Slater briefly touched his index finger to his lips. Liz nodded, almost imperceptibly, then held her phone in front of her chest, and tapped the top edge with a finger, then lowered it and looked away.

Did she want him to call her? No—she was miming a camera. She meant she'd be the one taking photos over the top of the restroom stall.

He hadn't expected to see her. If she'd told him she was working tonight, he would have read her in on his plan, told her to encourage Tanner to approach him. But it was too late for that now. At least it didn't seem like she was going to blow it for him.

From the direction of the bar, Tanner appeared, and strolled toward Liz, and set his drink on the table. He stood next to her but they didn't acknowledge each other. In the same jade-green suit he'd been wearing last night, he had his shirt open several buttons, revealing his pasty hairless skin and the curve of his pecs.

Slater went to the bar and ordered a gin and tonic. He should probably skip the booze altogether, but he could stay lucid if he stuck to one. With the drink in hand he walked to a patch of wall not far from the dance floor, and stood the way Bill had shown him, adjusting his back and his shoulders to achieve the look. The suit jacket felt tight around his ribs, and the pose felt like it made him look more relaxed than he normally was. It was actually uncomfortable, and he felt vulnerable, like he was exposed.

It didn't take Tanner long to act. Slater watched him make a circuit of the room, like a damn reef shark. He stopped beside Slater, and stood facing the room. When Slater glanced at him, the guy leaned in to speak.

"Not a lot of talent here tonight."

"I guess it depends on what you're looking for," Slater said.

"I hear you." He sipped his drink.

He was wearing a pinkie ring, Slater saw, a thick gold band with a green stone. Was that the one he'd taxed from Walter?

"Is that jade?" Slater said, gesturing to it.

"Good eye." Tanner briefly held it up. "Asians love this stuff. I like your watch. Is it real?"

Slater laughed. "I hope so. It was a gift from the wife. She's the one with the money."

"Where's she at?"

"In Aspen. On a ski weekend with her mother."

"While the cat's away, am I right? What does she do?"

"Works at Cudahy Mutual Insurance," he said. "Not C-suite but one of those big jobs."

"I've heard of that outfit." Tanner stood watching the room.

Slater slurped at his drink. He had to do more, he realized, had to look more interested. He made a point of looking the guy over.

"You're in good shape. Do you do sports?"

"I do," Tanner said. "What's your name, player?"

"John Van Ness."

"Tanner." He tapped his glass to Slater's. "So, John, what would the wife say if she found out you did molly? What's her name, by the way?"

"Della."

"What would Della say to that?"

"I'd definitely be in the doghouse. It doesn't matter anyway. I'm not going to do that."

"I thought it might loosen you up a little. We could have some fun."

As he watched him talk, the way Tanner was looking at him was a lot like Bill's version of a pick-up. Even without the coaching, this guy's intent was unmistakable.

Slater raised his eyebrows. "You're not shy."

"So how about it? I can blow you in the men's room. Nobody will see us."

"That seems a little sleazy." Slater looked around the room, feigning concern. "I mean, I'd hook up with you, of course. You're hot. But surely we can go somewhere comfortable."

"All right. I've got a pied-à-terre near here. We can walk."

Slater took a breath. "I don't usually do things like this."

"I spend two hours at the gym every day, John. I've got washboard abs, and I'm hung like a horse."

Slater nodded. "Sold."

Tanner set off toward the entrance, and Slater slammed his gin and tonic, then followed a few paces behind him. The guy might be overselling himself. It was hard to tell for sure, but from the way his pants fit he didn't really look stacked.

Liz was standing at the same table near the dance floor, and her brow furrowed at the sight of them walking out together. Once Tanner passed her, she met Slater's eye, and threw up a hand, and mouthed, *"What are you doing?"*

Slater winked at her and double-clicked his tongue. Out on the street he walked abreast with Tanner. The guy seemed bored now. Maybe he was—now that the deal was sealed, he just had to go through the motions.

"Why don't you have a partner?" Slater said. "A guy like you could take your pick."

"I like to play around."

"Picking up guys in a straight nightclub?"

"It's not exclusively straight."

In the next block Tanner turned into the lobby of a building. Slater had never been here, but he'd been in places like this. It was mixed residential, with hotel rooms and monthly apartments. From what he'd seen of these the units were modular and cramped.

Using a key card, Tanner called the elevator, and they stepped in. He was getting no warmth from this guy—he hadn't laid a finger on him or even looked at him twice. This really was a transaction.

They stepped off upstairs, and Tanner used the key card to open one of the numbered doors in the hallway. Inside it was smaller than a hotel room, with a lone bed and no space for much else besides a stretch of counter with a desk chair, and a separate little bathroom.

Pulling off his suit jacket, Tanner folded it over the back of the chair. "Let's get those clothes off."

Slater put his hands on his hips. "You first. I want to see the merchandise that was advertised."

He laughed and started to unbutton his shirt. It was clear now why he didn't smile very much—that perfect jaw line and chiseled look turned goonish the second he cracked a smile and his teeth appeared. It was like he'd put on a clown mask.

Soon Tanner was naked. His junk was maybe bigger than average but in no way approaching equine. Slater pulled off his jacket, and the rest of his clothes, and stroked his cock. Stepping close, Tanner pushed him back onto the bed, and straddled him, and mashed their mouths together, his tongue probing intently. After a minute he pulled back.

"I'm going to fuck you. Have you ever done that before?"

Slater made his eyes wide. "I'm willing to try."

"I'll take good care of you, John."

He grabbed a tube of lube from the nightstand and pressed his thumb into him.

"Whoa," Slater said. "Slow down, Seabiscuit."

"Relax." Tanner met his mouth again and pulled his knee up.

"You need to wear a condom," Slater said.

He growled in frustration but grabbed one from the bedside table and fumbled as he rolled it on. Watching him, Slater got a better look at the pinkie ring. It looked expensive, and old, the gold intricately patterned, the jade stone almost glowing even in the low light. That had to be Walter's.

Shifting closer, he pushed up Slater's knee. Slater moved onto his side, but Tanner pressed his shoulder back onto the bed.

"It works better if you stay on your back."

He was talking about the camera angle, Slater knew, and then yelped as Tanner shoved his way into him, moving way too fast.

"Dude," Slater said, and winced. "Seriously?"

"Just relax."

"You said that already."

Tanner ignored that and started to pound him. He leaned back, craning his chin toward the ceiling.

That was for the camera's benefit too, Slater realized. It would keep his face out of it, so only his torso would be visible, along with most of Slater's body. The camera had to be in the overhead light fixture, he decided, gazing up at it. The light was turned down dim but there could be a lens in the housing.

Seconds later Tanner made a choking sound, and his face contorted like he had an olive stuck in his windpipe. He strained into him and then collapsed. After a couple of breaths he rolled over and peeled off the condom. Slater was stroking himself.

"You want to smoke me?" he said.

"Why don't you do you?" Tanner said. "That's what you got two hands for. Be quick, though. I have to be somewhere."

Stepping off the bed, he walked into the bathroom, and Slater heard the shower go on.

Slater scoffed. The selfish little yutz. He wanted to tell him that was the worst sex he'd had in a long time, then punch him in his ugly kisser. But he had to suppress that. For a second he considered jerking off. It wasn't worth it, he decided. Despite the athletic build, the guy wasn't really a turn-on. As he got up and started to get dressed, he heard the shower go off.

Stepping out of the bathroom, Tanner's hair was wet, and he was naked except for the towel draped on his shoulders. He looked like such an idiot jock. At the counter he fished his phone out of the green suit pants.

"I need to get your digits, John."

"You want to do this again?" Slater said, buttoning his shirt.

"Maybe, yeah."

He recited the number he'd set up with the spoofing service.

"That's your cell?" Tanner said. "Where do you work, anyway? You never told me."

"I do some office work, but I'm mostly a man of leisure. My wife has the big job."

"Sweet deal."

He dropped the towel and stepped into his underpants. Slater pulled on his suit jacket and adjusted the fit.

"Will you really call me?" Slater said.

"Oh, I've got your number, big guy."

Slater walked out and went down to the street. Nosing the Continental out of the parking structure, he drove to his house. The freeway was moving fast, and when he rolled up on his garage, he saw Pike's SUV was parked at the curb. Upstairs he checked the bedroom, but Pike wasn't here. He went through the kitchen and found him on the sofa with that hardback, still wearing that ratty navy-blue sweater. There was music on, turned down low.

Sitting up, Pike set the book facedown on the coffee table. "I've never seen that suit before. It looks upscale."

"I got it today. To attract the attention of the blond."

"That's the suit you can wear to anything semiformal now. Doris's dinners and nightclubs and quinceañeras."

"It's not especially comfortable," Slater said. "But I know beauty is painful sometimes."

"Did it work?"

"With the blond? Yeah."

"Tell me about the sex."

He put his hands on his hips. "You don't want to hear that."

"You have to tell me." Pike raised his voice. "Have to."

Slater huffed. "Let me get a drink first." Walking to the kitchen, he called back, "You want a taste?"

"Scotch."

That gave Slater the green light to pour the good stuff for himself too, instead of his cheapo rotgut. He pulled out a couple of tumblers, and sloshed a heavy half inch into each, and carried them back to the sofa. Handing one to Pike, he tapped his own against it, then dropped into the chair opposite him, and took a slurp.

He told Pike about his evening, emphasizing the fact that the guy had left him hanging. "It was the worst sex I've had in a long time," he said finally.

"Blondie sounds like trade."

"I think so. I don't envy the women in his life if that's what they have to deal with." He held Pike's gaze. "So what did you do tonight?"

Pike swirled the contents of his glass. "I hired three rent boys and we all got fucked up on meth and trashed the place."

"I can see all the evidence of that," Slater said, and waved at the empty room.

"I went to Hollywood and got a tramp-stamp tattoo that says OPEN HOUSE in big gothic letters." He waggled his fingers to put air quotes around the phrase.

Slater frowned. "You did not."

"I read my book and thought about what you were doing."

"I was working," Slater said intently. "The guy was such a dud I didn't even get a woody."

"I can give you a woody." Pike rose and drained his glass. "Come on."

Slamming the scotch, Slater followed him down to the bedroom, and pulled off the suit jacket, and tossed it on the chair.

"Here's what I want to do," Pike said. "I'm going to hook you up, like a goddamn lowlife, and then I'm going to skull-fuck you."

Slater pulled off his shirt. "Works for me, if it'll get you to stop being mad at me."

He jutted his chin. "Shut the fuck up."

Stepping around the bed, Pike dug around in the bedside drawer and produced a heavy pair of hand-cuffs. Slater stepped out of the shoes and the flimsy suit pants and tossed them on the chair. He was chubby now, watching Pike, and stroked his cock. Pike's jaw was set as he stepped toward him, and grabbed his wrist, and deftly spun him around. He pulled his other hand behind his back, and Slater let him squeeze the cuffs on.

Pike stepped over to the closet to ditch his sweater and his shirt but left his jeans on. Watching him step closer, Slater sat on the side of the bed.

"No fucking way," Pike said. "On your knees."

He slid onto the floor, and Pike yanked his chin up. His mouth a tight line, he slapped him hard, turning his head. Slater could see he had a raging woody bulging in the denim. Opening his fly, Pike smacked his face with his cock, and eventually let him take him into his mouth.

Despite the way he'd phrased it, Pike wasn't too

hard on him as Slater worked him, resting a hand on the back of his head to guide him but not using force. When Pike first touched his hair it felt like he was wearing a hat, but he realized it was the hairspray, still holding the look together like an invisible net. Eventually Pike climaxed, straining into him, then pulled back.

Not pausing, he grabbed Slater under his arms and pulled him to his feet. Pike moved behind him and wrapped one arm around his chest, with the other hand stroking his cock.

"You like that? Huh?" Pike growled in his ear, and Slater came, straining into Pike's hand, his knees buckling.

Pike shifted him toward the bed, and he flopped onto his side. Stretching out beside him, Pike pushed his arm under his neck, and notched his knees into Slater's. He could feel his warm breath on his neck, and smell a faint trace of the scotch.

Sometime later he woke to Pike's voice.

"I should unhook you."

"You don't have to," he mumbled. "You know I'm trash, and I know I'm trash. Just dump me in the street on trash day."

Pike chuckled. "You're not trash. You're beautiful, and I love you."

"I know. I don't fucking understand why, but I know it's true."

TWENTY-THREE

S LATER WOKE TO THE sun streaming in the sheers. Pike was up already. He scrabbled for his phone on the bedside table. There was no word from Tanner yet. He checked the activity on Chad's phone, and saw a text exchange between the two idiots late last night.

Tanner wrote, "Landed one last night," and Chad responded "Finally." Tanner's follow-up was, "Guy's a wetback but married to money. I put the photos in the drive."

Rubbing sleep out of his eyes, he checked the other activity on Chad's device. Svetlana's app said that he had spent nine minutes on a cloud drive app. Slater couldn't see any images of it, but the first thing Chad had done was type his login credentials. He stared at the screen for a moment. This was it—the keys to their operation.

He thought about it for a minute. Chad had likely checked out the new photos, and there was a chance he'd recognize Slater as the person who'd returned his phone a week ago. But he'd looked different that day, with the stealthy glasses, and apart from when he'd slapped him, Chad hadn't paid him any attention. If he did figure it out, they wouldn't try to extort him. But maybe it didn't matter. Access to their cloud drive could be even more valuable.

Slater climbed out of bed and pulled on his clothes, then grabbed his laptop from his satchel and went up to the kitchen. Pike had left coffee in the pot, lukewarm now. That meant he'd been up and out for a while. He knew he had a gun-range date with some colleague. Slater couldn't remember who, but it wasn't that sleazebag Davis.

Once he'd poured himself a mug of the java, he took it out to the deck, and set the laptop on the patio table, facing the sun so that the screen would be in the shade.

There was a chance these idiots had set up their cloud drive to require an additional password when they used a new device, but if it came by text to Chad's phone, he could see that too. The problem was that Chad would likely notice it, and maybe get spooked, and lock him out. But when he tried to get into the drive, they hadn't set it up that way. As soon as he typed in the password the screen resolved into a grid of file folders. He had access to their cloud storage.

"Yes," he said under his breath, and felt his heart start to pound.

Slater spent some time digging around in it, parsing the array of folders and their contents. Each was labeled with someone's name and contained images, just three or four, the type that Walter had shown him, and Bucky had described—lurid toilet-stall photos of people with their junk exposed and syringes against their arms. Several sets had been taken from above in that micro hotel room. Tanner's pasty body loomed over naked men and women both, and some depicted a female torso straddling clueless-looking guys. Even though her face was out of the frame, that had to be Liz.

A few supporting documents were scattered among the folders, including the photo of the IOU Walter had signed. There was a folder each for Walter and Bucky, and one for Liz, and for Mara from the eyewear store. Another was labeled John Van Ness.

When Slater clicked on it, he found three photos, each depicting Slater's naked body with ghostly white Tanner looming over him, his head outside the frame. There was no mistaking what was going on. In one of the images Slater was wincing, his mouth in a puckered pout. Of course he looked like that. Moron Tanner had no idea how to fuck a man. He took a breath. Why did he look so stupid? The only thing that looked great was his natty haircut, still sprayed into place. Thank you for that, Gladys Rayon.

Besides the folders with the photos, there was a spreadsheet titled "Sucker List." When he opened it, he found all the same names with columns for the dates and the amounts they'd paid, and a column for notes about each person. In the last row, for Jon Van Ness, the note said "wife Della, Cudahy Mutual Insurance," with her job title and the company's street address. They had already done the research on her to work the grift—they must really need cash.

There were over a dozen entries on the list, and some had paid more than others. Slater didn't do a detailed accounting, but from scanning the numbers, it looked like they were pulling in several grand a month. These guys acted like nickel rats, but the operation definitely wasn't small potatoes. It was amazing that nobody had capped one of these idiots yet.

Slater spent a minute copying everything to his computer, the spreadsheet and all the photos, then sat back, staring absently at the screen. He could delete everything from their drive right now, but they almost certainly had backups. He'd only be slowing them down a little. If he was going to delete this stuff, it had to be synchronized with the other part of his plan.

Folding the laptop closed, he went inside to get some fruit from the icebox and toast a bagel. He was still eating at the patio table when his phone buzzed. The caller ID said WALTER YAN, and he picked up.

"That fucking psycho hit me up again," Walter said, his voice loud.

"You're talking about Chad?"

"I just paid him. It hasn't even been a week. He wants more now."

"Interesting," Slater said. "They're getting greedy."

"What are you doing in your investigation? Is there any way you can shut them down?"

"I'm working an angle. I'm right in the middle of it. But I can't promise anything."

"Fuck," Walter roared.

"Can you stall him? Tell him you can't get the cash until next week."

"I don't need that kind of help, Slater." He huffed. "I have to go."

The line went dead, and when he looked at the screen, Slater saw there was a text from a new number. It was just a photo—one of the John Van Ness images he'd just looked at. Of course they'd picked the worst one, where his face was all contorted.

Slater spent a minute configuring his spoofing service, so that Tanner would see the number Slater had given him come up as his caller ID, then he dialed the number the photo had come from, and listened to it ring. Tanner's familiar voice answered.

"How did you take that photo?" Slater demanded. "I didn't see any cameras in that room."

"I wanted a sweet memento of our time together, John."

"You need to delete that."

"Of course I will, big guy. Della never has to see it. I can make it go away for a small service fee."

"I'm not paying you."

"You don't have to do anything," Tanner said. "But then I can swing by Cudahy Mutual one day this week and have a chat with her. I know that building. Her office is on the thirty-fourth floor, isn't it?"

"This is an outrage," Slater said through his teeth.

Tanner held his tongue. He was letting Slater digest the situation, he knew. When it had been long enough, Slater spoke again.

"How much?"

"A grand," Tanner said. "That's nothing to a fancy guy like you. In cash, of course. Bring it to a bar in Hollywood called the Blue Dragon. Anytime tonight after eight."

"No way. You'll have to come to my office. It's in the Fashion District. I'll be there tomorrow."

"You're not calling the shots here, John."

"I understand that," Slater said, "but I can't go to the Blue Dragon. If you want the money, this is the way it has to be."

Tanner scoffed but said, "Fine."

Once he'd recited the address, he ended the call and sat back. The wheels were definitely in motion.

———◆———

SLATER WAS FINISHING HIS breakfast at the patio table when Pike stepped out onto the deck. He was wearing a plaid shirt and a pair of fugly lumpy cargo shorts. Leaning down, he kissed Slater's neck.

"You were out early."

Pike took the chair opposite. "Hopkins says you want to get there before all the yahoos show up. He says the hangover types come around noon, and tweaker time is after two."

He scoffed. "I get it. I definitely wouldn't want to be around a bunch of wastoids with loaded firearms."

"You remember we've got a quinceañera tonight."

"Fuck me. That's today?"

"The party starts at five," Pike said, "but the *vals* is at eight, so we can show up any time between those. The food is buffet style so there's no set time to eat."

"What's the *vals*?"

"The dance Amelia does with her chamberlain, and then with her father."

"How the hell do you know all this?" Slater demanded.

"You forwarded me the invite, and I called Lupe

to check on the details."

Slater stared at him for a moment. "You fit so well in this world. You know how to do it. Like a trout in a stream up in the Sierra. Maneuvering around, zero friction. I'm a damn rock that just sinks to the bottom where the slime is."

He laughed. "You can swim too. You just don't want to."

"So blondie hit me up already." Slater pushed his plate away. "The first installment is a grand."

"He sent photos?"

"Just one."

"Show me," Pike said, and raised his eyebrows.

"It's not flattering."

"I don't care. You have to show me."

He groaned and dug out his phone, and pulled up the photo, and handed it across the table.

"Why are you making duck lips?"

"I'm not. That's just my face."

"You look pretty turned on."

"Not by that guy," Slater said. "He was so bad at it. It's called playing a role."

Pike sighed and handed the phone back. "You're a lot of man, Ibáñez."

His phone buzzed in his hand—Etta.

"I can get you that item once Regina's workplace opens tomorrow," she said when he picked up. "I'll bring it by the office."

"That's great news. I owe you one."

"You owe her too. She said she'd do it for three dollars."

"Whatever it takes," Slater said. "Don't you have school tomorrow?"

"It's a professional development day."

"That's such a great gig. Two months off in summer and all those days out of the classroom."

"But when I'm actually there," Etta said, "I'm dealing with the raging hormones of middle schoolers. It's no picnic."

After he'd ended the call, Pike sat up. "I'm going down to Grace's later. One of her doors is sticking."

Grace lived in the ADU behind the garage and worked as his operative sometimes. She was sharp-witted and spry, but because of her age, she could feign the doddering frail old woman.

Slater frowned. "She asked you to deal with it? Why didn't she call me? I'm her damn landlord."

"We bumped into each other in front of the house," Pike said. "She mentioned it, and I offered. And I'm not sure you can call yourself her landlord when she doesn't pay rent."

"Why would she tell you that?"

He folded his arms. "She figured I already knew. The real question is, why aren't you charging her rent?"

"I asked her to come with me from Westlake because she was paying too damn much over there. We were both getting sucked dry in that building."

"You have such an odd relationship with money," Pike said. "It's like you don't really value it, but you still manage to accumulate plenty of it."

"By 'accumulate' I hope you get that I bust my ass working for it."

"You know Grace has her own dough, right?"

Slater gestured helplessly.

"The bigger question is, why wouldn't you tell me

that? Considering we trust each other and all."

"Why do you need to know?"

"It's not about that," Pike said. "You're not a spy agency. I live here too, and you didn't give me the whole story."

He looked away. "My instinct isn't to share and gossip and shmooze. One of the long list of shrinks Doris sent me to in my youth called it the social contract. You have to do all this work to make nice with everybody. Go to quinceañeras and make full financial disclosures." He waved at the city beyond the deck. "It's so much damn work to keep all this going."

"I think it's because you don't want to be judged," Pike said. "You don't want me to think you're a sap for letting Grace live rent-free."

"Now you sound like one of Doris's shrinks."

"I don't care about who's paying for what. I want you to let me in."

"I get it." He took a breath. "I told you about the blond trade up front, didn't I?"

"You did. That's definitely progress." Pike got up.

"I bought rugelach for Grace a couple days ago. I forgot them in my car. On the floor of the backseat. In a little pink pastry box."

"I'll tell her you sent them."

"Or just tell her they're from you," Slater said. "Listen, those doors are all solid wood. There's a block plane hanging on the rack over the workbench in the garage if you need it."

"I know there is." Pike leaned in to kiss him, and lingered in it a moment, then walked inside.

Why couldn't it just be the good stuff, Slater wondered. Handcuffs and blow jobs and hotcha blues clubs. All the bullshit, all the demands on him were inextricably intertwined with it. Looking at his phone, he dialed Andy.

"What do you need, Slater?" he said when he picked up. "It's the … weekend."

"You can cut the crap. I know you work when there's work. I need to talk to spouse B anyway, not you."

"About what?"

"I need perspective from his level of the economy."

"I'm not sure I like the sound of that," Andy said.

"It'll only take a couple minutes."

"We're at his place today. I guess you can … come over. You cannot punch him."

"If he chooses his words with care," Slater said, "and dials down the attitude, I won't get riled, and I won't have to." Not waiting for a response, he ended the call.

When he trotted down to the garage, there was no sign of Pike, but the red toolbox was gone from the workbench, and the pastry box wasn't in his car. He backed into the street, and saw that the gate to Grace's side yard was hanging open. That seemed like a great way to get a homeless camp set up in the yard. But he knew he needed to let it go.

Kyle's pad was in a high-rise in the bougie neighborhood around Grand Avenue, and he cruised downtown to Bunker Hill, and found a meter in front of Kyle's building.

When he got upstairs and knocked on the door, Andy pulled it open, wearing shorts and a T-shirt despite the weather, and flashed that beautiful smile. His red mobility scooter was parked along the wall next to the door.

"You live here now?" Slater said, gesturing to it.

"Not full time."

Kyle was on the sofa over by the big windows, with a broad view east over downtown and city hall. The blond-wood furniture gave the place a frosty Scandinavian vibe.

Wearing tan chinos and a sky-blue collared shirt, Kyle rose as he stepped in. He was lithe and wore his hair in a trendy cut. Slater hated that his shirt looked so good on him, accentuating his pecs, and hated the way his pants fit so well.

"Don't get up for me, cupcake," Slater said. "I won't be here long."

"That's a relief, at least," Kyle said.

Andy stepped over and sat next to Kyle. "Sit down."

As he dropped into the chair opposite them, Slater gestured to the view. "This place is so fancy."

"I know you mean that as an insult," Kyle said.

Slater held up his palms. "I've got nothing against rich folks. I'm sure your grandparents worked hard for all this."

"Slater," Andy said intently. "What do you want?"

He huffed and looked to Kyle. "What do affluent zombies wear? People like you and your father. I see them floating around but I'm not sure I can replicate the look."

"Why?" Andy said.

"I've got a meeting where I'm going to pose as somebody like them."

"You've got the haircut … pretty close already."

"I can loan you some stuff," Kyle said. "My

clothes might be a little small for you, especially in the crotch."

Slater laughed. "Because what you're packing is so impressive? You remember I've seen your junk."

"You couldn't keep your hands off it, as I remember."

"So what would your pop wear for a casual business meeting?"

Kyle heaved a sigh and rose from the sofa, then beckoned him to follow, leading the way down the hall and into the bedroom.

"Cedar closets," Slater said, and scoffed. "Of course you have cedar closets."

Digging through the rail of pants on clamp hangers, Kyle pulled out a pair of gray dress pants and a black belt.

"These should fit you." He tossed them on the bed and went to a drawer. Pulling out a burgundy sweater, he held it up to Slater's shoulders. "This will too. Just wear any light-colored shirt with a collar." He met his gaze. "A shirt from this century."

"You can't wear the boots," Andy said.

"I've got a pair of black derbies."

Kyle nodded. "That'll work. As long as they're not patent leather. Let me get a bag."

He took the clothes and walked toward the kitchen, and Slater followed Andy to the front door.

"I've been trying to get Kyle to get a pair of … boots like yours," he said. "So he can butch it up a little once in a while."

"That's kind of like putting a poodle on a skateboard," Slater said. "You can do it, but it's going to look stupid."

Stepping out of the kitchen, Kyle tucked the clothes into a paper grocery bag.

"What do I owe you?" Slater said.

"Are you going to give the clothes back?"

"I'm not going to need them more than once."

"Then nothing."

Slater took the bag from him. "I guess that's your call."

"How's that hunk of Pike?" Andy said.

"I thought you might have seen him last night. I had to fuck a guy for work, so he said he'd try to set something up with you two."

"He never called me," Andy said. "He just said that because … he knew it would piss you off."

Kyle raised his eyebrows. "I wouldn't be opposed to that. He's a nice guy. Good-looking. It's completely inexplicable that he's with you."

"Trust me, I don't get it either," Slater said. "By now he has to know I'm no damn good. But the dick wants what the dick wants."

"He's got my number," Andy said.

"I'd actually rather he fuck you two than one of his work colleagues. He might ditch me for one of those idiots, but I know he'd get awfully tired of your icy Nordic world." Slater swirled his hand at the room. "He'd come running back for the salsa."

Kyle scoffed. "You've got about as much salsa as a bowl of cottage cheese from an all-night Westside deli."

"Are you even allowed out after dark?" Slater said. "You can tell me all about the late nights once your mom graduates you from knee pants."

"Slater," Andy said intently. "Just go."

As he stepped out the door, Slater jabbed a finger at him. "Get a horse." It didn't make any sense, he knew that, but no way was he going to let him have the last word.

TWENTY-FOUR

WHEN SLATER GOT BACK to his house, Pike was in the bedroom getting dressed for the quince.

"What happened at Grace's?" Slater said.

"I didn't need to plane the door. I just tightened some screws. She said thanks for the rugelach."

"So do I wear the new suit? I've got that tux too."

"The tux is too formal. That suit looks great on you." Pike was buttoning his shirt. "I'm glad you're up for doing this."

He unbuckled his belt. "It's a transaction. If I show up tonight, things will go more smoothly next time with Gabe. In the long run it'll save me money."

Pike chuckled. "I just hope there's something for you to eat."

Once he had the suit on, Slater held up the

derbies and the weird-ass pointy shoes. "Which ones?"

"Not the rat-stabbers." He was pulling on his suit jacket. "They're too much."

"Is that what they're called in the federal shoe database?" he said, and tossed them in the bottom of the closet.

"I knew a guy who wore those. That's what he called them."

Once Slater was dressed, Pike stepped close and adjusted his lapels.

"With that haircut and the suit, you look like the other kind of godfather. Like from a syndicate."

"And you look like my wet dreams."

"Don't forget the gift," Pike said. "Do you have a few hundred in cash, or do you want to raid your bathroom stash?"

"That's for emergencies only." As he dug out his wad, he met his eye. "I know how much is in that bag, by the way."

"Damn." Pike put his hands on his hips. "That means I can't steal from you."

As he riffled off a handful of C-notes, Slater looked up. "OK, I can see how that sounds." He gestured with the cash. "I'm trying here. You know I'm not a right guy. You know I'm fucking crazy."

"I've got an envelope in my desk," Pike said, and went over to the other bedroom.

The party was at a banquet hall in Elysian Park, right around the corner but not quite close enough to walk. They took Pike's rig. Inside there were a lot of people, and they were dressed up, standing around and sitting at the banquet tables along the sides of the room. A DJ was spinning upbeat music.

Pike pointed out a clear plastic cube with a slot in the top, sitting on a table near the kitchen. "That's for the gifts."

Once he'd dropped the envelope into it, Slater eyed the buffet laid out on the nearby tables, a row of chafing dishes and platters. "We should check out the food."

"First we have to greet the elders." He gestured to one of the banquet tables. "They're over there."

"Did Lupe tell you to do that?"

"It's Latin culture. We'll just say hello. Then you can eat."

"You're like my reality sherpa," Slater said, following him across the room.

"I've seen Doris do it too."

"With her it's just my mother telling me what to do, despite the fact that I'm a grown-ass adult."

Even though he only spoke taco-cart Spanish, Pike introduced Slater as *padrino de pastel*. The grandparents and aunts and uncles seemed to understand, and smiled and squeezed his hand. After they'd run the gauntlet of Amelia's senior relatives, they stepped away and stood at the side of the room.

"Mission accomplished," Pike said.

Slater punched him on the shoulder.

"What's that for?" Pike said, and laughed, massaging his arm.

"You're such a boss. So confident about all this stuff. Like when Odysseus had to sail between the two monsters. Remember that? He went through at top speed, no fucks given."

"Those monsters wanted to kill the guy. These

people already love you. You're a *padrino*."

"It's about you. The elders love you, and I love you."

Pike put a hand on his neck and briefly met his mouth. "Let's get some grub."

He found some stuff at the buffet that passed as vegan, and on the next table was a big acrylic tank with a spout labeled MARGARITAS, and under that 21+. Slater filled a plastic cup for each of them, and handed one to Pike. He slammed his own, relishing the tart intensity of it, then refilled the cup.

The music stopped, and something seemed to be happening over by the DJ, on the open patch of floor. They stood at the edge of the crowd to watch. Amelia appeared, looking dramatic, in a pale pink gown with a voluminous spreading skirt and a tiara, and everyone clapped and hooted. There were six chamberlains, not just one like Pike had implied, in matching gray suits with bow ties the same color as her dress, all with perfectly groomed hair. They stood in a line at the side of the open floor.

The speeches were mostly in Spanish, and at one point Gabe acknowledged the godfathers, and Slater heard his name. Amelia's actual godfather danced with her after she danced with one of the chamberlains, and then with Gabe. After the formal *valses*, other people started dancing. Amelia briefly came over to talk to him.

"The cake is really nice, Slater. Thanks for doing that."

"You look so beautiful. I hope you're having fun today too."

She beamed and floated away.

Pike frowned at him. "You don't need a sherpa. You totally know how to do this."

"I looked it up online beforehand. 'How to talk to a quinceañera celebrant.'"

He laughed. "Bullshit."

A minute later Gabe and Lupe stepped over, accompanied by their son, decked out in a suit even though he wasn't old enough to be in school yet. The pair of them were dressed up too, and animated, and laughing. Maybe a little drunk, Slater decided.

"Everyone loved the cake," Lupe said. "I know you didn't try it. Did you have one of the cupcakes?"

"We missed those," Pike said.

"Gabe said you were vegan, so we got vegan cupcakes. The pink ones."

They chatted for a minute, and Pike squatted to talk to the boy, animated in his interaction with him. After they stepped away, Pike squeezed his shoulder.

"You've put in your time, *padrino*. I think we can go."

"Not without my cupcakes."

They found the table with the cake he'd ordered, half eaten now. Next to it was a tray of cupcakes with pink frosting, marked with a sign that said VEGAN. Slater unwrapped one and started to scarf it.

His mouth half full, he said, "It's good."

Pike took one, and when Slater finished his, he grabbed another.

"It was thoughtful of them to do this," Pike said.

"I can't be the only vegan here."

"It's nice that Lupe remembered you specifically."

"I'm sure it's just one of the long list of reasons

they think I'm a weirdo," Slater said.

"They think you're great. Why else would they make you pink cupcakes?"

———·———

In the morning Pike had left early for work, and after some java and a leisurely breakfast, Slater went to the bedroom to put on Kyle's clothes. The pants felt tight, but he had to believe that it was the right look. The sweater fit well, and when he checked himself out in the floor mirror, he liked the look. Kyle might not get these back.

He pulled on the derbies. They felt light and airy, like wearing nothing at all. Hustling downstairs, he climbed into the Continental and drove to his office. Tanner wasn't due until early afternoon but he needed to get things set up.

When he stepped inside, Etta was sitting at the front desk, and another woman stood nearby. With wild wavy hair, she was wearing a gray suit. Rey Pascual was positioned to face the pair of them.

"What are you wearing?" Etta said, looking him over.

"Fancy, right?"

"This is Regina. She works at the bank."

"You're not working today?" Slater said.

"It's my lunch break."

"I know it wasn't necessary," Etta said, "but she wanted to meet you."

"For my own peace of mind," Regina said.

"Did you bring the gadget?"

She pulled open her handbag, and fished out a thin gray box, and handed it to him. Smaller than a banknote, it was surprisingly thin, and had a patch of exposed blue circuit board on one side.

"Is it armed?" Slater said.

"Not yet. It's the kind that spews dye, not the kind that smokes."

"I didn't realize there were different models. What color is the dye?"

"Bright fluorescent green," Regina said. "It's intense. After a week or so it fades to a darker shade, but you still look green."

"Right on. It's not traceable to you, is it?"

"Not if you wipe off my fingerprints."

"Does it have a serial number?" Etta said.

"They're generic. Lots of banks use them." She looked from her to Slater. "I'm more worried that the cops or somebody will make you tell them where it came from."

"Nobody's ever going to hear about you," Etta said. "This is my world. I know how to make it all work smoothly."

Regina frowned. "You're a middle school teacher."

"I know what I'm doing," Etta said, holding her gaze.

"Etta's part-time here," Slater said, "but she's a highly skilled investigator. My partner and I call her a natural."

Regina waved at the device. "Let me show you how to arm it."

Slater handed it back, and she spent a minute explaining it, then set it on the desktop.

"I have to get back to work."

Digging out his wad of cash, Slater peeled off four C-notes and handed them over.

"I only asked for three hundred," Regina said, and frowned.

"That extra Ben Franklin is to keep your mouth shut. You can't tell anyone about me. Not your girlfriend and not your mama. You don't know me, and you never heard of me."

"You don't have to worry about that." She tucked the bills into her pants pocket. "I'd be way more exposed than you two. If the bank found out, they'd can me and prosecute." Gathering up her bag, she walked out.

"Are you going to use actual cash with that thing?" Etta said, eyeing the dye pack.

"Hell, no," Slater said. "This is just a message. Part of it is to say 'Back off,' and part of it is 'You're not getting paid anymore.' So no lettuce required. I do need to cut up printer paper to the size of cash. Do we have an envelope for it?"

"You should use one of those plastic ones. They're really hard to rip open. You have to use scissors. That way he won't open it in here."

"What did I just say?" Slater waved an arm. "You're a natural."

Etta chuckled. "Do you want me to go to the stationery store and get one?"

"That would be great. I'll start on cutting up paper."

As she left, Slater sat at his desk with the scissors. It was painfully boring, as he wasn't able to cut that many sheets at once, but eventually he had a thick stack of blank sheets the size and thickness of a rack. When Etta got back, they put the dye pack in the middle of the stack of paper.

"You should put real bills on the outside," Etta

said. "Otherwise he might not even open the bundle."

"Smart." He pulled out his wad, and found a fin and a sawbuck, and put them on either side of the stack. Finally they bound it up with rubber bands.

"It doesn't look like cash from the sides," Etta said. "The paper is too white."

"Maybe he won't notice that. Even if he does, I bet he'll take the bands off to check."

"Are they tight enough?"

"Let's hope so."

He gingerly pulled on the plastic thread to arm the dye pack. Nothing happened when it came out— Regina said it would only blow up once the pressure was removed from the sides. The envelope Etta bought was the size used for business mail, and he sealed the bundle inside, then put it in the top drawer of the front desk.

"You should vamoose," Slater said. "The grifter will be here soon."

"I really want to stay. If you're on the front desk, I can sit in your office. I won't make a sound."

"He's going to check."

"So I'll pretend I'm working," Etta said. "Obviously it's somebody else's office. Why not mine?"

Slater groaned. "I don't know."

"This is how I learn the trade—stooging you and Max. I have to be immersed. To study the work of the ascended great ones."

"I know your yanking my chain," he said. "Just make like you know nothing about what I'm doing. I'm your desk clerk."

A while later there was a knock at the door. Slater waited for Etta to hustle into his office and sit down, then pulled it open. Tanner was wearing jeans and a white T-shirt emblazoned with a big purple VOLES logo.

"You trash bag," Slater snapped.

"Settle down." Tanner gestured to the office behind him. "Are you going to let me in?"

He pulled open the door, then stepped around the desk and sat down, scowling at him.

"Your sign says investigations," Tanner said.

"I handle the paperwork and the accounting for the PIs. I don't work in the field."

"Why did you want me to come here? You think I'd be intimidated by some gum-heel? I eat people like that for breakfast."

"I had to work today, asshole. I wasn't going to invite you to my home."

"On Rossmore, right?" Tanner raised his eyebrows. "Nice neighborhood."

"You've done your homework."

The sound of movement came from Slater's office, and Tanner scowled. "Who else is here?" He stepped over and stuck his head into Max's office, then into Slater's. "Who are you?"

Slater got up and stood behind him. Etta was sitting at his desk, holding a sheaf of paper from his drawer. He'd forgotten about those—expense reports he was supposed to be filling out.

Etta frowned at him. "The name is Ibáñez. What are you doing in my office?"

"Are you monitoring me?" Tanner demanded.

"Son, I don't know who you are," Etta said, "but you're starting to interrupt my workday."

"I'm handling this," Slater called to her. "Come

out of there, you big mook."

"Why do you work here if your wife has dough?" he said, stepping back into the front office.

"Would you cool it?" Slater sat down again. "That's my boss. This doesn't concern her."

Tanner threw up his hands. "So where's my money?"

He rolled open the desk drawer and handed him the envelope. Tanner tore at it, but it wouldn't give.

"I can't open it. Why is it plastic?"

"If it's the wrong amount, I'm sure you'll track me down." Slater lowered his voice. "Now, delete that photo."

"As soon as I get home." Tanner looked around the room again, and waggled the envelope. "See you later, John."

Once he'd walked out, Etta came into the front office. "That was quite convincing. You sounded angry."

"It's not hard to conjure. It's always just below the surface."

"Being pissed at that guy?"

"I'd call it a more generalized persistent seething rage."

Etta nodded. "That rings true. Do you know where he lives?"

"Pasadena," Slater said. "He won't open it until he gets home, so I'm not going to hear from him for a while."

"I hope it works. With the blond hair it'll be dramatic."

TWENTY-FIVE

THEY WERE STILL IN the front office talking when they heard someone try the handle, then pound on the door. Slater got up and opened it a crack, his foot planted inside it.

Tanner stood there, wide-eyed, his white shirt now splattered with neon green. The lower half of his face was blotchy green, along with the left side of his hair. His hands and forearms were streaked with dye too.

"It looks like Purim came early this year," Slater said.

He shoved on the door, but it was blocked by Slater's foot. "I'm going to fucking kill you."

"No, you're not," Slater said. "You know I can take you, football boy."

"You can't fucking get away with this. You owe

me. I'm going to talk to your wife, like, now. I know where Della works."

"If I let you in, are you going to behave? I'd hate to have to break your nose. Mostly because I'd get that green stuff all over my fist."

He pulled the door open and sat behind the desk.

Standing back near Slater's office, Etta said, "Whoa."

"I'm told the color fades to jade green in a week or so," Slater said. "It'll match that beautiful suit you were wearing on Saturday."

His fists balled, Tanner stood in front of the desk, breathing hard. "Why would you do this to me, John, when you know I can blow up your life? I know your wife."

"Della's not my wife, and my name's not John." He waved a hand. "If you show her that photo, she'll laugh, and ask for a souvenir copy, then throw you out of her office."

"Who the fuck are you?" he shouted.

"I'm the guy who knows all about Bucky Mainwaring, and Walter Yan, and Mara Ortiz, and Liz Delgado. I have the whole list. My advice is to delete all the photos you have. That way the cops won't find the evidence when they search your electronics."

"You can't do this. I'll distribute that photo."

"You're not getting it, dipshit," Slater said. "I'm not who you think I am. You've got nothing over me. So you're going to do what I tell you, or I'll put you on the fast track to the hoosegow. Extortion is a felony with serious prison time." He jabbed a finger at him. "You and your degenerate brother are going over for it."

He knew he shouldn't have let the guy back in, or sat down, as it made him vulnerable, but he'd wanted Etta to take in the full effect of what the dye pack had done. As Tanner lunged at him, he had a split second to ready himself before the guy landed on top of him, throwing wild punches. Tanner landed a blow to his ear, but Slater quickly used a wrestling move to flip him onto the floor, throwing them both out of the chair. Tanner landed flat on his back, and Slater quickly straddled his torso.

It was easy to avoid his fists, as the guy didn't really know how to throw a punch. Slater punched his face, left and right, several times, until his eyes went glassy, and he looked dazed, and his arms dropped to the floor. A trickle of bright red appeared at his nose.

Rising to his feet, Slater massaged his knuckles. "What's with the glass jaw? It must be genetic. Chad went down like a crunk twink at Pride too."

Watching the guy recover his senses, he noticed the jade ring, and dropped to one knee. Tanner struggled to resist him, but he was still muddled, and Slater managed to pull it off his finger.

"I'm giving this back to Walter." He rose and briefly looked it over before he pocketed it. "You got dye on it, you moron."

Tanner sat up on an elbow and roared, "Bastard."

Standing astride his shoulders, Slater squatted to lift him by the armpits and dragged him to his feet, then frog-marched him the few steps to the door, and shoved him out into the hallway. Tanner stumbled, then turned to glare at him.

"It's over, Tanner. You need to get to work and

delete everything. Cover your tracks. It's time for damage control."

He closed the door and bolted it. Etta picked up the desk chair and set it back on its wheels, and Slater scooped up the blotter and the notepad Tanner had knocked off the desk. Luckily Rey Pascual had survived the scuffle unscathed, still at his post, watching the room with his empty eye sockets.

"Bro must have opened it in his car," Etta said.

"It definitely looked like it happened in an enclosed space." He checked his knuckles. "At least none of it transferred onto me."

"Pow." Etta mimed a punch. "What a beautiful good-night kiss. It was like watching the ballet. Why did you let him back in when he was that pissed off?"

"It was a safe bet. He's a jock, but nobody ever taught him how to brawl. I could tell from his body language."

"We should get lunch and debrief."

"I have some computer work to do," Slater said. "I need to delete all the blackmail photos from the Green Man's cloud drive."

She frowned. "How did you get access to that?"

"I'm running surveillance on everybody involved in this. Cars and phones."

"Tech from the Russian," Etta said. "I need to meet her at some point."

"You will. You'll like her—she's a no-bullshit type, like you." He stepped into his office and sat behind the desk, pulling his keyboard toward him.

Etta stood in the doorway. "Do you know how to permanently delete the files? With lots of those services it just goes into a thirty-day trash folder."

"Fuck me." Slater stared at her for a moment, then waved a hand. "Grab a chair."

She chuckled and wheeled the desk chair in beside him. Once he was in the cloud drive, Etta guided him on how to permanently delete the images and the spreadsheet.

"Don't you think they'd have backups on a flash drive or in another cloud account?" she said. "I would."

"Probably. But this is another component of the message: 'I can get to you when you don't expect it.'"

"I guess it would slow them down a little, even if they don't take you seriously."

He eyed her. "I turned him the color of a camphor tree. Wouldn't you take that seriously?"

"If they're making money doing this, it's going to be hard to just stop. Maybe you should take it to the cops."

"My client would never swear out a complaint, and neither would any of these other patsies. All their secrets would come out."

"I guess that's why blackmail works." She pointed at the screen. "If you want to accentuate your message, you could delete the entire account."

"Great fricking idea," he said, and they spent a minute closing it down.

After Etta left, he sat back in his chair, thinking about it all. It wasn't a perfect solution, and it wasn't as satisfying as seeing Chad and Tanner arrested, but he'd thrown sand on the fire. The blaze had been beaten back. Like those wildfire reports. It felt like their grift was eighty percent contained.

Picking up his phone, he checked the tracker on Bucky. The guy was at his house. He didn't seem to work very much. Locking up the office, he went down to his car and drove to Silver Lake and pulled into Bucky's empty driveway. When he rang the bell, Bucky pulled open the door, dressed the same way Slater was, in chinos and a conservative blue dress shirt, like he had a business meeting lined up.

Bucky gave him the once-over. "This is a new look for you."

"We need to talk."

"You can't hit me again."

"I never hit you. It was a slap. Open-handed. And it was self-defense, after you came at me."

He frowned. "I never touched you."

"That's your word against mine."

Bucky scoffed and waved him in, and led the way to the lounge furniture, where he sat on the sofa, extending an arm along the back.

"What do we need to talk about?"

"I was able to mess with Chad and Tanner today. I told them to lay off the squeeze play or I'd get the cops involved."

"Why would they listen to you?" Bucky said.

"I posed as an affluent mark, and let Tanner pick me up at Electric on Saturday. I let him photograph my bare ass." Slater gestured to his own torso. "Thus the square clothes. When they sent me the photo and asked for money, I told them I was going to the cops with the photo as evidence."

His brow furrowed. "Are you really going to do that?"

"It wouldn't work. I set a trap for them. I don't think the prosecutors would touch it."

Bucky sat up. "I'm going to need more detail."

Slater explained what he'd done in broad strokes. "The key here is that you don't talk to Chad or Tanner again. Block their numbers. Don't answer any unknown calls, and definitely don't pay them anymore. They might lay off for a while and regroup, but they could also play it as business as usual. You need to stand firm and not engage with them."

"If you think that'll work."

"Let me know if you hear from them. Especially if they threaten to distribute that photo. I can pay them another visit."

"It feels good to hear you say that. Like things are lighter now." Bucky took a breath. "Like a weight coming off me."

"Those idiots made you lose your freaking memory and wind up in Albuquerque. You don't need to let them get you that stressed out again."

Slater got up, and Bucky rose with him.

"Do you need any more money?"

"We're all square."

"You could hang out, if you want." Bucky raised his eyebrows. "I was going to have a shower."

"Another time, maybe." Slater waved an arm. "You should give L-Rat a call."

Walking out, he climbed into the Continental, and backed into the street. Once he was on the boulevard he phoned Walter but got his voice mail. When he called Mara Ortiz, she picked up.

"Where are you?" he said.

"Why are you asking?"

"We need to talk. Not on the phone."

"That certainly sounds sinister. I'm at my shop."

"I'm on my way out there."

"I'll be here all day," Mara said. "And this neighborhood isn't out anywhere, by the way. It's the center. The core. Ground zero for fashion."

"If you're an affluent white airhead, maybe." Not waiting for a response, he ended the call.

Crossing under the freeway as he headed west, he called Liz Delgado next.

"What the hell were you doing at Electric the other night?" she demanded.

"Posing as a mark."

"I figured. I hardly recognized you in that suit. Did it work?"

"You didn't see the photos?"

"I'm an employee, not a partner, remember?" Liz said.

"Tanner came to collect the first installment today. I punched him in the face and told him the cops were coming to search his electronics. If I were you I'd lose his number, and Chad's."

"Seriously?"

"It's that moment you talked about, Liz, where you get out of the way so that you don't get caught up in the fallout. The bunco is collapsing around them. Lose their phone numbers, and do not talk to them again."

"OK, Slater, I get it."

"They might pretend nothing's changed," he said, "and threaten you. You have to hold firm. Call me if you hear anything from either of them."

Once he'd ended the call, he dialed Walter again, and got no answer. Once he'd parked at a meter in front of Mara's shop, he took a minute to send Walter a text:

Call me. It's important.

The tattoo parlor guy was standing outside his place next door, a cloud of smoke around him. He was wearing the same white tank top. He must be proud of all that ink on his arms. Climbing out of the Continental, he strode past him.

"It's the rat man," the guy called to him. "Why are you dressed like an accountant?"

Slater paused on the sidewalk. "You say that like I brought the rats." He jabbed a finger at him. "That's on you. I just pointed it out."

"You're kind of a dick, you know that?"

"And you invited rats onto your block. I just assumed it was some quirky new trend that I wasn't sophisticated enough to understand. That you'd created an ironic immersive experience where the hep rats go to groove."

He walked toward Mara's shop, and the guy shouted after him: "Asshole."

"All that ink is going to look amazing in twenty years," Slater called back to him, pausing at Mara's door. "Enjoy it now before it all bleeds together and looks like prison tats."

As he stepped inside, no one was at the counter, but Mara soon stepped out of the back, and frowned at the sight of him.

"You cut your hair."

Slater absently ran a hand into it. "It's part of the game I ran on Tanner."

"So what happened?"

He outlined what he'd done on Saturday. "Tanner hit me up for the dough today. I punched him in the face and told him to expect the cops to search his electronics."

"Do you think they will? Have you reported it already?"

"Those idiots know it's a possibility now," Slater said. "They're going to delete all the images, but they might lie to you, and act like nothing has changed, and try to squeeze you for more cash. But you have to block Chad's number. Don't talk to him. Don't give him anything. If he comes over here, call the cops and tell them he's shoplifting."

"You think that's where it's at?"

"I don't think you're even going to hear from them again, what with the pushback from me, and what you and Gonzalo did." Slater chuckled at the memory and put his hands on his hips. "They have to see that it's getting dangerous for them."

Mara's eyes narrowed. "What's funny?"

"Remembering Chad handcuffed to that chair and drooling his way through a k-hole. It lifts my spirits and warms my heart."

"You sound like a sociopath."

Slater raised his eyebrows. "You know who's a sociopath? That Gonzalo guy. You need to stop hanging around with him. He was going to grease me without even blinking. He could easily do that to you."

"At this time I'm not in need of advice about men, or from men," she said, and frowned.

He pointed a finger at her. "No more contact with Chad."

"Got it, Papa."

When he walked out to the street, the tattooed

idiot was gone. Lucky for him—one more crack and he would have had to punch him in the face. But not even that stupe was going to bring him down right now. He felt too high from outmaneuvering the sleaze brothers. Was this how the world looked to Pike all the time? He felt light on his feet. Pink cupcakes instead of knuckle sandwiches.

Driving back to his house, the traffic was sluggish at the end of the day. There were other names on that sucker list. It might be an awkward conversation, but if he wanted to shut it down completely, he needed to talk to them, make sure all of them cut off communication and payments. The victims needed to present a united front. Conveniently the morons had put everybody's contact details in that spreadsheet. That had to be his project for the rest of the day—talking to the rest of the patsies.

TWENTY-SIX

PIKE WAS ALREADY GONE when Slater woke in the morning, and he went upstairs to pour a mug of tepid java and take half a bagel out onto the deck. He knew what Bucky meant when he talked about that feeling of a weight being lifted. He'd done all he could to shut down Chad and Tanner, and it was behind him now.

Slater was still enjoying the morning sun, letting the light and the crisp air wake him up, when his phone buzzed. The call was coming in on the spoofed number he'd set up—it was the chiseler in jade.

"Hey, little sprout," Slater said as he picked up. "How's the green life?"

"Asshole," Tanner snapped. "Where's my brother?"

"The fuck would I know that?"

"He's not where he's supposed to be. He's not

answering his phone. I found his car parked at the Blue Dragon in Hollywood. It makes no sense."

"Maybe he doesn't love you anymore," Slater said. "Or maybe he's going solo. That kind of makes sense, don't you think? He's the pretty one."

"Fuck you," he growled.

"I wonder if one of your patsies finally greased him? You can only push people so far before they snap."

The line went dead, and Slater looked at the screen. Tanner had hung up on him.

It was easy to see where Chad's phone was. He opened Svetlana's app and checked his trackers. The green dot on the map was crawling along the 10 freeway, eastbound in the Inland Empire. But Tanner said his car was in Hollywood.

He hadn't been able to connect with Walter in the last few days. The guy had sounded pretty upset with Chad when they'd talked on the weekend. As he thought about it, he could feel a vague queasy knot forming in the pit of his stomach. The vehicle tracker on Walter's Barracuda was still working, he found, and the imprecise circle for its location, as the device sniffed out Wi-Fi and cell towers, was hopping east through the Inland Empire. It was on the same stretch of freeway, on the same trajectory as Chad's phone.

"No fucking way," he muttered. If Chad wasn't answering his phone, he wasn't with Walter by choice. Dialing Walter again, it went straight to voice mail. What the hell was he up to?

Gazing absently out at the hazy hillside, he thought it through. *Ten acres of paradise.* Walter had said that. He owned land out in the Mojave. It was an ideal place to get rid of a body. The cartels did that as a standard business practice. He looked at the tracking map again, at the green dot for Chad's phone crawling along. With any luck Walter hadn't croaked the guy yet. Either way Walter had at least an hour on him.

Slater hustled down to the garage and backed the Continental into the street. He got on the freeway, and navigated to the 10, driving fast and hard, maneuvering around other vehicles when it gave him a speed advantage. Periodically he checked the trackers on the map.

Walter had passed the 15, so he wasn't going up into the Mojave that way. Eventually the map showed that he left the freeway on the road north out of the Coachella Valley. That was the way to Joshua Tree.

Following his path, Slater was soon in the high desert, rolling past the spiky Joshua trees that studded the arid pinky-brown landscape. Even more pervasive were the creosote bushes waving lazily in the breeze. He'd heard old-timers call them greasewoods, but the people who'd taught him horticulture called them creosotes. They were hardy, and drought-tolerant, and grew absolutely fricking everywhere up here.

Walter had turned off the highway, and the trackers for the Barracuda and for Chad's phone had stopped a few miles north of it. The route led him first onto an unstriped paved road, then a wide dirt road, and eventually a turn onto a dusty rutted doubletrack. Finally he could see the bright-green Barracuda up ahead, pulled off to the side.

Parking the Continental a few yards behind it,

he surveyed the landscape as he climbed out. Homesteads were visible in the distance, farther up the road, but no structures were anywhere close by. The land was studded with Joshua trees and Mojave yuccas and creosotes. It must have rained this winter—a fine green fuzz of matted forbs and delicate grasses carpeted the ground. There was no sign of Walter or Chad.

He walked up to the Barracuda and cupped his hands against the driver's window to look inside, but it was unoccupied. In the sandy earth behind the trunk was a scuffled mess of footprints on the ground, then two sets of prints led away from the car, in the pink-and-tan earth, among the sparse foliage.

Following the footprints, Slater climbed a gentle rise, and in the distance beyond it Walter came into view, standing with his back to him, an ugly black handgun dangling at his side. Slater had only ever seen him in a suit, but today he was wearing a black shirt and jeans.

In front of him was an arroyo, its fine gravel surface a couple of yards wide. The lowest point in the landscape, it was dry now. Nothing ever grew on those. Chad was in the middle of it, visible only from mid-thigh up, as he was standing in an oblong hole, working a spade, tossing loads of earth onto a pile behind him. His shirt was stained with dark patches of sweat.

As he got closer, Slater called to them, "Hey, fellas."

"Oh, thank god," Chad said.

Walter whirled around, eyes wide.

"Don't point your gun at me," Slater snapped.

He could see Walter didn't know how to use a weapon, with his index finger poised on the trigger.

That made him way more dangerous.

Not lowering the heater, Walter jutted his chin. "How did you find me?"

"Can you put that thing away? You're making me nervous."

"You're not going to stop me, Slater. If I have to blast you too, I'm fine with that. There's room for two down there."

"Before you do that, let me point something out." He flashed his palms. "I'm going to come closer. I'm not armed. Keep your finger off that goddamn trigger."

Chad stood now with both hands on the spade handle, using it to hold himself up. He was breathing hard, his mouth hanging open, watching them. The skin around his eye was yellowish now—that shiner Slater had given him had almost faded away.

"You didn't think to turn the knucklehead's phone off," Slater said, stepping closer. "Even if you bury it with him, the cops can trace it to this spot. On your land. Just like I did."

Walter stared at him for a moment, then roared, "Damn it."

"You're the one who messed with Tanner, you dick." Chad glared at Slater. "How did you track my phone?"

"What did you think would happen when you started extorting people, genius?" Slater demanded. "In my business there's a thing called the blackmailer's ultimate reward. You almost got it Friday night at Chalo's Rims. The big guy wanted to croak you. Mara and I talked him out of it." He waved at the hole in the sand. "And once again you're prepping for it."

"Maybe I'll revise the plan," Walter said. "If the

cops are going to find him anyway, I'll blast this fucker, then I'll blast you, then I'll do myself. Problem solved."

"Dude, think about it," Slater said. "Murder-suicide is going to look a lot worse to your family than that stupid drug photo ever would. And why would you deprive the world of your perfect little caboose, and those sweet lips, and your big heart? I'm thinking about those two dozen roses. You'd be cheating all the guys, and you'd be letting these idiots win."

His face contorted, and he waved the rod. "So this trash bag just gets away with it."

"I've already put a dent in their operation. If you'd answer your damn phone you'd know that." Slater chuckled. "I turned this moron's idiot brother into a Hindu god."

"You ruined his car," Chad said. "You'd better watch your back. He'll mess you up."

Slater cackled. "Him and what army?"

"You shut your mouth," Walter shouted at Chad, and waved the gun, then eyed Slater. "What are you talking about?"

"You know how at the Indian supermarket, on the candles and the little cards, some of the gods are blue, and some are lime green? I let Tanner pick me up at Electric, then I put a dye pack in an envelope instead of the payoff cash. He opened it, when he was in his car, if you can believe this lowlife, and turned himself green. For the next few weeks his ugly face is going to be the same shade as the Barracuda."

"That's a nice story," Walter said, "but you've lied to me before."

Digging in the pocket of his jeans, Slater pulled

out the jade ring and held it up. "I took this off him when he came back to complain. I'm pretty sure it's yours. It has a bit of the dye on it."

"OK, so you turned one of them green. Why would that stop them?"

"It's a way to demonstrate that I'm not messing around," Slater said. "I have proof that he was trying to blackmail me with a surreptitious sex photo, and I'm not afraid to take that to the cops. That's a couple of felonies right there, with actual hard evidence. I've got the photo and a witness in my office who overheard the demand for money. They'll definitely investigate it. And if Chad wants to get ahead of that, and get himself out of that hole, he's going to delete all the images and close up shop."

"I can do that, totally," Chad said quickly. "I'll delete everything."

"You'd say anything to save your skin," Walter shouted at him.

Slater held up a hand. "Here's the flip side of it. If Chad decides to go to the cops, 'Oh, poor me, that mean Walter kidnapped me,' my story is that I was here, and there was no kidnapping." He looked to Chad. "I saw the photo of Tanner having sex and doing drugs with Walter, and I've personally had sex with Walter, so I assume you two dimwits made up the kidnapping story because you were jealous." He met Walter's eye. "A man-man love triangle. It all fits together. No matter what this idiot says to anyone, you're golden. You go back to your office tomorrow, cruising the boulevard like a boss in that sweet Barracuda, and you never have to give this dirtbag another dime."

"It still feels like he's getting away with it," Walter said.

"His squeeze play is over. If he's not smart about damage control, he might be going to prison."

"What do you get out of it?"

"The warm feeling of shutting down a trash factory." He shrugged. "And like I told you, one of the other victims hired me. I'm all paid up for the work I've done."

Walter sobbed, his breath catching in his throat, and finally lowered the weapon. "I almost killed him."

"But you didn't, Walter. That's not you. You're about hot cars and natty tats and roses."

Chad set the spade aside and moved to climb out of the hole.

"Don't you fucking move," Slater shouted, and jabbed a finger at him, "or I'll shoot you myself." Stepping toward Walter, he extended a hand. "Let me take that."

He handed the weapon over, muzzle first, pointing it at him in the process. Slater frowned and took hold of the barrel.

"Where did you get this?" Slater said. "It's a lot of gun, and you clearly don't know how to use it."

Walter wiped at his eyes with his shirtsleeve. "A former client."

"I thought you did contract law."

"For about ten minutes after law school I worked as a public defender. You meet all kinds of people."

Slater eyed Chad and waggled the heater at him. "Step away from the spade."

He showed his hands and moved sideways. "I thought it was a shovel."

"That's because you've never used one before. It's a spade. Get out of the hole." He watched as he climbed out, clearly stiff from the manual labor. He'd been at it for a while, Slater realized, as it was several feet deep, and the pile of excavated sand was sizeable. "I bet you've got blisters right now."

"All over my hands," Chad said, wincing as he slowly stood erect.

"How did he get you out here?"

"I went to collect some money he owed me. He made me come over to his car. Then he clocked me, and pulled the gun on me, and zip-tied my hands." He glared at Walter. "Two hours like that. My wrists are shredded."

"I heard it was a sex thing," Slater said. "You wanted Walter to tie you up and fuck you. I've seen photographic evidence that you and Tanner were quite intimate with a number of men, and of course drugs were usually involved."

"Stop saying that," Chad shouted. "I get it. I'm not going to tell anyone."

Stepping over to him, Slater punched him in the face. Chad hadn't been expecting it, and grunted as his head spun.

"That's for trying to blackmail me," Slater said. He punched him on the other side. "That's for blackmailing Walter."

Chad collapsed to his knees, and a line of red trickled from his nostril. Why was that so satisfying to see?

Shaking his head to recover, he managed to wheeze, "Stop it."

"These fricking guys," Slater said. "Always with the glass jaw."

Watching them, Walter looked ashen now, his shoulders hunched, the anger drained out of him.

"On your feet," Slater said to Chad, and once he was standing, waved the weapon. "You first."

Wiping the blood from his upper lip with the back of his hand, Chad started to trudge toward the rise, following the footprints. Slater grabbed the spade from the hole and handed it to Walter.

As they walked, he popped the mag out of the heater. It was fully loaded. He scoffed and checked the chamber, then tucked it into the back of his belt, and stuffed the mag in his hip pocket.

"Idiot Tanner got green dye on it," Slater said, fishing out the jade ring and handing it to Walter. "I'm sure a jeweler can clean it up."

He slipped it onto his finger. "Is it crazy that watching you punch him gave me a giddy little boost? It felt like a shot of espresso."

"Considering you were about to grease the guy, that's not really a surprise."

"I feel kind of nauseous about that."

"I get why you were going to do it. But nobody is beyond redemption. You showed your true colors when you chose not to. Focus on that part. That you didn't do it." As they crested the rise and the vehicles came into view, Slater looked around and draped an arm on Walter's shoulder. "This really is a beautiful piece of land."

———◆———